GHOSTS OF THE
REVOLUTIONARY
WAR

THE JOURNAL OF A 21ST CENTURY MAN
WHO TRAVELS BACK IN TIME TO 1780

MAJOR (DR) JOHN VON ROHR

GHOSTS OF THE REVOLUTIONARY WAR
Copyright © 2026 by MAJOR (DR) JOHN VON ROHR

ISBN: 979-8994853528 (hc)
ISBN: 979-8994853504 (sc)
ISBN: 979-8994853511 (e)

**VON ROHR
PRESS**

Von Rohr Press
jmvonrohr@aol.com
(864) 764-4722

CONTENTS

Preface

Driven by persecution on account of their religious belief, from Scotland and Ireland they emigrated to an unknown wilderness, braving the dangers and disregarding the perils attending to the formation of feeble settlements upon the borders of fierce and warlike tribes of Indians, whose savage barbarity drenched the frontier with the blood of these adventurous emigrants, sparing neither woman or children, thousands of whom were victims of the scalping knife and the tomahawk. It was a perilous conflict that tries men's souls.

The little log cabins and rough puncheon floors first erected by these pioneers. became the funeral pile of its occupants. Struggling under these fearful surroundings our fore fathers drove back these cruel barbarians and laid the foundation for peaceful habitations and happy homes, where every man could worship God according to the dictates of his own conscience, and we find today the impress of the heroic valor, virtue and patriotic love of freedom possessed by our forefathers in their struggle against savage Indians and British oppressors stamped upon their descendants, who with pride can say:

"Let no mean hope your souls enslave;
Be independent, generous, brave;
Your Forefathers such example gave,
And such revere."

JOHN HUGH MCDOWELL 1918

Chapter 1

Prelude

Although David McDowell Steele was born and raised in Southern California, he would much later learn that his Scottish family roots were firmly entrenched in Northern Ireland and the Scottish Lowlands of Dumfries and Galloway. At six feet six inches in height and weighing two hundred twenty-five pounds while still in high school, he would go on to attend college in Kansas, where he blossomed as both athlete and scholar.

Upon completion of his undergraduate degree, he volunteered for duty with the U.S. Army, where he rose in the ranks from private to Major. While on active duty in a twenty-four-year military career he earned both master's and doctoral degrees in History.

Following his military career, he served in a myriad of educational positions, to include teaching college credit history classes at the high school level and serving as a history professor at several noteworthy colleges and universities. Dave often wondered what it would have been like to have lived in a simpler time than the 21st Century.

On a more personal note, Dave is a widower. His wife of twenty-five years, Ann, died five years earlier from a rare form of ovarian cancer. While still alive, Ann had done her very best to prepare him for the inevitability of her demise, but he held out hope to the very end that she would make a comeback via some new miraculous medical cure, but none ever emerged. Starting out with a large circle of close friends, the great majority of them other married couples, as the months and years went by, his universe of close relationships virtually ceased to exist.

After Ann's death, Dave often felt lonely, so he found comfort by exploring his mother's McDowell family history. By studying other people's lives, he could possibly avoid dwelling upon his own. One day in 2023, Dave came into possession of a seven hundred page plus book published in 1918, which purported to detail the history of his mother's family heritage under the surname "McDowell." As he read more, he came to fully recognize that the McDowells had been one of the most prominent Revolutionary War era families in the Carolinas.

Without further ado, Dave was determined to seek out all the information he could about his McDowell relatives in the late 1700's. His early research efforts gained traction when he came upon a copy of a letter written by George Washington to Joseph McDowell of North Carolina in 1758, the original of this correspondence maintained at the Library of Congress.

"Wait a minute, he thought, if my relatives were corresponding with George Washington, even before he became our first President, they must have been some very prominent people of their time, much more so that I could ever have imagined."

Dave discovered that his relative Joseph McDowell the elder, and his wife, Margaret O'Neil McDowell. a member of the Irish aristocracy, came to America from Ireland about 1739, about the same time as his grandfather, sixty-two-year-old Ephraim McDowell, who is recognized as the founder of McDowell family branches in Kentucky, Virginia and North Carolina. It was said of Ephraim that he was a descendent of Someril, Lord of the Isles, through his son, Dougald, founder of Clan McDougald.

Dave was aware, from previous research he'd completed, that the surname "McDowell" is, in Scottish and Irish, the Anglicized form of the Gaelic "MacDub-hghail," "son of Dubhgall." This name presented itself as a meaning for "dark stranger," which was used by the Gaels to distinguish the darker-haired Danes from the fairer-haired Norwegians. As well as in Ireland, "McDowall" was a common surname in southwestern of Scotland, in Galloway.

While living in Winchester, Virginia, Joseph and his wife Margaret were said to have lived in one of the "finest homes in the area. This clearly led Dave to the conclusion that Joseph Sr. and his family were indeed well off financially before they moved south from Winchester to an area in North Carolina already known as "Quaker Meadows. they moved south from Winchester to an area in North Carolina already known as "Quaker Meadows."

He read further that moving south several years earlier was his cousin, John "Hunting" McDowell, who received his own land grant for property about a day's ride away from Quaker, Meadows. near present day Marion, North Carolina. "Hunting John" McDowell would call his plantation "Pleasant Gardens." His son, also named Joseph, would carry the "Pleasant Gardens" moniker with him throughout his life to distinguish him from his Quaker Meadows cousin of the same first name.

Further reflecting on family names, Dave reminded himself that his mother's brother and son (senior and junior), like him, had "McDowell" as their middle name. With his research to date in mind, David understood that the "McDowell" surname had been passed down through generations for well over two hundred years by both male and female progeny. This was the first time anyone had ever explained to him the source of his middle name, nor had anyone even remotely inferred to him that his mother's family history could be traced back to Ireland almost a thousand years ago. Dave then had his DNA tested.

The results he received provided him with irrefutable evidence that he still possessed a very distinct connection to the McDowell 'clan," with 55% of his DNA showing a direct familial link to Northern Ireland and the Central Scottish Lowlands, both locations his McDowell ancestors had claimed as home.

Before Dave was in a position to be able to write even a preliminary report on his findings about his family history, he would first spend two years making investigative trips to Revolutionary War battlefields, interviewing National Park Service rangers, digging through reference material in library after library and traveling to sites in both Carolinas to search, identify and meet with present-day relatives of the men who fought loyalist forces at the Battle of Kings Mountain in 1780.

On one particularly sunny afternoon day in June in Morganton, North Carolina, he sat down under a large, well-kept oak tree, located at the corner of what is now an older strip mall, where the closest building is a steak buffet restaurant.

He was somewhat dismayed to learn that the original "Council Oak" that stood on McDowell property at Quaker Meadows in 1780 was no longer there. In its place was a replica oak tree, planted after the original tree was washed away in the Great Flood of 1916. Lost along with the great oak were the memories of the people who possessed knowledge about where the original "Council Oak" once stood. In determining the correct location of the" Council Oak" some guessing was required.

The replica tree therefore became the result of those inquiries. Within ten feet of the "new" oak tree was an unadorned rectangular bronze plaque attached to a large granite shaft. Dave could read the inscription that appears on the plaque, "NEAR THIS SPOT STOOD THE OAK/WHICH SHELTERED THE BRAVE MEN/WHO HERE MET IN COUNCIL/SEPT 30, 1780/AND MARCHED ON TO GLORIOUS VICTORY/AT KINGS MOUNTAIN/ERECTED BY COUNCIL OAK CHAPTER D.A.R./SEPT 30, 1916.

Dave remembered how this all began, that prior to the Spring of 1778, when the South Carolina Provincial Congress passed a law requiring all males over the age of 18 to swear allegiance to them or forfeit their right to vote, conduct business or participate in legal sanctions.

The law went even farther for it stated that if a man were to depart the state to avoid the oath, upon his return he would be subject to the penalty of death. At this point in time, the settlers had largely ignored the war being conducted to the north between their fellow countrymen and the Mother Country, but now it struck home.

The residents of the backcountry were further marginalized since they had no established court and law enforcement in place, with the result they had to depend on local justices of the peace to hand out judgment. In this same realm of governmental inefficiency, backcountry settlers were forced to travel all the way to Charleston to conduct any legal business.

In addition to neglecting its citizens, the Provincial Assembly taxed their property at the same rate as the cash-rich plantations of the Low Country. In North Carolina a similar problem materialized by their underrepresentation in the provincial government. Those who collected taxes for the colony demanded gold coins or British currency, while the backcountry settlers were used to the barter system.

Most annoying was the high levy of taxes on them, seemingly at the will of the eastern landowners. In 1767 an open revolt took place in reaction to public funds being used to build Royal Governor William Tryon's house in New Bern.

As a result of perceived absurdity for building such an expensive structure at the expense of the colonists, a group called the "Regulators" formed. Without any official authority being granted to them, they nevertheless harassed the frontier population by collecting their own taxes and administering the law as they saw fit.

By the time of the Cherokee War, backcountry settlers like the McDowells had developed a well-organized militia to take care of themselves, no longer dependent on British authorities in time of need.

It was a result of incidents like those described that caused them to resent the tight control of exhibited by British authorities. To further aggravate the situation, the British made no fruitful efforts at bringing the colonists into their fold, but instead caused great resentment of their rule. The outrage at the Stamp Act of 1767 is but one example of an event that colonists protested as their "rights as Englishmen."

It was these same settlers that had come to the Americas after receiving very generous land grants (for some, thousands of acres) from the English king to lure new settlers to the "backcountry," which Southerners defined as any area more than fifty miles from the coast.

The great majority of those arriving in the Carolinas, beginning in the mid-1700's, were of Scots-Irish descent. With them they brought their Presbyterian religion and a general tolerance for religious freedom.

It was from here, in this small rural town of Alder Springs (now Morganton), North Carolina, that Dave's ancestors and fellow patriots began their exhausting six-day journey to the low laying hills along the North Carolina/South Carolina border to battle those loyal to the usurper, Kings George III of England.

While he remained seated, the hair on Dave's arm suddenly stood on end, like there was static electricity in the air. In this same short timeframe, he experienced what he believed to be a change in air pressure, followed by his ears "popping," like when an airplane takes off or is landing.

Wondering just what was going on, Dave sensed someone was subtlety touching him on his right arm, just below the elbow joint. Without any hesitation, he peered down at his arm, saw there was no one anywhere near him, stood up feeling a bit uneasy, walked back to his vehicle, started the engine and began the journey back to his home near Greenville, South Carolina.

Once he arrived back at his home in the Upstate of South Carolina, convinced his research into family history to be complete, Dave decided it was his duty to write a very personal and detailed account of what his McDowell relatives and the Over the Mountain Men did before, during and after the tumultuous day in 1780 at Kings Mountain, South Carolina.

With you, the reader, now possessing sufficient knowledge of the man now known as David McDowell Steele, retired military man and educator, you can now more easily comprehend the events that would change his life forever.

Early one evening on a chilly winter night in late 2023, Major David McDowell Steele contacted this writer at my home near Greenville, South Carolina, alerting me that something "very, very unusual" had happened to him. I could hear the distinct ring of excitement in his voice, so I encouraged him to visit me that very evening. The events described henceforth are in Major McDowell's own words as I took note of them on that same date.

Chapter 2

Into the Forest

While I continued to do historical research on the McDowells at the desk in my office in late September 2023, I smelled what I believed to be the faint odor of smoke coming from the opposite side of my home, located in rural Spartanburg County, South Carolina. For this reason, I got up from my chair and began to take the twenty-five-foot journey toward the sliding glass door that led out onto the covered rear deck at the back of my house.

Along the way, I painstakingly checked every possible source for the smoke, but finding none, I opened the sliding glass door and walked out. Sniffing first to the left, then to the center and, finally, to the right, still, with no smoke detected, I returned to the comfortable chair that awaited me back in my office.

My next attempt to return to my research lasted only a sort while. Within five minutes of again being seated at my desk, I was certain I not only smelled smoke again, but I could also swear I could hear human voices coming from somewhere behind my house, out past the back gate, into the forest.

Maybe I just needed to be distracted for a moment, for my obsession with research on my family history had become all-consuming; for every available minute I could find during any day would be spent on research, research and more research, with the result that my head often seemed to be stuck in the year 1780. Regardless of the specific reason on this occasion, I rose from my office chair for the second time within ten minutes and again walked to the rear of my house.

This time, however, I first went through the sliding glass door, then the aluminum door leading down the thirteen wooden steps to the beautifully manicured green fescue lawn below. I made my trek across the grass toward the gate at the center of the yard on the south side of the property.

As I looked up from the gate, with its top and bottom hinges now released for exit, my eyes traveled upward, where I noted the magnificent stand of trees in the forest beyond, many of which stood well over two hundred feet in height, leading me to think aloud "these trees must well over two hundred years old. I wondered if they standing in 1780, when my relatives fought in battles here in Spartanburg County?" The forest in front of me was so deep, I could only see where it began, not end, out in the distance to the front of me.

I was acutely aware that eastern diamondback rattlesnakes might still be present here, at least the ones not going into "brumation" (hibernation for cold-blooded things). I shuffled across about 10 feet of low-lying shrubs when my attention was immediately drawn to the unnamed creek that flowed in a southwesterly direction along the back of my property.

The creek was now no more than twelve inches in depth and two feet in width, although when it rained heavily it could be up to three times as deep and ten feet wider. Taking a big leap across it, my feet quickly found solid ground, while in the same instance my nostrils were filled with the smell of burning wood, which reminded me of the many nights I'd spent out in the field around campfires while serving in the Army.

As I prepared to walk deeper into the woods, I heard the distinct sound of adult male voices wafting toward me through the dense forest directly in front of me. I pushed through thick bushes and vines for about fifty feet until I reached a clearing in the undergrowth.

My reaction was simple, I was startled to come upon a large, blazing campfire burning there in front of me. I squinted a bit due to the campfire smoke, but was able to count two men sitting around it, both dressed in what appeared to be some sort of "colonial era costumes." Before I could open my mouth to ask "Who are you? "or "What's going on here?'" the man who appeared to be the older of the two looked up at me and shouted out in what sounded like some form of old English, "Davy boy, what took ye so long?"

Shocked by the inferred friendliness of his statement, I squeezed out my own, "Who exactly are you and what are you doing here on my property?" A smile quickly came to the face of this inquiring stranger, followed softly by his proclamation "I am your uncle Charles McDowell. I have come here to your house, in your time, to take you back to my home in Quaker Meadows, with the intent to reveal to you the truth about what happened to your McDowell family members before, during and after the Battle of Kings Mountain in 1780."

He continued, "I've brought my brother Joseph along with me. Very soon we will be leaving for Quaker Meadows, where you can expect to meet some very important people, including several of my very well-known Patriot brothers."

"You will meet with these men at my home at Quaker Meadows on September 30, 1780, before we make our way south down to Kings Mountain to fight Major Patrick Fergusion and his loyalist troops." It was quite unnerving to me that this man, alleging to be my uncle, seemed to know that I'd spent the past two years researching McDowell family history about what roles they played in the Revolutionary War. Since I'd seen both Charles and Joseph's names on national battlefield monuments, I knew they would never fit any description of "an average person of their time."

Recognizing the uniqueness of this situation, I resolved to cooperate and keep my mouth shut, to listen and see what would come next. This man, who identified himself as Charles McDowell (age thirty-seven), reaffirmed to me some information I already knew about him, to include that his parents were Joseph McDowell, Sr. a Presbyterian Ulster-Scot immigrant from Ballcarry, Ireland and Margaret O'Neill, daughter of Laird Samuel O'Neill of Country Antrim, Ireland. Margaret was raised at Shane Castle, home of the ancient McNeill family, which meant royal blood flowed through her veins.

Aha, I thought, no wonder my DNA test results identify me as being 14% Irish. It was very rewarding for me to finally know the origin of my Irish ancestry." Another 41% indicated a birthright connection to the lowlands of Scotland.

My memory faded back to over a year ago, when I first became aware of my mother's family heritage, which pointed out that the Scots-Irish were the blood descendants of Lowland Scottish ancestors from Galloway. In the 1600's the English induced them to migrate to property the English had confiscated from Irish rebels in Northern Ireland, where these lands were known as the Ulster Plantations.

There was an apparently good reason for the English encourage this migration, for it was their belief that it would help them maintain control over the Irish, who have been anti-English throughout the history of their relationship.

The English King and his representatives did little to assist the Lowland Scots who settled there, for in fact they began mistreating them by imposing the collection of higher taxes. In addition, and highly insulting to the Scots-Irish Presbyterians, was the enforcement of the doctrines of the Church of England, which included the requirement that any legal marriage had to be officiated by a clergyman of the English church.

Economically, as the Lowland Scots began to prosper through their production of excellent woolens and linens, the English imposed even higher tax rates on these items in order that their own English products would appear to be more attractive for foreign investment.

Tired of what they considered to be abuse at the hands of the British government, many of these Lowland Scots made the decision to migrate to America in their quest for economic, political and religious freedom. Their treatment at the hands of the British government provided them with a predisposition, some might even characterize as a "hate" and a justification for the consequence of revolt once they set afoot in the American colonies in the 1700's.

I would be remiss if I did not point out an important point that came to my mind on this subject; that one should be careful to pointedly distinguish my Scots-Irish McDowell relatives from both real Irish-born and those Highland and Lowland Scots who migrated directly to America.

It is now the appropriate time to more formally introduce you to my two newly discovered relatives.

The first of them is my "Uncle" Charles McDowell...

CHAPTER 3

CHARLES MCDOWELL

Charles McDowell spoke first, stating "I am a direct descendant of a Scots-Irish family. My father was Joseph McDowell the elder, a Scotsman, my mother Margaret O'Neil McDowell, born an Irish woman." In an effort to more formally introduce himself, he made it quite clear he knew I was a former military officer, in fact, at the rank of Major, while he clearly identified himself as attaining the rank of full Colonel as Regimental Commander of the Burke County Militia." He was emphatic when he remarked "I am their first and only Commanding Officer."

He continued, "I was born in 1743 in Winchester, Frederick County, Virginia, as was my brother, Joseph "Quaker Meadows" McDowell Jr. in 1756." Feeling like a high-voltage light bulb had gone off in my head, from this second on I accepted the fact the Charles McDowell standing in front was my six to seven times removed ancestor.

Charles was a proud man and a highly successful one at that, for by October 1780 he had secured numerous land grants in western North Carolina.

To illustrate his prominence as a man of standing, he made sure I recognized this by making the following statement, "I own a thousand acres surrounding my "Quaker Mountain" tract; three hundred seventy-six acres on the northside of the Catawba River, including four islands in the river and mouth of Canoe Creek; and three hundred sixty-five acres on the southwest side of Upper Creek, on both sides of Will's Creek."

"Besides that, he said, I am waiting for approval for a four-hundred-acre plot in eastern Burke County and another one thousand acres on the Mulberry Fork of John's River." I added it all up. The total acreage he owned now, or would shortly own, would exceed three thousand acres.

Whether or not Charles was my cousin or uncle made little difference to me, for the man now in my presence would be two hundred forty-four years "old." Of course. he did not look that old for a man of thirty-seven, but at about six feet in height and around one hundred eighty pounds, the demands of life in colonial America in the 1700's had no doubt taken a high physical toll on him. It was obvious he did not have a full head of hair on his head, which made me wonder if he was the long ago relative who passed on to me the undesirable physical trait of early male pattern baldness. If this were true, it was something I could not thank him for!

It was at this this juncture in our interaction that I reached the point where I had absolutely no problem referring to this man as my "Uncle Charles." I did know from my review of multiple literature sources, that the McDowells were recognized as the most prominent family in the western Catawba Valley of North Carolina in the late

1700's. That was good enough for me, although I still had no logical explanation as to how all of this was happening, or even possible for that matter. I just continued to experience it.

Charles McDowell went on to advise me "My military career began in November of 1775, when I was appointed to the rank of Captain in the Rowan County Militia. From then on, my duty performance was consistently recognized as exceptional, with the result that by April of 1776 I was promoted to the rank of Lieutenant Colonel." I had read that his reputation as a leader in the militia was further embellished by the performance of his troops at "The Skirmish at McDowell Station."

He went on to reveal to me that in that same year, 1776, he accompanied Brigadier General Rutherford, with a force of two thousand five hundred men, on what is known as the "Cherokee Expedition." This was an attempt on the part of colonists to wipe out the presence of troublesome Cherokee Indians on the western frontier.

McDowell proudly announced that what came next was a very important event, one that transpired on the 9th of May 1777, when "I became a full Colonel, the Regimental Commander of the Burke County Militia." He noted that his peers "always praised him to the highest degree possible for his demonstrated duty performance in the areas of organization and supply." In the language of the 21st Century, his area of success would be characterized as "Logistics."

In the early months of 1780, he again demonstrated his well-tuned logistical skills by recruiting troops in both North and South Carolina and by directing community efforts to fortify and increase the number of forts in their local proximity. In this same time frame, Colonel McDowell led his troops to victories at the enemy works on the Pacolet River, at Musgrove's Mill and at Cane Creek. The leadership he demonstrated in battle against both the British and Loyalists was well earned as he skillfully led his Burke County Regiment in numerous guerilla warfare encounters with their British adversaries.

Charles McDowell continued, "My Patriot superiors identified my most important mission to be that of continually harassing both British and Loyalist forces, to put pressure on them while weakening popular support for them in the Carolinas." In several sources I'd read about Uncle Charles, it noted that "his efforts to organize and lead men in the South Carolina backcountry during this time went a long way toward securing America's independence from Great Britain." This was quite some praise, it gave me an immense feeling of pride in knowing I was related to an individual who helped found our fledging country.

In the months leading up to the gathering at Quaker Meadows in late September of 1780, my Uncle Charles had been quite busy, combat military action-wise. His successful leadership skills were on display at three successful battlefield encounters with the British, most notably at Thicketty Fort on July 31st, Cedar Springs on August 8th and Musgrove's Mill on August 18th. To avoid enemy reprisals after the last of these engagements, McDowell and his militiamen traveled back up the Catawba Valley and over the mountains to the Watauga settlements, where they found safety away from the eyes of their British oppressors.

Isaac Shelby and his militiamen went there because they needed a safe place to regroup, while at the same time substantially increasing their numbers in preparation for battles to come. Uncle Charles noted "there were several legitimate reasons for us to temporarily halt any aggressive action toward the enemy at this time; to include the summer heat; the need of our militiamen to attend to crops on their land and, even more of an issue; to counteract the continued presence of any neighboring, marauding Cherokee Indians." He said, "We called this plan Watchful Waiting."

They would soon be aware of Major Patrick Ferguson's bold threat to "march his Army over the mountains, hang their leaders and lay their country waste with fire and sword." The Patriot leaders knew the time was soon coming for them, with their newly augmented numbers in tow, to march back over the mountains to once again locate and fight Ferguson.

As soon as details for the new expedition became known to him, McDowell provided "We quickly made haste to my home at Quaker Meadows. When I returned home, I sent out messengers to all the settlements at the heads of the Catawba, Broad and Pacolet Rivers, with the intent to both recruit new militiamen and gather intelligence on enemy positions." His next comment could surely be considered prophetic, "the wait should turn out to be a short one."

Military triumphs aside, it was my Uncle Charles and his brother, Joseph "Quaker Meadows" McDowell, who first conceived the concept of a force of militiamen that would be, over two hundred years into the future, be referred to as the "Overmountain Men." I took a big breath and once again sighed with pride, with knowledge in hand that both my uncle and cousin absolutely deserved the honor of being memorialized on the battlefield monument at Kings Mountain.

I couldn't figure out, with his many earlier victories in mind, how anyone could possibly believe that my Uncle Charles had shortcomings as a commander in the field.

A POSSIBLE CAUSE?

After hearing Uncle Charles' personal introduction, my mind raced back to what I had read about an account of his involvement in the "Affair at Earle's Ford," which occurred on July 15th, 1780. It was that summer that my uncle led a force of about three hundred militiamen into South Carolina, settling in at Earle's Ford on the North Pacolet River, near the state line in what was then Spartanburg County, South Carolina, about twenty-seven miles southwest of current day Rutherfordton.

It was during that encampment, not believing any Loyalist or British troops were in their vicinity, that Colonel McDowell chose to set up his security with static defensive positions, versus "videttes," or moving patrols, which were more were commonly used in that day. He took several things into consideration when making his decision; the first being that the enemy had not been sighted in the area; while the second was the plain fact that his men had just completed a very tedious march and were in need rest.

Although feeling secure at his current physical location, he did initiate some degree of concern for security when he gave his brother Joseph the following instructions: "Take a party of men with you and reconnoiter the local area for the enemy. If you encounter any, report back to me immediately!"

Unfortunately for all concerned parties, my cousin, Major Joseph McDowell, did, along with his men on horse-back, wander off in the wrong direction, thereby failing to detect nearby British and Loyalist forces under the command of Colonel Alexander Innes.

First suspecting, and then in possession of knowledge of a Patriot presence, Innes was smart enough to send a spy into the Patriot camp.

The spy reported back to him that the Patriots were present there under the command of Colonel McDowell. In the evening, the Loyalist Colonel proceeded to send his subordinate officers, Major James Dunlap, in command of seventy Dragoons, and Lieutenant Colonel Ambrose Mills, commanding a party of sixty from the Old Tryon County Regiment of Loyalist Militia, to attack their enemy's camp. They were not aware of the true strength of the Patriot force encamped there.

There was only one Patriot guard posted that evening near the ford along the Pacolet riverbank. His sole duty was to sound the alarm if any enemy forces were detected. When he did become aware that British and Loyalist troops were quickly approaching, this same sentinel abandoned his post and ran back to the camp, yelling "They're coming, they're coming!" in what was a futile attempt to awaken his fellow militiamen.

It would be too late to save them all. No doubt sensing the Patriot vulnerability, Dunlap and Mills' troops immediately drew their swords and went on a killing spree amongst the militiamen encamped there, the great majority of them still soundly asleep when all hell broke loose.

Militiamen from Georgia were the first to die in the attack, with two killed and six more wounded. Among the dead was Colonel John Jones, who was the recipient of the British "gift" of eight saber stabs to the head for his past success in battle against them.

Aware they were being overrun, my Uncle Charles and Colonel Andrew Hampton, Commanding Officer of the Rutherford County Militia, formed up their main body of suddenly awakened militiamen to their right, along with Major John Singleton, and ordered a counterattack. Shocked to find themselves encountering an enemy in much greater number than expected, Dunlap, with but one of his troops killed, decided to make a hasty retreat across the Pacolet River, leaving six of McDowell's men dead and twenty-four wounded.

Very likely a contributing factor in the making of a significant leadership decision in the future, was the death of Lieutenant Noah Hampton, Colonel Andrew Hampton's son. Tragically, young Hampton, when aroused from sleep by the Tories, was one of the first to be slain. When challenged as to who he was by enemy troops, his reply was quite simple, "Hampton."

Unfortunately for him, his family name was well known in Loyalist circles. His relatives included both his uncle, Colonel Wade Hampton and his father, Colonel Andrew Hampon, both of whom were staunch supporters of the Patriot cause. Most likely a result of his known family connections, while Noah Hampton was on his knees before his captures, begging for his life, the Dragoons ran him through with bayonets. His fellow militiamen and friend Andrew Dunn, only a few feet away, met a similar fate.

It has been said that this very same Major James Dunlap exhibited a great deal of enthusiasm while watching his troops mortally dispatch this member of the famous Hampton family. It is doubtful Dunlap could have contemplated that his public expression of joy at Hampton's demise might someday come back to haunt him.

This event, the loss of his treasured son Noah, would greatly influence Colonel Andrew Hampton, giving him an extremely adverse opinion of his superior officer, Colonel McDowell. Hampton believed McDowell had been grossly negligent when he did not follow up favorably on his own, personal recommendation to establish guard posts in "patrol day" fashion, out beyond the ford, versus "picketing" in static guard posts along the river. From Hampton's perspective, the dye had been case in reference to what he believed to be McDowell's inability to lead from that date forward.

THE PROVOCATEUR

I read about Andrew Hampton while conducting my research. His life presents several mysteries of their own, the first being that there is no one truth about where he was born in 1730. Some sources report he was born in England, while others claim in the American colonies in either New Jersey, Pennsylvania or Maryland. The closest guess anyone has appears to be "Kent, Maryland." I could not find any veritable information as to where he was educated. Efforts to obtain confirmable information became more complicated since there were two Andrew Hamptons living in the Carolinas at the same time, only two hundred miles apart, both running grist mills as an occupation.

Researchers inherently had a difficult time separating one Andrew Hampton from the other. What is believed is that our Andrew Hampton first settled in Virgina before later moving south to live on Dutchman's Creek on the Catawba River. It appears that prior to the Revolution he moved southwest to what later became Rutherford County, North Carolina.

Andrew Hampton's rise in the military ranks was indeed quite fluid. He went from militia Captain in 1775, to Major in 1776, to Lieutenant Colonel in that same year and, finally, to full Colonel in 1779. His military records indicate he participated in battles at Charles Town, Earle's Ford, Thicketty Ford and Cane's Creek. I found Colonel Andrew Hampton to somewhat of a "mystery man," one to be careful to associate with.

In McDowell's defense, it was well known that he'd proven his mettle in combat at the Peach Trees, Wofford's Iron Works, Fort Thicketty and Musgrove's Mill. Although not "officially" designated as commander of troops other than his own Burke's County Regiment, he routinely led militiamen from other locations into battle in the Carolinas, where they excelled under his command. McDowell did have one blemish among all his achievements, that event taking place at Cane Creek, where his leadership abilities were characterized as "indecisive." It was here that his brother Joseph, my illustrious cousin, would save the day.

Historians have noted that Charles McDowell was often overlooked in reference to the important role he played in the American Revolution in 1780. It was during this year that he continued to perform his leadership duties in a truly outstanding manner, by continually demonstrating his success in recruiting, organizing and leading a very disparate group of men to victory in the backcountry of South Carolina.

I wondered, taking into consideration McDowell's well documented leadership experience, if it could be that the death of Colonel Hampton's son Noah was the impetus behind the decision to oust McDowell from the senior leadership position at Kings Mountain and instead send him off to Hillsborough to confer with General Gates?

Would it be possible for me to ever find out what the "real truth" is on this topic since it has been glossed over in all or most all published accounts? If I had learned anything in my time in the Army as a military intelligence officer, it was that human intelligence (HUMINT) is the most valuable and reliable source information.

With this thought in mind, I set a goal for myself, to use my learned military skills to eavesdrop on as many Patriot leadership conversations as I could, from Quaker Meadows on to the journey south. I could now identify my personal mission: to be in a position to determine how and why my Uncle Charles was ousted from command.

It is now time to hear from my new cousin, Joseph McDowell...

CHAPTER 4

JOESEPH MCDOWELL

Uncle Charles pointed toward the man beside him, who just a few minutes earlier had been sitting to his right on a small boulder by the campfire. "This is my brother, Joseph "Quaker Meadows" McDowell, age twenty-four." When I asked him about the meaning of the "Quaker Meadows" moniker, he remarked "It is to distinguish him from a second cousin, also named Joseph, age twenty-two, who resides at his own plantation, which he calls "Pleasant Gardens." Because of where he lives and to avoid confusion, everyone refers to him as "PG Joe." I don't wish to confuse you, so from now on, unless I note otherwise, when I speak about "Cousin Joseph," or even just "Joseph," I am speaking about my brother who resides with me at Quaker Meadows."

I looked over to Joseph "QM" McDowell, put forth my hand as he stood up and declared "It's a pleasure to meet you Cousin Joseph," to which he enthusiastically countered "The pleasure is mine Cousin Davy, I hope you and I can become good friends, after all, we're cousins, so just call me Joe or Cousin Joe."

Since I didn't know anyone named "Joe" in my life in the 21st Century, using the formal "Joseph" was my preference. Cousin Joseph said his second cousin's land was in Marion, North Carolina, a full day from Quaker Meadow. He estimated the distance between the two properties to be about twenty-two miles and that the two cousins would often spend weekends at each other's homes. In literature, this cousin, Joseph "PG" McDowell, is identified as being both "highly educated and gifted," with some even characterizing him as "brilliant."

Given this information, it is quite evident the two Josephs got along so well because they apparently shared at least one common character trait, high intellect. Personality aside, I knew that both cousins would be joined together in the baptism of fire that would be known as The Battle at Kings Mountain. I was eager to observe how each of them performed their duties that day.

Uncle Charles' final words to me were indeed forceful in nature when he added "I want to make it clear to you that your cousin Joseph "QM" McDowell is a Major in my Burke County Regiment, whereas your other cousin, Joseph "PG" McDowell, serves him in the chain of command as a Captain and Company Commander."

Now standing up beside Joseph, I guessed him to be about six feet one to two in height and around one hundred seventy to one hundred eighty pounds, with not an ounce of fat visible on him. Based on what I'd already heard about my Cousin Joe and now seeing him standing facing me, he reminded me of the stereotypical Army Ranger of the 21st Century. In other words, he looked like one hell of a tough soldier.

Historically speaking, Joseph had made a name for himself by demonstrating his leadership skills in making quick raids on the enemy, whether Indian or Tories, and conducting reconnaissance missions while in command of mounted troops, most often referred to as "light horse."

I looked closely at my new cousin Joseph and could see he is a quite a handsome young man, one who in correspondence of his time was reported to be "wonderfully magnetic, outspoken, universally popular and of more than ordinary ability." Another source referred to him "a born leader of men, a man both loved and respected by his soldiers," while still others reported his men had "unbounded confidence in his leadership abilities, while all felt affection toward him." It was pretty much "official," Joseph was admired by those who served with him.

From my own personal experience in the military, it was no stretch of the imagination to conclude my cousin Joseph was the type of leader the U.S. military sought out to serve in leadership positions throughout its history. Joseph absolutely fulfilled the adage "Leaders are made, not born." Joseph would, at the youthful age of only twenty-four, be recognized by his Patriot peers as a leader "who could and would inspire his men to fight."

I looked into Joseph's eyes and could see a depth of maturity well beyond his youthful appearance, which could explain how he had achieved recognition as a man of substance at such a young age. By achieving the rank of Major while so young, he made me a bit jealous, for I had spent seven years as a Captain before I reached that higher rank.

Joseph went on to advise me "My military career began in 1776, when I was but twenty years of age, when I was fighting both Tories and Indians alongside my older brother Charles. I helped support him while he was driving off the Cherokee Indians that were attacking up and down the western frontier. I learned a lot from him."

"In the fall of that same year, we both accompanied General Rutherford from the Salisbury District in his campaign against those same Indians. In early 1777, with the creation of Burke County, I was promoted to the rank of Major. My brother Charles was assigned as second in command to Lieutenant Colonel Hugh Brevard, who commanded a force of about one hundred and fifty mounted riflemen."

"In 1779, I joined the Stono expedition and in 1780 I fought with my brother's regiment at Ramsour's Mill." I was aware that Joseph was commended for his performance of duty in that later battle, which began with his discovery of a Tory gathering on Indian Creek on July 10th. The battle would end ten days later with a decisive Patriot victory.

Some sources highlight the battle at Ramsour's Mill as significant, while others overlook its decisive role in weakening Tory influence in the Catawba Valley. As a result of Ramsour's Mill, local support for Cornwallis' domination of the Carolinas was seriously diminished. For this one battle alone, Joseph would earn a reputation "as one of the most ubiquitous officers of the North Carolina Militia during the Revolution." In this same timeframe, Joseph would distinguish himself at Cane Creek, now called "Cowans Ford," where he and his troops fought with distinction against their primary British nemesis, Major Patrick Ferguson.

When I read about Joseph's personal exploits at Cane Creek, I was immediately drawn to thinking about how, in battle, he exposed himself to serious physical harm on numerous occasions as he rode amongst his militiamen, swearing and exclaiming to them "I will never yield, nor should you Burke County boys," quickly followed by a subsequent declaration to "Stand your ground and die with me if necessary."

During that day at Cane Creek, the Patriots were able to strike a personal blow for past infractions when they wounded British Major James Dunlap, the Loyalist leader who had led the sneak attack on them while they were sleeping at Earle's Ford. Dunlap earned his disreputable reputation as he was defined by all those sympathetic to the Patriot cause as "a man whose severities incensed people against him." With him being wounded that day, many felt he was finally getting a dose of his own medicine.

THE CHARACTER OF A HERO

The motto on the McDowell family crest is translated from Latin to English as "Virtue Lies Beyond the Grave." Throughout time, it has led later generations of McDowells in only one direction, to the front, to lead the charge, and to lead with distinction. Joseph McDowell, through his continual display of insightful leadership on the battlefield, was a perfect example of a man who incorporated the family creed into his daily life. He was a man whose ego was not impacted by either his aristocratic ancestral ties or his familial wealth; he was prepared to deal with all the hardships or victories that life might present him.

Following the examples set by many of his ancient McDowell ancestors, he was, at times, not necessarily a silent hero, but one who helped shape his own destiny. Joseph McDowell would pass on to generations of unborn McDowell's propensity to display a "flawless character and unconquerable will."

In my opinion, Cousin Joseph's words and deeds without question identify him as one of the finest Patriot battle leaders in the Revolutionary War. I was literally without words as I came to conclude "My cousin was a Revolutionary War hero!"

I could sense something wonderful was going to happen...

CHAPTER 5

TRANSFORMATION & JOURNEY

MY TRANSFORMATION

While still holding Joseph's sizeable hand, I felt a tingling from head to toe. Looking down towards my feet I was patently shocked when I saw I was now wearing the same buckskin outfit as my cousin and uncle. Most profoundly, I not only looked younger but felt it too, my creaky joints no longer playing their own symphony, most likely titled "your days are numbered old man."

Short-circuiting my comprehension, my body felt like I was a twenty-five-year-old again, in my first military assignment in Texas. Like lightning had struck, I now inhabited the "lean, mean, fighting machine" body the United States Army had produced, later to nurture through trial and combat during a twenty-two-year career.

It would be a gross understatement to say I would fall short of providing a logical explanation to myself, or to anyone else for that matter, about what was happening to me. What I can say is that it was indeed an exhilarating, life-altering event. I was in awe as I observed for myself what was happening, body part after body part, so I verbally acknowledged the startling changes.

"Twenty-five and I'm alive!" I declared, glancing wistfully at my Uncle Charles. With an amused grin on his face, he whispered "Davy boy, how could we expect you to join us on this journey at fifty years of age? People would think we'd brought along some old codger. You are now my nephew, Major David McDowell of the Burke County Regiment."

Still somewhat bewildered, I directed my complete attention toward my Uncle Charles, who was taking a huge breath as I turned toward him. I could clearly see his lips unfurl, immediately followed by these now unforgettable words, "And now it is time to go home!"

In the blink of an eye, the three of us found ourselves travelling back in time to the "Council Oak" on the McDowell family plantation at Quaker Meadows, two miles from 21st Century Morganton, North Carolina, in the year of our Lord 1780.

THE JOURNEY

It felt like flying through thick clouds, not toward a familiar airport, but nearly 250 years into the past. I felt a bit queasy, as if positioned in the front seat of a roller coaster, just as if it reached its' highest point, the global maxima, before plummeting downward faster, faster and even faster.

The entire trip back could have taken but a few minutes from start to finish. As the mist below me began to clear, I was able to make out below the outline of western North Carolina in the year 1780. Slowly, but surely, I was able to see some type of crude military encampment below, populated by what appeared to be hundreds of men and women dressed in Revolutionary War era clothing.

Before I was fully capable of regaining my senses, maybe a few heartbeats later, I found myself sitting under what I knew was the "famous" Council Oak, with seven commonly clad colonials seated in a circle around it.

CHAPTER 6

THE DISTINGUISHED GENTLEMEN

The first question that came to my mind as I sat under this beautiful, red oak tree on this rainy day was whether or not the 2023 location was accurate? I vividly recalled a conversation I had in 2023 with Rebecca Heacock of the Burke County Foundation, who during one of my trips to Morganton made a passing comment to me that no one was sure of the exact location of the Council Oak in 1780, since the original tree was washed away in the Great Flood of 1916.

I did, however, remember that local Revolutionary War historian William Brown III conducted extensive research into this very topic. Brown's conclusion was that he was satisfied that the Council Oak's location after 1916 is as close as possible to being historically accurate. Since I highly respect his opinion, this was good enough for me.

In a way, it seemed tragic to me that the replacement Council Oak was now sitting next to commercial businesses in the strip mall. The only saving grace is that the current owner of the property, where the tree is located, is aware of and recognizes its historical significance.

It is well known that my Uncle Charles, Cousin Joseph, William Campbell, Isaac Shelby, John Sevier, Benjamin Cleveland and Joseph Winston came together here at Quaker Meadows in late September 1780 after traveling overland from the mountains of Western North Carolina, Eastern Tennessee and Southwestern Virginia to prepare for a major military engagement against Major Patrick Ferguson and his British Loyalist forces.

They would later be joined by militiamen from the South Carolina and Georgia colonies. More than two centuries later, these seven men and their followers became known in U.S. history books as the "Overmountain Men."

COLONEL WILLIAM CAMPBELL

The man sitting next to Cousin Joseph stood up and offered me his right hand. He proceeded to introduce himself as Colonel William Campbell of Virginia, a Scots-Irishman, 35 years of age, a Virginia planter and military officer who was among the 13 men who signed the Fincastle Resolutions in 1775. That document, he said, promised armed resistance toward the British Crown should it continue to trample their civil liberties.

With a distinct look of pride on his face, Campbell commented "I married Elizabeth Henry, sister of Virginia Governor Patrick Henry, that same year." He provided more details when he reported "I inherited a large property in southwestern Virginia I called "Aspenvale.""

Before Campbell spoke another word, I stood in shock when I realized he was quite tall, like me, standing six feet six inches in height, which identified the two of us giants in this time. Campbell possessed the ruddy complexion typical of a Scots-Irishman and along with it a penchant for a quick temper. Educated by private tutors and eventually at the Augusta Academy (later renamed Washington and Lee University), he was noted as being a very courteous as a young man.

Campbell hesitated for a moment and then addressed me directly, "Now where in the world did you come from? I thought I was the only man of my stature in the entire Southern colonies." He then inquired of me "Have you ever heard of Patrick Henry?" My reply was quite simple, "Give me liberty or give me death!" to which Campbell replied "yes, that's him. Quite an inspiring man, wouldn't you say?"

I could only think of one answer, that being "Indeed he is!" I asked myself, "where in the world did that phrasing come from?" I decided to ponder that question sometime in the future, if I was ever able to determine whether the past, present or future existed anymore.

Campbell went on to advise me that he has been involved in fighting in the colonies since Lord Dunmore's War in 1774 and he was promoted to the rank of Colonel recently, in fact, just this year. I remembered that he had earned the title "the Bloody Tyrant of Washington County" for the battlefield leadership he displayed in fighting British forces.

A significant part of that reputation must have come about as a result of his documented lack of concern for his own personal welfare during these engagements, in particular when he continued to slash away, with unrelenting vigor, at loyalist soldiers with his broadsword, resulting in a great number of them being found on the ground, a bloody mess, most often dead, after his intervention. I was quite impressed by what I had heard about his swashbuckling exploits, so I could not help but ask him if the "rumors" were indeed true.

Campbell's reply came quickly, "My objective was to put as many loyalist soldiers as possible under my blade so that decent folks in this country could live their lives without a king telling them what to do." I felt honored to be in Campbell's presence, now comprehending at least one reason why he might later be chosen over my Uncle Charles to lead the Patriot forces at Kings Mountain. There was no doubt, Campbell was charismatic.

At the same time, I resumed my personal mission, that being to determine exactly how my Uncle Charles had lost the confidence of his peers before the battle, only to end up as what I could only describe as a 'glorified messenger boy." All the source material I had read led me to what I considered "murky conclusions."

In my head, repeatedly, rolled the thought "Is "finding out an answer to this question my real reason for being here in 1780?" At any rate, I felt honored to be in Colonel Campbell's presence, just as I was in my 21st Century military career when I met any organization's Commanding Officer.

I would be remiss if I did not comment about Colonel Campbell's and my height at 6'6,"as it compares to the "average" male of this time. My memory of events "back in the future" reminded me that it was again William Brown III of Nebo, North Carolina that brought clarification to this issue when he did a deep dive into the records of men in the "Morgan District of North Carolina" in the early 1780's.

Brown was confident he was able to validate that whereas the height of the average U.S. male in the 21st Century United States is 5'9," it was 5'8" in the late 1780's. Brown summary contradicts the almost universal assumption that men who lived over two hundred years ago were considerably shorter in stature.

Brown's conclusions came about as a result of his examination of the records of fifty men, average age twenty-four, all of whom resided in either Lincoln, Burke, Rutherford or Wilkes County in North Carolina. He reported that the tallest man was 6'7," while the shortest was but 5'1/2."

What I found to be quite profound about his research was that of the fifty men whose physical attributes were examined, twelve had black hair, eighteen brown, two "fair," two grey, fifteen "light" and one yellow" and that of this same grouping, thirty-five had complexions listed as "fair," four-teen "dark" and one "yellow." Our leader, William Campbell, was indeed somewhat of a "breed apart" at 6'6", with his red hair and fair complexion. He is, undoubtedly, a prime example of a man with a significant amount of Scots-Irish blood running through his veins!

COLONEL ISAAC SHELBY

As soon as Colonel Campbell retreated to his seat, the man next to him stood up and immediately extended his hand toward mine, announcing "I am Isaac Shelby, of Welsh heritage, 34 years of age and hail from Hagerstown, Fredrick County, Maryland. My parents immigrated to America from Tregaron, Wales in 1735. I was commissioned as a lieutenant in the Virginia militia and fought against both the Shawnee and Mingo Indians for Virginia's Royal Governor. When I completed that service, I worked briefly as a land surveyor until 1777, when Virginia Governor Patrick Henry appointed me Captain of a company, with my duty being to resist the British, forcibly if necessary."

"Furthermore, the understanding was that I would secure provisions for the army in frontier areas. I also served in similar roles in 1778 and 1779, when I pursued the gathering of provisions for the Continental Army. In 1779, I supported John Sevier's expedition against the Chickamauga Indians with my own money. The Chickamauga were a band of the Cherokee nation who were resisting a colonial presence on the western frontier. Until we had the Indians under control, lives would continue to be forfeited."

Shelby continued, "In 1779, Virginia Governor Thomas Jefferson promoted me to the rank of Major and directed me to lead several more expeditions to the west to establish a frontier border line between the colonies of Virgina and North Carolina. From the fall of Charleston on, I led forces against British attempts to control the South."

I recalled that soon thereafter Shelby became both a Colonel in the Sullivan County Regiment and in the same time frame a magistrate. I almost forgot that I would be related to Colonel Shelby through marriage within a few years, but I knew that passing that information on to him now would only cause a great deal of confusion, head shaking and questioning about how I could possibly know this.

Shelby's primary mission was to lead his assigned militia against the British. After hearing of the fall of Charlestown, he hurried to North Carolina at the request of my uncle, Charles McDowell. It was at that time that Shelby received orders to defend the borders of North Carolina against British intrusion.

Shelby proved he possessed superior battlefield skills when he led Patriot forces to a significant victory over the British on July 31st at Fort Thicketty, with the result that without a shot being fired, ninety-four enemy Loyalist prisoners were captured. From this point forward, Shelby was characterized by his peers as one of the finest militia leaders in the southern colonies.

At a subsequent battle near Cedar Springs, South Carolina, Shelby was once again triumphant. When he heard about the Patriot defeat at Camden and with the news that Cornwallis and Ferguson had joined forces to defeat him, he retreated over the Appalachian Mountains. Upon receiving a request from my Uncle Charles for military support, Shelby contacted John Sevier.

Between the two of them they were each able to raise a force of two hundred and forty men, to go along with a four-hundred-man force led by William Campbell of Washington County, Viginia. They were joined there at Sycamore Shoals, near present day Elizabethton, Tennessee, by my Uncle Charles, with one hundred sixty men from Burke and Rutherford Counties.

Shelby described to me how they then traveled over the Appalachian Mountains to McDowell's property at Quaker Meadows. Shelby continued, remarking that "At Quaker Meadows our overall military strength was improved when Colonel Cleveland and Major Winston arrived with three hundred -fifty-five men from Surrey and Wilkies Counties." He went on to state, quire firmly, that "When these troops joined our force we were in a position to go south to the border area to engage Fergusion."

I was aware that Shelby would join my McDowell relatives and a thousand others to "fight at a South Carolina terrain feature identified on maps as "Kings Mountain." At that locale Shelby would undoubtedly be a very familiar figure to his British counterpart, Major Patrick Fergusion, who had become a constant thorn in Shelby's side in previous military encounters.

In the past, Shelby had moved his troops in and around the South Carolina colony, leading up to September 1780. From my research I knew that for many years after the Battle of Kings Mountain it would be Shelby himself who would proclaim to anyone who would listen, "I led men at the Battle of Kings Mountain!"

I also knew full well that the bravery Shelby exhibited at Kings Mountain would earn him the deserved nickname "Old Kings Mountain," a title he would retain throughout the rest of his life. Once again, I kept this "future information" to myself.

COLONEL JOHN SEVIER

As Shelby sat down, I looked toward the gentleman next to him, who was in the process of rising. He took the few steps required to reach me and extended his right hand. In a very calm and eloquent voice (perfect for future politician) he looked me up and down, possibly with as hint of apprehension, and stated "I am John Sevier, born in Augusta County in the Virginia Colony of the Watauga Association in 1745.

I knew Sevier's family roots included French Huguenots. From my research, I knew he had been married twice, originally to one Sarah Hawkins when he was only seventeen years old. That marriage produced ten children, whereas his second marriage, to "Bonney Kate" Sherrill bore him eight more, for a total of eighteen. This number of children may have been a bit atypical for the times, but it wasn't at all unusual in the 1780's, when babies often died shortly after childbirth. I recalled that my McDowell grandfather had produced ten children, seven who lived, in the early 1900's, so even then childbirth was a dangerous event.

He continued, "I fought against the Cherokee and was chosen as a member of the Committee of Safety, which later became the Washington District." I implored of him, "Please tell me more." Sevier stated that on this date he was thirty-five years of age, the son of a tavern keeper, fur trader and land speculator who immigrated from England to Baltimore in 1740, before later moving south to the Shenandoah Valley in Virginia.

Shelby took special pride in one family member, his father, who founded the Virginia town of New Market. He continued to provide me with more background information about his exploits. Sevier reviewed details about the many trips he and his brother Valentine had made to colonial settlements on the trans-Appalachian border. I felt that Sevier could be classified, hundreds of years later, as the equivalent of a "Colonial GPS" for his extensive knowledge of terrain in the Carolinas.

Sevier continued, "In 1773, I moved farther south to the Carter Valley settlements along the Holston River and from there even further south to the Watauga Settlements." Sevier noted, with great regret, that the Royal Proclamation of 1736 forbade English settlement on lands west of the Appalachian Mountains where Indian tribes of the Cherokee Nation resided.

This Proclamation made it quite clear that anyone who attempted to settle in this area would do so in legal defiance of British authority and that the Watauga District was an example of colonial defiance against just such threats.

By this time, I now more clearly understood that the British were attempting to control the colonists by keeping them within arm's reach and, furthermore, that they would not hesitate to utilize their Indian allies on the western frontier to assist them in enforcing this mandate.

In 1776, the Committee of Safety, including Sevier, sought permission to settle these lands but was denied by British authorities in Virginia. In this same year, this refusal led the Wataugans to attempt this very same petitioning effort in the North Carolina colony. Successful with this second effort, the "District of Washington" was created, later to be identified as the current State of Tennessee. Sevier proudly boasted "I was appointed Lieutenant Colonial in the new Washington County Regiment of militia."

COLONEL BENJAMIN CLEVELAND

As the conversations were becoming less emphatic and with the introductions heading toward an end, a tall and quite rotund man, soon to be identified as Benjamin Cleveland, age thirty-four, got up to his feet and just missed stepping on the foot of the one other still unidentified gentleman. Cleveland spoke first, apparently attempting to gauge my reaction to the sum of all the previous introductions.

He informed me that he was of English and Irish descent, was born in Orange County, Virginia and eventually moved to Wilkes County, North Carolina at age thirty-one. Although he did not brag, I remembered that during my earlier research I had read an article authored by the American Battlefield Trust, which purported that at the onset of the Revolutionary War, Cleveland was the richest and most prominent citizen in Wilkes County.

In regard to his physical features, sources concluded that Cleveland stood around six feet tall, while tipping the scales at around three-hundred-thirty pounds, which earned him the nickname "Old Roundabout," Although Cleveland was considered tall in his time, he was still a good three inches shorter than me and I would guess at least twenty pounds heavier than noted in literature. I saw no reason at all to make mention I was cognizant of his "nickname." I did, however, make an internal note that "he surely earned that nickname based on what I could see."

Cleveland provided additional information about his military career, to include the period 17875-1777, when he served as an officer in the Surrey County militia. Now speaking in a somewhat more forceful voice, he noted he now serves as Colonel over the Wilkes County Militia. Cleveland made it clear to me that he was particularly proud of his earlier military service by pointing out that prior to Lord Cornwallis' invasion of South Carolina in 1780, he had fought along with the rebellious "Whig" forces who successfully resisted the British Loyalist forces. I knew the tactics he was describing to me would later be characterized as "guerilla warfare."

I saw Cleveland's eyes light up even brighter just a moment later when he unexpectedly shouted out "I am known as the Terror of the Torries!" I couldn't help but ask him what he was meant by this comment, to which he replied, "I showed our enemies little or no quarter and they deserved none!"

He completed his enthusiastic introduction by adding a second credit to his fame, "I led my Wilkes County men into battle and got my horse shot out from under me!" Upon hearing this remark, my Uncle Charles, as well as the others, looked toward Cleveland with raised eyebrows, with Charles quickly exhorting under his breath, "Enough Benjamin, we're here for several reasons, none of which includes hearing you brag about your military exploits."

MAJOR JOSEPH WINSTON

The final "distinguished gentleman" to introduce himself was Major Joseph Winston. Winston informed me that he had, like several of the others, been born in Virginia, in his particular instance in Louisa County and that he was related to Sarah Winston Henry, Patrick Henry's mother. Winston put forth that he was born on June 17, 1746. I calculated that he was now thirty-four years.

Hesitating for just a moment, Winston first sniffed, took a deep breath and then divulged that he had represented the Surrey Committee of Safety in 1776 when they voted to encourage the North Carolina Provincial Congress to vote for independence from the British. Furthermore, for what must have been a short period of time, he worked as a register of deeds for his home county, where he became well known for his close friendship with the local Moravian community.

Winston proudly reported that at the Hillsborough Congress in 1775, he was appointed as a Major in the Surrey County militia. After having listened to the other gentlemen introduce themselves, in what appeared to be a rare moment of candor, Winston surprised me when he somewhat dramatically inferred there was a personal connection between us. "This, he said, is based upon the fact that each of us serve our country at the rank of Major."

I wasted no time in getting Winston's "message," so I instantly engaged in close contact with his eyes. He once again offered his right hand, this time for a second shake, which this time around was like putting my hand into a mechanic's vice.

It was so strong, this joining of digits, that I instantly calculated that most men would have done anything they could to avoid such a manly grappling. The two of us, Joseph Winston and David McDowell, mutually agreed that we were "brothers in arms," which was quite miraculous since we two men were from different centuries.

The mass of men would gather next at Quaker Meadows....

CHAPTER 7

THE MEETING

My cousin Joseph advised me that earlier, before our "departure" from my South Carolina home, that Isaac Shelby, John Sevier, William Campbell and Uncle Charles had mustered their men together at Sycamore Shoals (current Eastern Tennessee) on their way to crossing the Blue Ridge Mountains to arrive at "Fort McDowell." Shelby and Sevier had each brought with them two hundred forty men, Campbell four hundred and his uncle Charles one hundred sixty men.

I was also aware that on this same date, September 30th, that Benjamin Cleveland and Joseph Winston had arrived with a militia force of three hundred and fifty men. Calculating these numbers in my head, I came up with a total of one thousand three hundred and ninety militiamen on hand to go south as representatives of the Patriot Army.

I surmised that many of these men had left their homes, farms, wives and children fully recognizing they might never see them again. I remembered the many times I had experienced this same apprehension about being "deployed" during my own military career, noting to myself that some things never change in the life of a soldier.

Over a thousand militiamen and their horses were now bivouacked in the verdant meadow laying directly below Fort McDowell. I was quick to note that this group of militiamen did not look like any traditional army I had ever seen, for they were seriously short of logistical support in the form of wagons, cannons or even tents.

With no barracks for them to sleep in, they would be sleeping out in the open in the meadow, in my mind leaving them uncomfortable with this season's chilly weather. I estimated the temperature would get down to about thirty-two degrees Fahrenheit in the early morning here in the hills of the Piedmont region of North Carolina. I was shocked that these very militiamen, who would through direct rebellion sever colonial American ties with the British, could function independently, for they provided their own horses weapons, gunpowder and bullets. The great majority of the men were attired in clothing very similar to that worn by their leaders, a linen hunting shirt, buckskin breeches, moccasins and a wool hat, usually broad rimmed.

It was impossible for me to personally count all the one thousand plus militiamen spread across the vast expanse of McDowell property here at Quaker Meadows, however it was abundantly clear to me that not even one Continental Army soldier was present, for I couldn't see even one dressed in the official Continental

Army-produced uniform. I was aware there were several marked differences between the Continental soldier and the militiaman who were present here.

A significant difference between the two involved times of conscription (length of the time they agreed to be under arms) and training. Combatants recruited by the Continental Congress were prepared to serve for longer periods of time and were furnished with both uniforms and weapons.

As a result of good organization, Continental Army soldiers were well trained in for the traditional form of open field warfare popular on the European continent. In general, they were thought to be highly organized and responsive to their higher-ranking officers.

Militiamen, on the other hand, anticipated service for short periods of time. These shorter intervals of service allowed them to address the need for them to return home to care for their crops, animals, and for other personal needs. There were about thirty-five thousand settlers living in the "backcountry" at this time, which equaled about seventy-five percent of the white population. These settlers lived a significant number of miles inland from the coastal markets, which resulted in them obtaining their sustenance from the livestock they raised on their farms of two-hundred acres or less. What they would consume daily was largely determined by how much livestock they had on hand and their hunting and fishing skills.

There was no uniform required for the militiamen who had gathered before me, they wore whatever they could produce for themselves. In contrast and regarding battlefield "etiquette," these militiamen found great success in rough or forested terrain, where a great marksmen could use their skills to duck and hide behind trees while shooting at their enemy from a distance.

From my personal observations to date, there would undoubtedly be trouble if these militiamen, who lacked adequate training in open (European style) combat, were ever forced into that position without additional training.

Uncle Charles stood up and directed me to a spot about twenty yards away from where the other six were six were previously engaged in some very "colorful" conversation about battle plans and strategies they would implement to locate Fergusion and his troops. My uncle made it quite clear to me that any other McDowell family member I might meet on this journey would only know me as a visiting relative, a Major in the Burke's County Regiment. Uncle Charles added that the only exception other than himself to the truth was his brother, my cousin Joseph.

Most of these men who lived on the frontier had for years ignored the conflict going on between the Mother Country and the colonies to the north, but now it was in their backyard. The South Carolina colony had ignited controversary in the Spring of 1778 when the Provincial Congress passed a law requiring men over the age of sixteen to swear allegiance to South Carolina or forfeit many of their rights. If a man were to flee the state to avoid the allegiance pledge and were to then return, they were subject to the death penalty.

While Cousin Joseph, Colonels Campbell, Shelby, Sevier, Cleveland and Major Winston continued talking, Uncle Charles and I were far enough way to be out of earshot of their conversations. Now standing about twenty yards away from the oak tree, with my hearing now more fine-tuned, I could clearly hear these militia leaders speaking

51

about what must have been the first hint of dissent about who would command the militia army in pursuit of Ferguson.

I was able to discern that while there was no outright refusal to serve under Uncle Charles, they were using words and terms like "he's too old, he's just not a good battle leader" and "he's a better organizer than a fighter." In relation to the "too old" comment, I wanted to interject "he's only two years older than Colonel Sevier," but I kept my comments to myself. I felt a palpable negative climate beginning to establish itself, one I was not eager to endure.

It now occurred to me that it was right here, under the Council Oak, that the first seeds of discontent began to grow in relation to eliminating the man who would, under normal circumstances, be the obvious choice to assume the overall mantle of leadership at Kings Mountain. This was somewhat puzzling to me since my Uncle Charles was the most experienced leader among them; truly an experienced officer who routinely fought against the British and Loyalists in this specific geographical area.

History books claim that the decision-making process about who would be the commanding officer for the Overmountain Men came up for the first time on October 2nd, when they spent their second day in a row encamped in a gap of the South Mountain. I wondered why history had brushed this command issue aside without any further discussion. I now assumed it to be my mission to further investigate the truth about how my uncle was passed over for command of the Overmountain Men.

I was acutely aware, because of my purposeful eavesdropping on the men under the Council Oak tree, that my Uncle Charles was the subject of interest as soon as they arrived at Quaker Meadows.

Colonel Shelby seemed to be the member of the group most concerned about who would lead. I came to the conclusion that each of these complex men, Campbell, Shelby, Sevier, Cleveland, Winston and my even my cousin Joseph, had very high opinions of themselves.

However, not desiring to "stir the pot" any more than what was already in motion, I moved away from the Council Oak and out into the fields where the militiamen were going about their duties in preparing for the march south. Taking into consideration what the textbooks had to say about the leadership decision made on "October 2nd," I endeavored not to tell my uncle about any of the conversations I now had knowledge of.

I was fascinated by all the hustle and bustle, what some might call "organized chaos," going on around me at Quaker Meadows, with many in the great force of the militiamen in the great expanse of meadow engaged in enthusiastic, highly animated conversations. These militiamen showed remarkable energy, especially after trekking over twenty miles from North Cove to Quaker Meadows.

I was very proud to see my McDowell family members make every possible effort to be gracious, welcoming hosts to the thousand plus Overmountain men. Cousin Joseph displayed his individual hospitality when he offered up the dry rail fencing on the property for the Overmountain Men's bonfires. He was circulating among the men in his regiment and shortly thereafter initiated a conversation with a man later known to me as Captain Edmund Fears, one of his regimental company commanders. "Edmund, is all well with you and your men? Have they had their fill of my beeves and the sweet water in our spring here at Quaker Meadows?" Captain Fears looked up at Cousin Joseph and in an obviously respectful voice replied, "Yes sir, we are well fed and prepared to move out upon your command."

With the sun setting, I personally experienced the outside temperature here in western North Carolina wherein late September/ early October 1780, I imagined it often dropped to thirty-two degrees Fahrenheit in the early morning hours. It was obvious to me that the warmer temperatures I'd become exposed to in winter 2023, a result of climate-change, were not a factor in the weather for this day in the late 1700's.

Both Uncle Charles and Cousin Joseph made sure the Overmountain Men and all others assembled had every convenience possible at their disposal, to include offering them food stocks collected from their plentiful harvest this year. As an example of their hospitality, I could see an unidentified man, who by sight obviously had very huge forearms and biceps, walking around from campfire to campfire, offering up his services as a blacksmith. At the same time, a willowy looking woman dressed in austere clothing, almost Quaker-like, accompanied him as he made his rounds, passing out blankets to those militiamen who appeared to have none.

Clearly placing myself at least thirty yards from where these conversations among the Overmountain Men were taking place, I was now blessed with a hearing capability that far exceeded any norm. I then walked another ten yards away and could hear these buckskin-clad militiamen speaking as if they were standing right beside me. The add-on to this condition was that I could turn on my new "super hearing" whenever I wanted, by merely focusing on a voice or voices in my immediate presence. I assumed that any further application of this gift would remain unknown to me until some later date.

I continued to be impressed by these patriots, who were the first "foragers" in our country's military history; for they could survive off the land without receiving logistical support from a higher-level organization. Contemplating back upon my own past military experience, I walked up to one such militiaman, who looked to be middle aged, while he was securing the saddlebags on his horse.

I asked him, "Please sir, can you tell me, do you get enough support to successfully fight against the British Army and Loyalist forces?" The answer he gave to me was remarkably simple, "We have what we need, but we do sometimes ask for more supplies of gunpowder. We all know what we're here for, to get those damn British out of our country!"

I couldn't move on without asking what this young man's name was, to which he replied "I sir am James Rogers, I'm thirty-four years of age and I was born in Lynchburg Ferry, Virginia. Since June of this year, I've served in Colonel McDowell's Burke County Regiment!" Thinking about this, I realized that as a man of thirty-four years of age, Rogers could be considered by many people to be close to "old." With this thought in mind, I was indeed happy to now be twenty-five years of age, one-half my real 21st Century age of fifty.

Pondering my current situation for a few seconds, I decided I would no longer waste time attempting to figure out how or why I had been plucked out of the forest behind my house in 2023. With determination, I turned my attention to my surroundings while my

McDowell relatives prepared for the upcoming battle that I knew would take place at King's Mountain.

There would no more internal discussion about what I knew about the battle from history books, I would transform my very existence into a "blank slate" on which to write what I would hopefully soon see, hear, smell and personally experience, if that was possible.

Unaware of my eventual role in this adventure, I would have to be very careful whenever I conversed with anyone, lest they come to portray me as anything other than a fellow 18th Century militiaman....

CHAPTER 8

WHIGS VS TORIES/LOYALISTS

Here I experienced a conundrum or sorts, for I wondered if I had addressed to you a understanding of the terms "Whigs," "Tories," or" Loyalist." Captain Thomas Patton, a Company Commander in the Burke County Regiment, cleared this up for me earlier when he related the term "Patriot" refers to a person who "loves, honors and defends their country." His reference to "their country" pertains to a country independent from Great Britain.

Furthermore, that Southerners like him, who supported independence, were called "Whigs." With a stern look on his face, Patton stated that both "Tories" and "Loyalists" opposed independence and avidly supported both their supreme monarch, King George III and the Anglican Church of England. The Whigs felt that it was "retribution from high above" that the Tories/Loyalists needed to suffer for not supporting independence from the British government.

Most of these men present had lived on the frontier for years and while doing so ignored the conflict going on between their Mother Country and the colonies to the north. Now that it was in their own "backyard," they felt quite differently. Dissent in the South Carolina colony ignited in the Spring of 1778 when the Provincial Congress passed a law requiring all men over the age of 16 to swear allegiance to King George III or forfeit many of their rights.

For example, if a man were to flee the state to avoid the allegiance pledge and were to then return, they were subject to the death penalty. Legal struggles with the ruling British became increasingly common. Most locals believed they faced discrimination, with some describing British rule as outright "tyranny."

In addition to enacting legally punitive laws, British officials directed both British regulars and their Tory/Loyalist counterparts to perpetrate atrocities in South Carolina, western North Carolina, Southwest Virginia and the Overmountain area which would later become the State of Tennessee. Some historians would later compare these actions to those of Attila the Hun. Cruelty on the part of the invading British forces would become commonplace, for they could not remotely fathom the idea that the colonists would want self-rule.

The British encouraged their own Cherokee Indian allies to conduct surprise attacks along the frontier to promote fear. These same Indians went on to commit unspeakable massacres, at which they scalped and killed both women and children. With this "barbarity" in mind, it is likewise note-worthy to point out that there were several

British officers who became infamous for the gross lack of humanity they displayed.

The person most often described as "the most hated British officer" was Lieutenant Colonel Banastre Tarleton, who served under General Cornwallis in the Carolinas. It is written that Lieutenant Colonel Tarleton did his very best to terrorize Patriot families in South Carolina. Loosely controlled by Cornwallis, his superior officer, Tarleton went about committing atrocities against the Scots-Irish population in the state, to include exhuming the grave of respected Whig Brigadier General Richard Richardson. Adding insult to injury, after the exhumation, Tarleton directed his troops to herd Richardson's cattle, swine and poultry into barns, which he then had set on fire.

Tarleton's increasingly erratic, inhuman behavior was vividly exhibited after engaging in combat with Patriot troops, when he not only failed to give quarter, but instead gave the order for them to be slaughtered for merely resisting him on the battlefield. This behavior earned him the inauspicious title of "Bloody Ban." Tarleton's reputation for being evil would spread far and wide, with the result that when Patriot troops came upon captured British and Tory troops they would shout "Remember Tarleton's Quarter."

Sadly, in war and in the presence of killing, even a good man's conscience could find itself falling prey to a disappearing act, with equally aggressive behavior being exhibited on the part of militia forces. As I made my way through the sea of militiamen, I could hear many of them expressing violent thoughts about the sane people who had just a few years ago been their friends and neighbors, whom they now held in the highest possible disregard.

In the same timeframe, in the same month as the meeting at Quaker Meadows, another British officer, Major James Weymess, would, along with his Tory counterparts, wreak havoc in an area seventy miles long and fifteen miles wide along the Black River, Lynches Creek and the Pee Dee River. Weymess would earn the title "The Second Most Hated British Officer" (one spot behind Tarleton) for attacking Whig homesteads, robbing them of their valuable personal items, stealing their horses, burning their churches and randomly hanging anyone he suspected to be a "rebel."

The extremely aggressive behavior served up by both Tarleton and Weymess did not obtain the result either of them had hoped for, in fact, the settlers in the Carolinas became even more resistant to British rule. **Two events in particular....**

CHAPTER 9

TWO EVENTS

Two events that shaped the Patriot mindset against British rule immediately came to my mind. The first occurred with McDowells in North Carolina, the second to our McDowell relatives in Mecklenburg County, South Carolina. Uncle Charles provided a context for me.

"Of course, he said, "I have many reasons to dislike British rule. The crown has sought to deny us personal freedom to settle where we want and then to tax us unfairly. Moreover, in the months before our meeting here at Quaker Meadows, soldiers serving under Ferguson's command came here to Quaker Meadows when my brother Joseph and I were away. These brigands ransacked my house and stole clothing that belonged to Joseph and me."

"While the soldiers were doing their best to give me personal insult by their actions, they were confronted by my mother, Margaret O'Neill

McDowell, fifty-seven years of age. To intimidate her, they reminded her that "if we catch Charles, we would kill him outright. "When this threat did not seem to intimidate her in the slightest, they tried a second time by stating "We will kill Joe on bended knees after humiliating him by making him beg for his life." Hearing these words, this Irish mother, in most disrespectful terms, then countered "You had best be careful lest you British do all the begging."

Uncle Charles was obviously quite proud of his mother, who was the daughter of Laird Samuel O'Neill of Tyrone, County Antrim in Northern Ireland. She was raised at Shane Castle and was an ancestor of Irish kings. She had left Ireland with Joseph, a weaver by trade, not of her aristocratic social class or religion (she Catholic, he Presbyterian) to move to the American colonies.

Regarding her personality, Uncle Charles said his mother was characterized as a "striking, intelligent, articulate woman with a tendency to speak her mind born of a deep-rooted hatred of the English." This dislike for the English likely resulted from her Irish father's imprisonment by the King, which included the confiscation of his land. Uncle Charles' reminiscence reminded me that his mother was such a strong advocate for the rebellion in the colonies that she would later be recognized by the Daughters of the American Revolution as an American Patriot.

I was proud to be related to such an outstanding, patriotic American woman. Hearing this tale about her made it clear to me that why, two hundred and forty years later, that Irish stubbornness was still carried on in fourteen percent of my DNA.

In this same timeframe, the issue of family loyalty and who would serve the Patriot cause, or support the King of England, was plainly displayed in the South Carolina colony in September of 1780, when foraging British troops under the command of a British Captain, went to the Steele Creek settlement in southwestern Mecklenburg County, to what they anticipated would be a Patriot plantation. The major crops were wheat, cotton and corn. The events that took place there emphasize that it wasn't unusual at all for one McDowell family member in America to be pitted against another.

The intent of the British soldiers at this plantation was to steal whatever they wanted and could carry away. Shortly after their arrival, they were unexpectedly approached by a woman who identified herself as Mrs. Jean McDowell, wife of the property owner. She proceeded to approach one of the officers on foot and looked up at him on his horse, where she could see the epaulettes of officer rank on his shoulders.

She appealed of him "And have you no women and children at home?" Surprised by the woman's boldness, he asked of her "What is your... name?" Proudly, she replied "McDowell, that is my name. Where are you from? Our family came from Scotland, sir." Without any hesitation, he responded, "I am Captain McDowell and very likely ye are kin of mine; I have some in America" he reported to her.

He then shouted out to his men, advising them they had taken enough from this property. Captain McDowell then glanced down toward Jean McDowell and proceeded to utter his final words, "And likely you have some of your family among the rebels, but that is the fortune of war." Captain McDowell and his men then rode away, most likely back to Cornwallis' headquarters at the home of Thomas Polk in Charlotte Town.

Matters were not getting any better....

Chapter 10

The Seeds of Discontent

Setting aside the topic of family relationships and warfare behavior for a moment, I turned toward Uncle Charles, who had been listening to my comments about events happening up to this date. He reminded me that he did not himself have any first-hand knowledge as to what took place at Kings Mountain, but only actions thereafter, such as his journey to Hillsborough to see General Gates.

Now aware of my place in this time, it was not at all difficult for me to assume that my presence during these events occurring in the fall of 1780 could be of eye-opening historical significance.

While Cousin Joseph, Colonels Campbell, Shelby, Sevier, Cleveland and Major Winston continued talking, Uncle Charles and I were far enough away to be out of earshot of their voices. For myself, now standing about twenty yards away from the oak tree, with my hearing now more fully focused,

I could clearly hear these militia leaders conversing about what I initially believed were some of the first expressions of concern about my Uncle Charles' leadership abilities. Like a rock striking me on the head, it now became obvious to me that I was poorly informed by historical summaries about the actual decision-making process, for the truth would soon come out.

I recalled that while there was no outright refusal from any of them to serve under Charles McDowell, their voices used words and terms like "he's too old" (Sevier). "He's not a good battle leader" and "He's better at organizing than fighting" (Shelby).

In familial defense of my Uncle Charles, I desperately wanted to walk up to them while they were sitting under the Council Oak and interject into their mistrustful conversation "He's only two years older than you, Colonel Sevier." Instead, I kept my mouth shut, barely, and kept these comments to myself. I could feel a palpable, undoubtedly negative momentum moving toward their eventual rejection of my Uncle Charles as commanding officer for the multi-state force aligned against Major Patrick Ferguson.

Following normal leadership protocol, my Uncle Charles would have been named as commander of the entire force. However, from my eavesdropping on the conversations of the Colonels themselves, it appears that the dye had already been cast by his fellow compatriot Colonels. Listening in again. I heard Colonel Shelby remark, with distinct disregard, "Colonel Hampton says that after Earles Ford, where his son Noah died, he felt that McDowell was unequal to the job of leadership."

Shelby continued "From my perspective, at Cane Creek, McDowell showed himself to be an ineffective leader, one who failed to take advantage of our position." Colonel Shelby could now be identified as a major stumbling block regarding Colonel McDowell's ascendence to command of the Patriot militia army. Almost instantaneously, the "piling on" continued, with Sevier quickly noting that although he was not present at either the event on the Pacolet River or Cane Creek, concerns about McDowell's leadership had been expressed to him, often, on a second- hand basis.

It was Shelby who once again took the lead in the group discussion as he chimed in "You all know McDowell takes for granted that as the senior Colonel he expects to be in charge." If not already making his position on McDowell clear, he added "Let's hope that as we continue to alternate command that on the day of battle it will not be McDowell's day!" Campbell, the more innocent (my opinion) of the participants in the discussion, offered his own question "Isn't it his prerogative as the senior officer?

I wondered if these Colonels had forgotten about all the successful military ventures my uncle had participated in across both sides of the Carolina's borders, against the Indians and the British? I wondered why history books had so often brushed aside this information without any further discussion.

Numerous history books I'd read asserted that the decision-making process about who would be the commanding officer only came up as topic of discussion on October 2nd, when they spent their second day in a row encamped in a gap of the South Mountain at Bedford Hill. It would become my personal mission to further investigate the truth about how my uncle was passed over for command of the Patriot army.

I was acutely aware, because of my purposeful eavesdropping on the men under the Council Oak tree, that my Uncle Charles was the subject of interest as soon as they arrived at Quaker Meadows. Colonel Isaac Shelby seemed to be the member of the group most concerned about who would lead. By now I had concluded that each of them, Campbell, Shelby, Sevier, Cleveland, Winston and even Cousin Joseph, had very high opinions of themselves. I was most concerned that at no time did I hear my cousin, Joseph, defend his brother, Charles.

Not wanting to "stir the pot" any more than was already in motion, I moved away from the Council Oak and walked out into the fields, where militiamen were going about their duties in preparing for the march south. Taking into consideration what the textbooks said about the leadership decision made on "October 2nd," I endeavored not to tell my uncle about any of the conversations his leadership peers had engaged in.

It was time to view the "organized chaos" in the meadow...

CHAPTER 11

THE MEADOW

I was fascinated by all the hustle and bustle in progress in the meadow, what some might call "organized chaos." Here at Quaker Meadows was this great mass of humanity, all engaged in very enthusiastic, highly animated conversations amongst themselves. It was beyond me how these militiamen could possess an energy level so high it likely surpassed any I had ever encountered with my own soldiers prior to deployment.

How was it possible they could be this energetic and happy-go-lucky after just completing a twenty mile plus trek over the mountains from North Cove to meet up here at Quaker Meadows?

I was very proud to see my McDowell family members make every possible effort to be gracious, welcoming hosts to the thousand plus Overmountain men. Cousin Joseph displayed his own individual hospitality when he offered up the dry rail fencing on the property to the Overmountain Men's bonfires. Joseph was circulating among the men in his regiment and initiated a conversation with a man later to be known to me as Captain Edmund Fears, one of his regimental company commanders.

Joseph asked of Captain Fears, "Is all well with you and your men? Have they had their fill of my beeves and the sweet water in our spring here at Quaker Meadows? Captain Fears looked up at Cousin Joseph and in an obviously respectful tone, replying "Yes sir, we are well fed and prepared to move out upon your command."

With the sun setting, I personally experienced the outside temperature here in western North Carolina in the fall of 1780. I imagined it often dropped to thirty-two degrees Fahrenheit in the early morning hours. It was obvious to me that the warmer temperatures I'd become used to in my time were influenced by climate change, which was not a factor in the weather for this day in the late 1700's. Both Uncle Charles and Cousin Joseph made sure all the Overmountain Men had every convenience possible at their disposal, to include offering them food stocks collected from their plentiful harvest collected this year.

As an example of their hospitality, I could see an unidentified man, who by sight obviously had very huge forearms and biceps, most likely a blacksmith, walking around from campfire to campfire, providing services as a blacksmith. At the same time, a willowy looking woman dressed in austere clothing, almost Quaker-like, accompanied him as he made his rounds, passing out blankets to those militiamen who appeared to have none.

Clearly placing myself at least thirty yards from where these conversations among the Overmountain Men were taking place, I was now blessed with a hearing capability that far exceeded any norm. I walked another ten yards away and could still hear the buckskin clad militiamen speaking as if they were standing right beside me.

The advantage of this condition was that I could turn off my newly improved hearing whenever I wanted, I merely had to focus on a voice or voices in my general proximity. I assumed that any further application of this gift would remain unknown to me until some later date.

I continued to be impressed by these Patriots, who were the first "forgers" in our country's military history; for they could survive off the land without receiving logistical support from a higher-level organization. Thinking back to my own past military experience, I walked up to a militiaman, who looked like he was middle aged, while he was securing his saddlebags on a roan-colored horse.

I asked him, "Please sir, can you tell me, do you get enough support to fight successfully against Fergusion? His reply to me was remarkably simple, "We have what we need, but we do sometimes ask for more supplies of gunpowder. We all know what we're here for, to get those damn British out of our country!" I had almost forgotten that it was a well-kept secret that my Uncle Charles produced gunpowder of his own in a nearby "hidden cave."

I couldn't move on without asking what this young man's name was, to which he replied "I Sir am James Rogers, I'm thirty-four years of age and I was born in Lynchburg Ferry, Virginia. Since June of this year, I've served in Colonel McDowell's Burke County Regiment!"

Thinking about this, I realized that as a man of thirty-four years of age, Rogers could be considered by many people of his time to be "old." With this thought in mind, I was now indeed happy to be twenty-five years of age, one-half my real 21st Century age of fifty.

Pondering my current situation for a few seconds, I decided I would no longer waste any of my time attempting to figure out how or why I had been plucked out of the forest behind my South Carolina home in 2023. Determinedly, I would now focus on what was going on around me as my McDowell relatives made ready to fight at what I knew would be King's Mountain.

There would no more internal discussion about what I knew about events leading up to the battle from history books; I would transform my very existence into a "blank slate," one on which to write what I would hopefully soon see, hear, smell and personally experience.

Unaware of my eventual role in this endeavor into the past, I readily acknowledged that I would have to be very careful whenever I conversed with anyone, lest they come to portray me as anything other than a fellow 18th Century militiaman.

I was interested in knowing more about the history of the McDowell's property…

CHAPTER 12

A CRY FOR HELP

At some point during the many confrontations with the Cherokee Indians, Uncle Charles sent a letter to General Griffith Rutherford, Commanding Officer of the Salisbury District. In it he requested military support. Rutherford and his militia were encamped at Salisbury with two hundred sixty men. I thought for a minute about what I knew about this General. I recalled he had been born in Ireland about 1731 and later traveled with his parents, of Scottish and Welsh heritage, to America by ship in 1739.

Tragically, both of his parents either died during the long voyage or shortly thereafter. Rutherford was later adopted by a German couple, whose identify has not been disclosed. John added, "He was not a tall man, only five feet five inches, but in good physical condition at one hundred-eighty pounds."

Obviously not one to dwell on his earlier misfortune, Rutherford was eventually appointed to the rank of Brigadier General in 1776 and he went on to represent the Salisbury District in North Carolina. John went on to tell me that there was a lot of activity on at the western frontier while Colonel McDowell was waiting for a reply from Rutherford. As a safety precaution, McDowell sent Robert Penland, a pastor in the communities Presbyterian Church, to contact as many settlers in the area as possible to encourage them to seek refuge at the fort.

This was Fort McDowell. Ignoring McDowell's plea, even Penland's mother-in-law refused to relocate to the fort, with the result that both she and one of her guests were scalped by the Indians. Hearing this, I put on hand on my now fully restored head of hair and thought to myself, "At twenty-five, or at any age, I definitely didn't want anyone lifting the hair from my head with any sharp object."

According to Cousin John, "Five to six hundred Cherokee Indians attacked the fort at Quaker Meadows. It only lasted one day, but there were significant casualties. We killed one hundred fifty to two hundred Indians but lost fifty to sixty of our white settlers that same day." General Rutherford and his troops did not arrive at Quaker Meadows in time to stay the siege. In the back of my mind, I recalled that historian William F. Brown III had done extensive research into what was the most accurate designation for the gathering place of the Over the Mountain Men in late September 1780.

Brown's review of pension records in the Colonial Records of North Carolina, Vol. X. concluded that the defensive position near Morganton was most accurately described as "Quaker Meadows Fort" and that the term "McDowell's Station" was very likely not used in colonial times. I was quite impressed that in a summary of his research Brown was able to include a letter from General Rutherford to the North Carolina Council of Safety about the 1776 siege of the fort, noting his inability to offer aide. Rutherford's letter, in his own words and spelling, reads as follows:

July ye 14th, 1776

Honorable Gentlemen,

I am Under the Nessety of sending you by Express, the Allerming Condition, this Contry is in, the Indins is making Grate prograce, in Distroying & Murdering, in the frunteers of this County, 37 I Iam informed was killed last Wednesday & Thursday, on the Cuttaba River. I am also informed that Colo McDowell 10 men more 120 women & Children is Beshaged, in sume kind of fort, & the Indins Round them, no help to them before yesterday, & they were surrounded on Wednesday. I Expect the Nex account to here, that they are all Distroyed. Colo Blackmans is the frunter of this County, pray Gentlemen Consider oure Distress, send us Plenty of Powder & I Hope unde God, we of Salsbury District is able to stand them, but, if you allows us to Go to the Nation, I Expect, you Will order Hillsborough District, to Joyn Salisbury, three of ouer Captans is kiled & one Wounded. This Day I set out with what men I Can Raise for the Relefe of the Distrest.

I am Gentlemen in hast, Youre Humble sert

———————————————

GRIFFITH RUTHERFORD

Once Rutherford did reach Quaker Meadows Fort, they rounded up and killed as many Indians as they could. General Rutherford then pledged to march through western North Carolina and into the Smoky Mountains to eliminate the Cherokee threat once and for all. Two thousand five hundred strong, this became known as The Cherokee

Expedition of 1776, during which time they burned to the ground thirty-six to forty Indian villages.

Both Uncle Charles and Cousin Joseph accompanied Rutherford on the expedition. Reports indicated that "Rutherford's venture did not totally eliminate the threat to white settlers on the frontier and Cherokee raids continued for several more years."

I asked a nearby militiaman if there were other forts near Quaker Meadows. He replied "Of course, many of us settlers need protection, which is why similar places of refuge can be found at Samuel Davidson's Fort at Old Fort, James Edmiston's Fort west of Old Fort, Wofford's Fort at Turkey Cove, Cathy's Fort at Pleasant Garden, White's Fort on John's River, and Fort Grider and Fort Defiance near Lenoir."

A man standing nearby, who by the look of him had possibly just joined McDowell's militiamen, blurted out "Quaker Meadows Fort is located here on the bottom lands of the Catawba River." I thought back to my previous trips to the Morganton area to pinpoint the location of the original McDowell homestead. The information I had read placed the location of the 1780 house to the far-right end of the current day strip mall. I wondered what "current day" meant anymore; did it mean in the year 1780, or some-time in the 21st Century?

I looked around and could see that a man sitting nearby had been eavesdropping on our conversation. I asked him if his last name was McDowell, to which he answered, "No sir, my name be Enoch Berry and I am a proud member of the Burke County Militia." Upon listening to this decidedly short introduction, I formally recognized Enoch as part of our brotherhood in arms, so I bid him a friendly farewell.

Now on our feet, it was on to "Quaker Meadows Fort"…

CHAPTER 13

THE NEED FOR REFUGE

Uncle Charles and Cousin Joseph were again plotting strategy with the others under the Council Oak, so I decided I would take a personal tour of the immediate area around Fort McDowell. I was fortunate enough in this instance to find another similarly clothed colonial soldier sitting a few feet away, astride a tree stump. Walking up to him and extending my right hand, I found myself in a temporary state of disbelief as I gazed into the eyes of what appeared to be yet another McDowell.

My "guess" quickly became a reality when this solider looked up, got to his feet from the tree stump and presented himself. "Welcome, Major McDowell, or should I say, Major Davy McDowell. I am your cousin, Captain John McDowell. I serve under both your uncle Charles and his brother Joseph, who are my older brothers. I moved here from

Virginia in 1765 and own six hundred forty acres, located on both sides of Silver Creek.

"If the opportunity presents itself Cousin, I'd like you to meet my wife, Hannah, who is from Virginia. I also believe that somewhere around here we might be able to find our adopted brother, Henry Highland, who we call "Harry." He is an Ensign in our Burke County Militia. If you'd like to see our little gathering place here on God's good earth more clearly, it would be my pleasure to show you around." I returned John's robust grip, followed by my words "Lead on, Cousin."

These four words exchanged, as we began walking, I realized that John's words brought one crucial fact to mind; it was quite apparent that all the McDowell men here at Quaker Meadows were at least aware of my reason for being here at Quaker Meadow, to fight alongside them against the British. It was equally apparent that aside from my uncle Charles and cousin Joseph, no one else understood the true circumstances surrounding my arrival.

Forsaking all other thoughts, I was now feeling more "revolutionary" than ever before. There was one unexpected "small" issue I was going to have to deal with, for at six feet six inches in height I was at least six inches taller than about ninety-five percent of the thousand plus militiamen assembled here at Quaker Meadows. I worked hard not to tip my hand as to where I really got my height from (a six foot four inch father and a five foot nine inch mother).

Being tall really me made me stand out in a crowd so, of course, I became the subject of many repeated innocent inquiries such as "How did you get so tall?" I figured I would humorously deal with this issue, so I would consistently reply "I had tall very tall parents." As the days went by, their curious stares no longer concerned me.

Cousin John initiated his unofficial briefing to me by passing on background information about how Fort McDowell came to be in the first place. He began by relating that, by the summer of 1776, white settlers established small settlements at the top of the Blue Ridge and that their peace on the cusp of the frontier did not last long at all, for one specific reason. John provided further clarification while we continued to walk through the fields of hot lips turtlehead and fall swamp sunflowers.

DRAGGIN CANOE

Cousin John continued "Their somewhat idyllic existence was shattered when Cherokee Chief Tsugunsin, known to settlers as "Draggin Canoe," proclaimed his fervent opposition to whites relocating on his tribal lands, promising that their blood would flow for their intrusion. He was born circa 1738 near present-day Chattanooga, Tennessee to Cherokee chief Attakullakulla. When he was a young, inexperienced warrior, his father first denied his request to fight against their enemies, the Shawnee.

Undeterred, Tsugunsin hid under a canoe, with the intent to join his fellow warriors in battle. The Cherokee warriors discovered him there and alerted his father, the Chief, who told Tsugunsin he could join the war party only if he could carry his canoe. Finding the canoe too heavy, the young boy began dragging it, thus earning him the nickname "Draggin Canoe."

He provided Davy with more insight when he reported that back in 1775, Draggin Canoe told Daniel Boone, famous in his own right, "You have bought a fair land but there is a cloud hanging over it, you will find its settlements dark and bloody." Draggin Canoe did his best to live up to his words of warning by continually making the lives of the white settlers on the western frontier thoroughly miserable by directing one Indian attack after another.

Their conversation became even more interesting as John and I reviewed the events that took place after Lord Cornwallis' capture of Charles Town in June of 1776. It was at this time that the British gave the Cherokee Indians tacit approval to harass the colonists. Draggin Canoe acted promptly by directing his great horde of Indian tribesmen to leave the Smokies and conduct raids on settlements all along the western frontier. These white settlers, most of Scots-Irish stock, had little or no choice but to build and then take refuge in forts along the frontier. John hesitated for a minute as a man walked by behind him.

While I was not paying attention to this individual, John suddenly raised his voice and proclaimed "Here is yet another McDowell seeking safety here at Fort McDowell. This is our cousin, Captain Joseph "Pleasant Gardens" McDowell. He brought his family members here from his own plantation after Indian raiding parties abducted and killed many women and children back home in his community."

Now becoming used to meeting even more McDowell's, I again extended my right hand and offered "Nice to meet you Cousin Joseph, I hear everyone calls you Joe "PG" McDowell," to which he replied "That's right, we wouldn't want to confuse me with my cousin, Joe "QM" McDowell. Dave knew that "PG" stood for "Pleasant Gardens" and "QM" stood for Quaker Meadows. I remembered that it was this same man, Joseph "PG" McDowell, who would become a highly controversial figure in the annals of McDowell family history due to his actions after the Battle of Kings Mountain. I imagined I would be exploring this matter later; there was no way it could be forgotten.

With further Indian attacks surely coming, and fearing for the lives of his family members, my new cousin Joe "PG" made it clear he believed his family would be much safer here at McDowell's Fort than back on his plantation. In quite a forceful voice, he interjected, "It is my intent to ride with my fellow Burke County militiamen to defeat those damn Loyalists."

Now, yet another McDowell relative had been introduced to me. I did not like to appear either impolite or confused myself and I wondered if I would ever be able to remember the names of all the McDowell's I'd already met, or were to yet meet, knowing they would be risking their lives to fight for God and country at Kings Mountain.

John related that by the summer of 1776, many of the settlers fleeing the Cherokee had traveled down either the Linville or Catawba Rivers to "find respite at Fort McDowell." Believing the settlers were safe, my Uncle Charles then moved his regiment south to protect the border between North and South Carolina from both the British and marauding Indians.

Uncle Charles had with him most of the available able-bodied men in the immediate area as he maneuvered around the Carolinas. When Draggin Canoe found out about McDowell's absence at Quaker Meadows, he sent two of his best chiefs, Raven and Old Abram, to attack the white settlements, which were often, overwhelmed.

I recalled from my research that Draggin Canoe would eventually be defeated and carried from the field after a battle at Island Flats. While attempting to recuperate from his wounds at Sycamore Shoals, Draggin Canoe revealed this prophecy,

Whole nations have melted away like balls of snow before the sun. The whites have passed the mountains and settled upon Cherokee lands.

New cessions will be required, and the small remnant of my people will be compelled to seek a new retreat in some far distant wilderness. When the whites are unable to point any further retreat for the miserable Cherokees, they will proclaim the extension of the whole race. Should we not therefore run all risks, and incur all consequences, rather than submit to further laceration of our country? Such treaties may be all right for men too old to hunt or fight. As far me, I have my own young warriors about me. We will have our lands."

I found Chief Draggin Canoe's threats to be expressed quite elegantly.

That history now reviewed, it is time to look more closely at the Fort at Quaker Meadows...

CHAPTER 14

THE FORT AT QUAKER MEADOWS

As I began to move through the meadow toward the fort, a particularly attractive, close to what I'd call "beautiful" young lady appeared out to the front of me. Looking into her eyes, which were either blue, green, or a combination of both as hazel, I found myself completely dumbfounded. It was quite evident she was a real beauty, of any age or time.

I felt my heart beating faster, with perspiration quickly forming on my forehead. The only words I was able to mutter while stumbling forward in her direction were "Good afternoon young lady." She stopped in her tracks, smiled, made a short curtsey and then spoke in the voice of an angel, "Good Afternoon to you too Major Davy McDowell."

Now standing in front of the main gate at Quaker Meadows Fort alongside Cousin John, I felt compelled to ask her, "Would it be possible to know your name Miss?" Setting down the bucket she was carrying in her right hand, a big smile once again lit up her face. She looked straight into my eyes and replied "My name is Mary Elizabeth Dysart and I am the daughter of James and Margaret Dysart. My father serves in the Burke County Regiment."

Finding it practically impossible to get the next words out of my mouth, I paused, somewhat stunned, and said, "It's a pleasure to meet you, Miss Dysart. Would it be possible for you to join me for dinner this evening?" "Oh my" immediately came to mind, for I had no idea if I was following 18th-century dating protocol, or for that matter in possession of any conscious thoughts about where we might consume a meal this night. I could not help myself; she was so thoroughly enchanting.

"Yes, Davy," flowed quickly from her lips, followed by, "But I have a better idea—why don't you join me and my family for a meal? We're camped out here on the meadow." She added, "We will all be together tonight for our last meal before Father rides south with you and the Burke County Regiment tomorrow morning."

She must have seen the glint in my eye, for she added, "Having a member of the McDowell family share dinner with us would be a great honor, even though it will not be as fancy a meal as it would be if we were eating at our house in Alder Springs, some two miles from here."

"From now on, you have my permission to address me informally. Major Davy, so please call me "Lizzy" the name all my friends use when speaking to me." Once again, I looked at her face, so beautiful, illuminated by the light provided by the half-moon in the sky this date. The next thing I was aware of was that Cousin John was pulling me forward with my left elbow, momentarily startling me. There was absolutely nothing I could do to restrain my impulse to respond, without the slightest hesitation, back to her so, I blurted out "Yes, yes, see you later this evening."

As I walked away, I could not take my eyes off her, the thoroughly enchanting Miss Lizzy Dysart. Almost in shock, I realized I needed to confront the dilemma being presented to me: "Could, I, or would I, ever forget those beautifully formed lips, her welcoming smile and those eyes of a yet undescribed color, that set my heart on fire? Her fine features, along with her friendly nature, were sending, without any discernible effort, signals to parts of me, to include my despondent heart, which I believed had withered away and died long ago.

Cousin John advised me that he had heard that the original fort had been built by Captain Joseph McDowell, Sr. around 1756-1757, to provide refuge against Indian attacks. This Joseph McDowell the elder was the father of my fellow travelers Charles and Joseph. I trudged around the fort itself for about two hours and while doing so calculated that it was about eighty feet long by fifty feet wide, these measurements taken by the military pacing technique I'd learned while doing land navigation exercises in the swamps around Fort Benning, Georgia.

The fort itself, which some described as the "largest on the frontier," could support up to one hundred twenty people and was surrounded by wooden palisades composed of vertical halved cut logs standing approximately eleven to twelve feet in height above the ground. I assumed that at least another five feet of the log's length were sunk into the ground for support. The top of the palisade featured logs carved into points at the top to discourage enemies (I suspect Indians) from climbing over them and into the fort.

The front gate was quite unique in that it was over ten feet in height and tilted open (in half) from bottom to top, rather than opening like a normal gate from the middle and out to the sides. I'd never seen anything like this before. Many gunports, which they called "loopholes," had been cut into the timbers at eye level all around the fort in a very organized pattern. They were each about twelve inches in height by twenty-four inches in length and were meant to serve as both observation points and rifle ports to engage hostile enemies.

At the back of the fort, in the left corner, stood a two-story log blockhouse with a chimney framed in river stones. On the left side were two windows and on the right side a door and porch. The left and right rear of the blockhouse took the place of palisades and its walls, in total, were approximately eight feet higher than the palisades surrounding the fort. The floor of the blockhouse was raised up from the ground and could easily be described by me as having a "crawlspace."

The blockhouse itself measured a square twenty-four feet by twenty-four, with a second-floor overhang extending out about six feet over the first-floor porch. With an understanding that the fort's primary mission was to serve as a defensive stronghold, I did not expect there to be any "wow factor" to the blockhouse, with the belief that it would be classified as "primitive" even by settlers in the eastern part of the colony.

I had one question about the fort's construction, so before I stepped down onto the ground outside the blockhouse, I asked a passing militiaman "What is the substance that's placed between the logs to close the gaps between them?" "Howdy do sir, shake hands with me, now knowing me to be Meshack Birchfield. Regarding your question, most folk around here would consider my answer obvious; it being that these logs don't by their nature fit together in the long run because the wood gets larger when it's hot and goes in when the weather changes."

He continued, "Logs only touch at them notching points. Those gaps are called "chinks." We fix up a substance made up of clay, mud and sand to fill in the places where it need be. It works real good." Meshack followed this up by identifying why he was here at Quaker Meadows, "I'm here to fight for Colonel McDowell's Burke County Regiment" and "I'm a damn fine shot with my musket! You look like one of them McDowell fellows! Which one are you?"

With a distinct feeling of familial pride, I replied "I'm Major Davy McDowell." Once more I realized I had become a colonial era citizen for no one in my real-life timeframe ever called me "Davy." I was feeling very fortunate to be meeting such a wide variety of true American patriots.

Stepping inside the blockhouse door, I could see that first floor was just one big open space running the entire length of the cabin, with a fireplace, framed with large river stones, located to the left in the middle, undoubtedly used for both cooking and as a heating source.

I observed that the now familiar loopholes would again be found on both the front, rear and sides of the blockhouse. Two windows had been cut out of timber in the front to the sides of the front door, while on the left side there was but one.

At the very rear, I could see what I would have predicted to be a stairway leading up to the second floor. While there was only one door at the front of the house, to enter and exit from, I suspected that in the event of an emergency, like a fire, or being overrun by Indians, the occupants would be able to escape through the gap under the cabin floor.

On my earlier trip around the outside on fort, I observed there was a two foot by two-foot opening that reminded me of a "doggie door," only this was much larger, enough in size for an adult person to get through and outside the fort. Of course, this colonial "escape hatch" was one feature of the cabin no one ever wanted to have to use.

Since no one appeared to be present in the blockhouse at this time, I decided to traverse the narrow staircase up to the second floor. Standing at the top of the narrow, one-turn staircase, I found a large open room. It was explained to me this is where the occupants sleep, in shifts, when the fort was under attack. This dry, open upstairs area provided a place for the militiamen to sleep and kept them warm and dry. Seeing enough of the empty room, I went downstairs, walked out the front door and came upon a militiaman sitting on a wooden rocking chair on the right side of the front porch, where he was smoking a corn cob pipe.

"My friend, I am Davy McDowell, and I have a question for you." Not hesitating for even a moment, this individual cleared his throat and replied in an almost indecipherable 18th Century "country" English, "My name is James Blair, I serve in Major Joe's regiment as an Ensign. I previously served in both the Wilkes County and Rutherford County militias and began my service in 1778. With introductions completed, I then asked him, "Could you please tell me where the privy is?"

James whimsically remarked, "Outside the fort, wherever you want it to be, most prefer behind a tree or bush." After thanking James for this "vital" information," I moved on to begin my search for the location of the McDowell family residence at Quaker Meadows.

As I walked away, I had a difficult time not laughing about the privy feedback I'd received, so I gave up and did, smiling at James Blair the entire time I was walking away from the blockhouse. Inadvertently, I flashed James the peace sign, which drew a blank look on his face. I had apparently forgotten that I was now positioned near Morganton, North Carolina in 1780.

Walking back toward the front gate, I could see people cooking food over fires, repairing personal gear, tending to horses, packing supplies onto horseback and dealing with rambunctious little children. I was surprised by how many women were present inside the fort. I surmised they were the wives of militiamen, since they seemed to be doing a lot hugging and kissing; keeping in mind this was all done in a PG-rated fashion.

I knew from personal experience with my wife Anne that goodbyes could be even tougher on a soldier's soul than the actual fighting. As these men prepared to leave Quaker Meadows Fort on their way south to fight the British, I knew some of these men would never see their loved ones again.

Across the courtyard, I could see several people walking in my direction...

CHAPTER 15

MEETING A BEAUTIFUL WIDOW

Always a friendly person in anyone's company, I found myself be taking every opportunity presented to me to make new friendships while here at Quaker Meadows. One quite attractive woman caught my eye while on my way out of the fort. She was maybe thirty yards away when I first spotted her, very likely due to the more formal attire she was wearing compared to the other women present.

I guessed she was about five four inches in height and of medium build, with rather pale white skin. For clothing she was wearing a light blue gown with pink flowers sewed onto it. The sleeves of her gown were three quarters in length, with ivory lace at the elbows, with a large pink bow in the front, about eight inches long, cascading down from her neckline.

I had no idea how to describe what kind of earrings she was wearing, only that they "dropped down from her earlobes" and appeared to be round. As she got closer, I observed she was carrying a pink fan in her right hand and that her hair was up in a bun on top of the brown hair on her head.

When she was twenty yards from me, I was able to see her eyes were, like mine, dark brown. I realized that in addition to my newly acquired improvement in hearing I was blessed with, I could now vividly view details from a far distance that would be impossible for the average man to see. While continuing to walk in this direction, still at least fifteen yards away, the lady stopped and struck up a conversation with a grizzly-looking old militiaman who was sitting down, leaning against a wood pile in the yard.

With my newly found "gift," I was able to clearly hear the conversation between the two of them as my eyes were able to focus on the details of their presence. Looking in their direction, I could hear they were discussing the availability of gunpowder in the local community. I had not thought about possible applications of these "new skills" might have for me in the future, but I had a gut feeling they had been given to me for a purpose to be revealed to me sometime later.

My attention continued to be drawn to this woman, not because of any physical attribute she possessed, but because of the highly cultured and sophisticated presence she exhibited while interacting with those inside this wooden fortress.

While this lady continued her walk around the fort, I felt a strange tingling sensation, this time like a twitch, in my left ear. Was this to be an indicator that I would encounter the presence of someone special or that something significant was going to happen to me? If this were true,

I might be able to identify the subject of this "early warning system" with some predictability.

Observing that I was acting a bit awkward, the lady walked up to me and gracefully introduced herself. "My name is Grace Greenlee Bowman. Whom do I have the pleasure of meeting today?" Without hesitation this time, I replied "I am Major David McDowell. I hail from the South Carolina colony. I serve in Colonel McDowell's Burke County Regiment." This was about as "secretive" as I could be, considering my background story is, as you already know, mostly fabrication. Okay, but not all of it.

Grace quickly processed this information and added "Oh, you must be related to Charles and Joseph, they are both good men and great leaders." I nodded, feeling a bit self-conscious, with no clever comeback available to my tongue. I did not know where my shyness came from. After a few seconds of silence, the lady offered "I was married to John Bowman, my dear husband, who died this past June 20th at the Battle of Ramsour's Mill." I did not hesitate to express my condolences to the lady, whom I knew to be thirty-years old, by promptly offering these words "I'm very sorry for your loss ma-m."

At Grace's request, I relayed a bit more information about my family to her, to include that I had lost my wife to an undiagnosed disease five years earlier. I was careful to avoid any references about my life in the 21st Century. I did repeat I was the nephew of Charles McDowell and cousin of Joseph "Quaker Meadows" McDowell, that I am twenty-five years of age and that I led a relatively quiet life in South Carolina while opposing the Whigs, before coming north to fight with my McDowell family members.

Of course, this was a lie, but a "white lie" for sure in that it had to be said to avoid what would have been a very uncomfortable situation for me under my truly unique circumstances. I had no desire to become an eighteenth century "Bigfoot" to these people, so I dispensed my words carefully.

I added some subterfuge when I was brought up that I was also related to another branch of the McDowell family located near Charlotte, just north of the South Carolina border, close to Steele's Creek, where Captain John McDowell and his wife Jane Parks McDowell lived on their two-thousand-acre plantation. I had, "ahead" in my time, been to the former plantation site on at least one occasion, where it was once located near 7001 S. Tryon Street in Charlotte. I was quite aware that after the McDowells owned the property it had later been turned into a golf course, their original home no longer existed.

A monument dedicated to Jane Parks McDowell is located there in the 21st Century, with a crest at the top of the monument with three stars representing the knighthood of three of McDowell ancestors for bravery in battle. It notes that in October 1780, at age thirty-four, after British troops attempted to pillage her property, she used her verbal skills to scare off the soldiers and then made a trip on horseback described as "ten perilous miles with infant in tow" to notify the American encampment at Sugar Creek that the British had evacuated Charlotte Town." For her actions, Jane Parks McDowell earned the title of "The feminine Paul Revere."

My conversation with Grace continued, with each of us acknowledging the grief we mutually shared with the loss of a spouse and how difficult it was some days just to get out of bed in the morning. Before heading off in different directions, we changed topics and expressed our shared enthusiasm for the impending journey south to fight Ferguson and his loyalist troops.

At no time did I reveal to Grace that I was well-read on the tragic sequence of events surrounding her husband's death at the Battle of Ramsour's Mill. I was aware, from my research on Revolutionary War history, that after Grace Greenlee Bowman discovered that her husband John had been wounded at Ramsour's Milll, she rode on houseback, with a toddler in tow, on a two-day, forty-mile trip over the South Mountains to Lincolnton.

When Grace finally reached him, he was in the final throes of death. I further recalled that I had once seen the personal papers of John Bowman in Raleigh, to include a profoundly heart-warming poem written by his wife Grace after his demise. I tried to remember it as best as I could and that it went something like this…

Like the sun rising in the morn
He went away, left me forlorn
And saw the tears I shed,
My boding heart did then fortell
That fated evening heard the knell
That my dear John had bled,
Tears that must ever fall,
For Ah! No lights the past recall,
No cries awoke the dead,
Weep not Polly for I will be a Mother
And father unto thee Oh!

The battle at Ramsour's Mill had pitted British Lieutenant Colonel John Moore against Patriot Colonel Francis Locke in what has been characterized in literature as a "fierce and disorganized military engagement." It only lasted about two hours, with the result that the Loyalists were overwhelmed and forced to retreat.

After her husband's death, Grace Bowman proceeded back to her family farm at Hickory Grove, located near Quaker Meadows, where she utilized the services of her chattel laborers to secure and then transport supplies (gunpowder) for Patriot use. I knew "chattel laborers" was a term they used in 18th Century South times to describe "enslaved peoples." On a more pleasant point for me to hear, Grace was decidedly very well known in the local Patriot community, this reputation resulting from an earlier incident that occurred at her home in Hickory Grove.

When loyalist soldiers came onto her property and attempted to illegally confiscate her prized horse, she reacted quickly. After one of Ferguson's Loyalist officers remarked to her "Madam, the King hath need of your horse," she went into her house and returned with a loaded musket, which she pointed directly at him. His next few words were quite simple, "Madam, the King hath no further need for horse," followed by him ordering his men to return the horse to her stable. In my opinion, Grace Greenlee Bowman earned her reputation as a woman of high moral character and grit.

Grace had indeed come a long way since her birth in Rockbridge County, Virginia in 1750. Married to John Bowman in 1778, she later moved south to North Carolina with her brother James Jr. and other Greenlee family members. With Cherokee Indians on the warpath there in North Carolina, they proceeded to the South Carolina home of their McDowell relatives (her father had married Mary Elizabeth McDowell) during which time her brother James Jr. met and married

Mary Mitchell. This was just but one example of "cousins marrying cousins" during the 18th Century.

Finally arriving in North Carolina, the Greenlees and Bowman's were entertained at the Quaker Meadows home of Joseph the elder McDowell and his sons, Charles and Joseph. Son John lived on his own property elsewhere. Not long after their arrival in North Carolina, Grace's brother, James Jr., became somewhat of a "land baron" himself when he acquired land located on Cane Creek, fronting the Catawba River, by winning a wrestling match.

This was just the first of James Greenlee Jr's. land purchases, as soon thereafter he came into possession of the land known as "Alder Springs" in the hills south of the Catawba, literally next door to Quaker Meadows." This would later be known as current day Morganton. James Jr. would eventually become a member of the ruling class of prominent property owners in western North Carolina, holding title to what were described as the best properties, not only around Morganton, but others in Yancey, Mitchell, Rutherford and McDowell Counties. Grace, through both her familial and marital ties, was a member of the patrician class of wealthy landowners in Revolutionary War era society.

Knowing far more about Grace Greenlee Bowman than I could ever reveal, I filed this information far back into the recesses of my gray matter. What I did find incredibly fascinating was that just after I finally bid Mrs. Bowman farewell, I saw my uncle Charles approach her in the fort's courtyard to engage in what the average 21st Century man would characterize as of a "very flirtatious nature." Grace Greenlee Bowman was actually a kinsman of Charles since her mother was Mary Elizabeth McDowell Greenlee, the first white woman to settle in Rockbridge County, Virginia.

Previously unknown to me, but now acknowledged, I was not only related to both Joseph the elder McDowell and his sons Charles, Joseph Jr. and John, through the Rockbridge, Virginia branch of the family, but also through the same lineage to Grace Greenlee Bowman McDowell, who would be recognized as a American Patriot in her own right by the Daughters of the American Revolution (DAR).

I was looking forward to taking a more expansive tour of the McDowell property…

CHAPTER 16

THE MCDOWELL PROPERTY

It was about a half a mile walk outside the fort to Charles and Joseph McDowell's home at Quaker Meadows, about two miles from present day Morganton, on the eastern boundary of the Catawba River. It was once described in literature as both a "magnificent and lordly estate."

The house was situated up on a hill, overlooking yet another great expanse of meadowland. Below lay a great field of fall-blooming perennials, including ginger lilies, chrysanthemums, asters, goldenrod and bright yellow sunflowers.

It was a truly wonderous sight to see. This tranquil setting would only a day or so be one filled with the sound of crashing hoofs, gnashing teeth and very impatient Overmountain Men.

As I walked toward the McDowell home, about one hundred yards in the distance to the south, I could see a watermill; used for grinding, rolling or hammering, these processes needed to sustain daily life in colonial times.

The mill would have been responsible for the production of material goods like flour, lumber, paper, textiles and even some metal needs. I had no doubt the McDowells owned quite a bit of property, up to three thousand acres, so I was not at all surprised to see what I calculated to be a herd of at least one hundred feeding on grass in a nearby field.

At least an equal number of grazing sheep could be seen in yet another field, and while up closer to the house were several hog pens. Around one hundred yards away (remember my superior sight made about anything visible to me these days) I observed what looked like a large tobacco shed, although I did not get close enough to it to verify whether tobacco was present in it or not. Smoke was coming from the chimney of what I could identify as a smoke house, located about fifty yards from the main house.

About half a mile to my right, I heard horses and saw a racetrack with nearby well-built stables. I knew that throughout history, on any continent, that horse racing was a sport for the landed gentry. If I had previously had any questions about how McDowells fit into colonial society, they were now answered.

Taking into consideration my previous understanding of their extensive property holdings in Virginia, before moving south, and that they were no doubt successful in selling that property for a large sum of money, their patrician lifestyle in North Carolina at Quaker Meadows was surely guaranteed. I believe I could now be considered somewhat of a minor expert about how the McDowells acquired their personal wealth.

Walking toward the McDowell home, I came upon a twelve-foot by twelve-foot outbuilding being utilized as a blacksmith shop, while a rudimentary brickyard set adjacent to it. Inside was a stone forge and bellows, in use daily for the repair of farm equipment. Working at the forge was a very large man, weighing at least three hundred pounds, holding a huge hammer in his right hand, striking down on what appeared to be a wagon wheel. He looked familiar.

Seeing the curious look on my face, he identified himself as Brian McKenzie, an indentured servant, who had two more years to serve the McDowells before gaining his freedom. He passed on to me that he had traveled to North Carolina from Galloway, Scotland in a seven-year contract of servitude, which had been transferred to the McDowells because of his occupational specialty.

When I asked him how he was treated as an indentured servant, his only reply, under muffled breath, was "Fairly," then he went back to work. I noted there was kiln for firing bricks, positioned relatively close to the blacksmith's work area. Brian McKenzie was a man of few words. I did not press him to answer any other questions as he did not seem to be in the mood for conversation.

I next passed a twenty-foot by twenty-foot structure that even I was able to identify as a "loom house," built out of pit sawn lumber. Sitting at one of the three looms was a woman who introduced herself as "Barbara McKenzie, Brian McKenzie's wife." She advised me she had come, along with her husband, from Scotland, also in the status of an indentured servant. She seemed happier in this setting than her husband, although this is just conjecture. I found it troublesome to make an attempt at calculating what "happiness" meant to an indentured person.

The "social dynamics" of colonial life in America were now becoming much clearer to me. Standing beside her in the loom house was a little baby crib, with a sleeping baby laying on its back inside it. To avoid waking the baby, I left quietly.

I was now fully aware that not all the people on the McDowell's property were present here of their own volition. Encountering two sixteen-by-sixteen-foot, single-story log houses near the blacksmith's building made me confront the harsh reality of life in the 18th century. With a high degree of apprehension, along with some curiosity, I peered into one of them, where I could see it had packed down dirt floors and a chimney to one side.

Inside, beds sat on crudely constructed raised pedestals, just above the floor at opposite sides of the cabin. There were obvious signs that people lived in these buildings, because I could see a few ragtag clothing items on the top of the beds. A little girl's homemade doll lay on one of the beds, which immediately got my attention. Looking around, I would characterize their actions as manual labor. I could also see a few cooking utensils in a corner by a wall, accompanied by some cups and a teapot.

My "morality bell" rang quickly, now realizing what I was seeing for myself. Honestly, I could not think of anything but getting out of the structure before I "lost" the lunch I had consumed earlier that day. The "big picture" of life in colonial North Carolina was revealed to me without any hesitation, that being that even without large cash crops such as rice or cotton, there would remain a need for manual labor, or "help," on a property this size.

I recalled that researcher William Brown III had concluded from his review of "property records" that Quaker Meadows would have had around ten enslaved people working on it in this particular year. From the personal research I had conducted I recalled that one in five people living on the frontier were enslaved. I could not help but think of that word, "property" and how it had an entirely different meaning to me than to my colonial ancestors.

If I did not disclose this "discovery" to you, I would not be an honest man; but one merely sugarcoating what I came to see. Within the next few moments, right after my head protruded out of the cabin door, my newly gifted superior eyesight focused in on what had to be at least seven identifiable people of African descent. Of course, they did not use the term "African American" to describe enslaved people in 1780, instead using the term "Negroes" or something even more distasteful. Four of the enslaved males were tending to the large number of animals kept in an enclosure by a barn, in relatively close proximity to what was the main residence.

These enslaved men were not performing the type field work traditionally shown either on television and in movies, where they were portrayed working on either rice or cotton plantations. I could also see three enslaved females performing their assigned duties; one churning butter, one washing clothes on a washboard and a third, who was "dipping candles." I was very pleased to see there was no malevolent "overseer" in place to direct any of their actions, although one white man was within thirty yards of their work area, but not armed with any kind of weapon, to include a firearm or whip.

I remembered an article I read in a history magazine that "proposed" that enslaved people on the frontier were treated more humanely than those on the plantations in the eastern part of North Carolina. I sincerely hoped this was true and that my McDowell relatives were of the benevolent type of owners of enslaved people. Although I still felt extremely uncomfortable, I kept my feelings of disgust for owning another human being to myself, barely, when I later spoke to any of the McDowell family. It was their time, not mine, yet my feeling of uneasiness would never again be free of my consciousness.

It is now time for me to see what Charles McDowell's house looked like circa 1780…

CHAPTER 17

MEETING MISTRESS MCDOWELL

At long last, I was finally able to see it, the McDowell's Quaker Meadows home (originally built by Joseph McDowell Sr. in the mid 1700's). The house might have been less dramatic in appearance compared to some of the more majestic colonial homes I'd seen on my 21st "Century trips to North Carolina cities like Charlotte, Raleigh and Tryon, but it was unquestionably beautiful.

The McDowell House, circa 1780, was designed in true American Colonial style. It was, indeed, a very large and attractive two-story home. I read that the house itself had gone through many changes since Charles McDowell became its owner upon the death of his father. For example, painted pit-sawn clapboards now covered the outside of the house and glass could be found in every window (eighteen in all, evenly spread; five each in front and back on the first floor, three each on the sides of the first floor and one each side upstairs).

It was my intent to first reconnoiter the outside of the house. Walking outside and periodically peeking inside, I was able to see planed wood flooring and planed wood paneling on interior walls. There were two brick chimneys, one on each side of the house. All the planed wood on the floors and walls had been sanded and either sealed or painted. I found the color scheme for the interior walls to be quite calming. The main house was connected to the highly functional kitchen by way of a "dog trot" porch.

I am no color expert, but the outside color of the house would best be described as "saffron," not yellow, not brown, but something in-between. The shutters outside each window were painted what I'd refer to as "midnight blue." I never asked any of the McDowells to describe the color, as they might have considered me uneducated.

To the rear of the house was a fenced-in, well-kept garden, which was home to a wide variety of actively growing vegetables, including sweet and Irish potatoes, pumpkins, melons and cabbage. About forty yards behind the main building, I saw a large barn.

My mind flashed back to the television series "Outlander," to the beautiful two-story home the family occupied on the fictional "Fraser's Ridge" in western North Carolina. One day back in my office in 21st Century South Carolina, I'd read a magazine article asserting it was unlikely that a house like the one in "Fraser's Ridge," with its clapboard siding and professional looking paint job, would have existed in this part of North Carolina during the 1780's.

This, the article emphasized, was due to the general unavailability of building materials such as siding and, in particular, good quality paint. It appears to me that those providing their opinions on home construction in 1780 western North Carolina did not comprehend what one of the most affluent men in the colony could construct. I saw it for myself.

The two-story house I was looking at was built of timber frame construction with a typical quadrant style layout. I believed the house's main staircase started around the center of the house. There was a wooden overhang running from midway up the second floor outward toward the front of the house over the porch.

I knocked on the front door and in seconds was challenged by an undoubtedly enslaved young woman who I'd guess was in her late twenties. She politely inquired of me as to my name. Upon hearing me reply "I am Major David McDowell," she welcomed me in, noting I was expected by the lady of the house, "Mistress McDowell."

Being polite, I then asked my greeter her name. She was quite befuddled as I stood there in front of her, at which time I realized that in 1780 the "ruling white people" did not, by their very nature, interact on a personal level with the "help" or "property" of their owners. With this inference in mind, I could not refrain myself and commented "Have a nice day."

I can assure you I was quite uncomfortable interacting with another human being in this manner; where one is worthy of their humanity, the other not. I did regain a bit of my own when the young lady identified herself as "Maebell" and replied to me "And you too Sir." I had to smile.

Miss Maebell then directed me to a comfortable looking chair in the parlor, located to the immediate left as I walked in. She asked me if I would like anything to drink, to which I replied, "No thank you." She advised me "Mistress McDowell will be with you shortly," to which I once again responded "Thank you."

It must have been less than three minutes until the grey-haired sovereign of the McDowell clan in North Carolina walked into the parlor. I'd read she was born in 1723, so I knew her current age to be fifty-seven, no small feat to reach that age in this time period. Mistress McDowell appeared to me to be about five feet four inches in height, slim in build, with brown eyes, like mine, however her's looked like they had already lived through a very tumultuous lifetime.

I stood up as she welcomed me, "We are very happy to have you join us here at Quaker Meadows, Cousin Davy. It is my hope that you are treated well by everyone here and that your efforts to defeat Major Patrick Ferguson are successful. I am sure my sons, Charles, Joseph and John will do their very best to see that you have every opportunity to deal the British a blow they cannot recover from. I have no love for the English and if anyone were to ever imply otherwise, they certainly don't know Margaret O'Neill McDowell!" My only thought upon hearing this was "What a truly magnificent woman." She made me very proud of my Irish ancestry.

After a short conversation, during which time I explained, in 18th Century terms, about my wife Ann's demise, Mistress McDowell excused herself, saying she had some last-minute work to do in preparing clothing for her sons to wear on their trip south. She directed Miss Maebell to make me comfortable and assist me in any way needed.

Before she crossed the threshold into the next room, I commented that I'd heard so much about her magnificent house that I would really like to have a first-hand look at it. In her delightful Irish brogue, she replied "Major Davy, we are pleased you are so interested in our lives here at Quaker Meadows. While you're upstairs, please choose one of our guest rooms for tonight." She followed his with "Excuse me now Davy, I have things to do. I'm sure I will see you later this evening at dinner."

As she slipped away, she looked toward Maebell and remarked "She will be happy to show you around the house." I gave Mistress McDowell a look of thanks and softy remarked "Thanks you so much Auntie." Since I acknowledged Charles McDowell as my uncle, surely Mistress McDowell would be my great aunt.

My 21st Century brain must have needed recharging since when my Auntie spoke about seeing me at dinner this evening I had forgotten I had a "date" with Miss Lizzy Dysart! I reminded myself that "military duty comes first."

My heartstrings were now in conflict with my warrior lifestyle....

CHAPTER 18

MCDOWELL HOUSE

I began my personal inquiry into the upper-class lifestyle of 18th Century colonial North Carolina. After walking out of the parlor to the front door, I could see a central hallway running from the front door to the rear of the house. There was a back door straight ahead of me to the rear. I would be remiss if I forgot to describe to you the room where I met with my Auntie, Mistress McDowell.

A few feet in, on the left, sat two couches and several chairs. Built-in cabinets covered a large percentage of the wall space, holding what must be family heirlooms and other items from their personal lives. A large fireplace was situated on the wall to the left about midway, framed in brick from the floor up to the ceiling.

An eight-foot-in-length table was positioned in the center of the room, with eight sturdy and expensive-looking wooden-backed chairs around it. Along the walls of the room at similar distances were some very well constructed and beautiful period furniture pieces, to include a pine hutch with a China cabinet above it, filled with glassware. Located nearby were several other base units of similar size, with cupboards, most likely used to store pewter dinner plates and dishes.

Upon closer examination, I could tell that each of these classic pieces of furniture had been hand-made somewhere in a more industrialized environment, either in Eastern North Carolina or Virginia. I was impressed by their remarkable appearance, concluding that this type of quality and pride in workmanship had disappeared well before my time in the 21st Century. On the right back wall of the room, sat a single spinning wheel, with a clothing item laying on a nearby rocking chair. Upon closer examination I could see it was a man's white linen shirt, very likely the property of either Cousin Joseph or Uncle Charles.

It was obvious to me that a wealthy family resided here and that there were female "touches" added to what could have been a thoroughly male-dominated setting. There was little doubt in my mind that it was Mistress McDowell who oversaw the décor of McDowell House.

I took a right turn through a door across the hall from the spinning wheel and when crossing the threshold saw what must have been the back door to the house. While in the hallway, I peered into a room right across the hall and ascertained it had to be their weapons storage facility; for in it I could see eight muskets, along with a wide variety of flint-lock pistols in an elaborately carved weapons rack.

Down the hallway to the front of the house and to the left, I found a door ajar, so I looked in and could see a large table, chairs around it, with numerous maps spread out on top. Along two of the interior walls were built-in bookcases, each shelf filled from end to end with books, leading me to believe this was my Uncle Charles' office or study.

Once again traveling toward the front of the house, I came to a second parlor, where couches and chairs were strategically arranged for seating and entertaining guests. I would add that in each room there were multiple candle holders. A ball of yarn set on one chair, leading me to believe this was Mistress McDowell's domain.

Believing I knew the layout downstairs; I walked back down the hallway to the center of the house and took the first of twenty steps up to the second floor. You might ask why so many steps? The answer is quite simple; the first-floor ceilings were at least twelve feet in height.

Standing in the hallway upstairs, I was able to identify six rooms, three on the left and an equal number on the right. The three rooms on the right gave me the impression they were occupied by full-time residents. This opinion was based on my view of the physical presence there of several pieces of very high quality, very well-made furniture, to include four-poster-beds, dressers with mirrors, a variety of clothes cabinets and writing desks with chairs pulled up to them. One of these rooms had their own fireplace, while the other two had wood-burning stoves.

I assumed that it would be the more important residents that would reside in these three rooms. It made complete sense to me that the rooms on the right, which were larger than the ones on the left, would serve as permanent sleeping quarters for Uncle Charles, Cousin Joseph and Mistress McDowell. Only one of the three rooms on the right side had feminine touches to it, with me concluding it was surely occupied by my Auntie Margaret. The other two rooms were quite plain compared to it, very likely occupied by the bachelor brothers, Charles and Joseph.

I was met by another obviously enslaved female coming out of a room on the left in the upstairs hallway, who upon my inquiry advised me her name was Cynthia. I asked her, "How long have you lived here at Quaker Meadows?" Her reply made me cringe, "Since 1770, Sir, when Master Joseph the Elder purchased me from a planter near Hillsborough."

I guessed Cynthia to be somewhere around twenty-five years of age, which meant that she had been a slave, owned by my family, for going on ten years, beginning when she was but fifteen. I did not have the personal courage to ask her where she was born, or what her life had been like before her sale to my great uncle, Joseph McDowell the elder.

The only emotion available to me at this time was sadness. I thanked Cynthia for her time and walked away, wanting so much to tell her personally I was sorry for how her life had turned out. However, comprehending my own "place" here in 1780, I instead bit my tongue as I continued to retreat from her presence.

Continuing my own personal "tour" of the upstairs, I was able to identify two sleeping rooms on the left side of the second floor, which were quite austere in comparison to the three on the right, each with only a single bed, small writing desk and stand-alone coat hangers. The middle room of the three had a fireplace, while the other two had wood-burning stoves. The middle room seemed to be used as a parlor for the upstairs. This room had built-in bookshelves on one wall. I suspect this room was set aside for reading. It also had a multitude of candle holders in it. I assumed these rooms were for short-term visitors, like me. I chose the room closest to the stairwell for my stay tonight.

I wondered if there could be any other family members, such as Captain Joe "PG" McDowell, or others, living here temporarily? While outside earlier, I confirmed that my cousin John McDowell did not live here, but elsewhere on his own property, which was not far from Quaker Meadows. I knew that Cousin Joseph also owned property nearby; but that he was now headquartered here at Quaker Meadows.

My final question about the construction of the McDowell's residence manifested itself once more in relation to my own "personal needs." This question was answered almost immediately when I went back downstairs and walked out the back door, only to see a traditional "out-house" in position about twenty yards to the rear.

Every human in the 18th Century had personal needs and I, certainly a human, although from another century, was determined to make a personal visit to what some of my very rural South Carolina friends, or even ex-military buddies might refer to as the "wooden throne."

Once inside the house, I was surprised to see the presence of a large scattering of leaves and more than a dozen dried corn cobs lying on a shelf on the left side of this one-seat "outdoor toilet." As a result of my "successful" experience in this 18th Century facility, I concluded I might never again eat corn-on-thecob at a barbeque. With my personal business taken care of, I walked back toward the Fort at Quaker Meadows, where a frenzy of activity was in progress.

I was hungry and in need of companionship...

CHAPTER 19

DINNER WITH THE MCDOWELLS

The final time I would see Mistress McDowell before our journey south the next day would be at dinner that same night. The guests we expected to be present included the leaders of the Overmountain Men and state militias: Charles and Joseph McDowell, William Campbell, Isaac Shelby, John Sevier, Benjamin Cleveland and Joseph Winston. Mistress McDowell was present with us for about thirty minutes as our gracious hostess, after which she excused herself, explaining she was tired and was going to bed.

As she departed, in a somewhat unsteady manner, I noticed a white pallor to her skin. I found this to be concerning, although I had no idea what could be causing it. As she was crossing the threshold of the doorway, I turned my head in her direction and called out "I look forward to seeing you again Auntie." My Great Aunt Margaret then looked back over her shoulder, smiled at me, and in her thoroughly delightful Irish brogue responded, "I too, my dear nephew Davy."

Feeling like a big brown grizzly bear had suddenly pounced on my back, I realized that although I could not turn down their dinner invitation at the McDowell House, it was equally impossible for me to forget the earlier invitation extended to me by the Dysart family.

I quickly tracked down my cousin John, whom I located at the rear of the house, in the garden. John was engaged in conversation with a young man who identified himself as Captain Dysart of Colonel Campbell's regiment. All this said, I'm sure John could easily tell from the expression on my face that I needed help, now!

I didn't need to ask John to find the local Dysart family, especially Miss Lizzy. John understood my situation and was willing to help. I asked him to pass on to the Dysarts my sincerest personal regrets, with the understanding that as a militia officer my first obligation was to honor my professional responsibilities under the command of my McDowell relatives.

Cousin John reported back to me he had given my message to the Dysarts. He commented that Miss Lizzy Dysart seemed to be particularly disappointed I was unable to join them.

Enough with the romance for right now, it was more important for me to figure out "What was to be my place here this evening?" Although I had earned the rank of Major, I was not an Overmountain Man nor a militia commander. Uncle Charles explained to those assembled around the eight-foot- long dining table that I was present to serve as his "Adjutant" for the evening. In 21st Century terms this position would best be described by the title "Executive Officer."

I was eager to assume this role since it would allow me to gain insight into the personalities of those involved in the leadership of the Overmountain Men. I did not sit at the "big table" with them, but at a smaller side table, located in the south corner of the room. I was there to serve at Uncle Charles' bidding.

Before their conversations became too complicated, Uncle Charles asked Benjamin Cleveland how his younger brother, Lieutenant Lark Cleveland, was doing. Lark had been accompanying his older brother Benjamin as they crossed the Bushy Mountains and reached Lovelady's Ford on the Catawba River. Benjamin disclosed that a small band of Loyalists attacked them from a rocky outcrop on the other side of the river. While watching them cross, the Loyalists misidentified the younger brother as the older and directed their firepower in his younger brother's direction.

Benjamin, the older brother, was not injured, while Lark, the younger, was struck in the thigh by a musket ball, causing serious injury. Sent up the river by canoe, Lark was eventually transported the remaining distance to Quaker Meadows, where he could receive medical care and rest. Upon further inquiry, Cleveland would only remark, "He is doing well, considering the injuries he received." There was no more to be said on this topic.

From then on, the evening was cheerful as they avoided discussing the trip south to fight but instead shared wild stories about their own personal exploits, while in the same breath vividly expressing their dislike for English rule and Major Patrick Ferguson. The meal itself, quite satisfying, consisted of pork as the main dish, complimented by side dishes of corn, beans, sweet potatoes and bread. For dessert we had "Moravian Sugar Cake." From my own personal perspective, I would not refer to it as "sugar" at all, with the closest comparison being to German pastries, which use a different type of sugar.

The sharing of personal "stories" over, the leaders at the table somewhat reluctantly turned to the topics of searching out and then engaging Ferguson in battle. I could tell the mere mention of Ferguson's name left a very distinct, bad taste in their mouths. The dinner meeting then came to an end.

In summary, they were determined to "plan along the way," or what I'd call "on the fly" as they moved south, with all of them having one common goal, to drive the British out of the Carolinas once and for all.

Feeling a bit tired myself after the long day, when the meeting reached its end, Uncle Charles looked up at me, keeping in mind I'm five inches taller than him, and directed me to my bed upstairs. I did my best to hide my overabundant enthusiasm for spending the night at the same Quaker Meadows house I'd read about in history books!

I knew that morning would come early, so I made my way upstairs with a candle secured in my right hand. Upstairs, I entered my room, sat on the bed, and started to undress. It was so quiet here at night, I could hear what had to be hundreds of jubilant bullfrogs croaking outside the house. Their rhythmic sound reminded me of the many nights I spent listening to the fog horns while on temporary duty at what used to be known as "The Presidio of San Francisco."

I drifted off, knowing that unless Miss Lizzy Dysart was present n them, there would be no dreams tonight...

CHAPTER 20

THE JOURNEY SOUTH

Upon waking up early on the morning of October 1st, I gathered my personal belongings and went downstairs for a biscuit and tea. I saw my Uncle Charles and Cousin Joseph for but a few minutes before they were out the front door, no doubt preparing themselves for the journey south to first find, then fight, Ferguson and his Loyalist troops. As they walked out, I commented "It's going to be a great day for us!" to which Uncle Charles replied "Yes, lad, it truly will be! Be prepared for a long day's journey." Upon hearing this comment, I thought "Oh, oh, I haven't ridden a horse in ten years, this could be a problem."

It was quite apparent that Uncle Charles had already arranged for me to ride one of the finest horses in his stable, for when I went out the rear door of the house a very impressive looking dark brown horse stood there, saddled and waiting. The reigns were presented to me by

Samual, an enslaved man on the Quaker Meadows property. I asked if the horse had a name and he replied, "Gunpowder."

After putting my personal items (also thought of and provided by my new McDowell relatives) onto the horse's back behind the saddle, I anchored my left foot into the stirrup and pulled myself up into the saddle. I was indeed ready to move south with my fellow Patriots. It was a truly magnificent sight to watch over fourteen hundred men traveling in sync in what I expected would be a well organized formation, their regimental commanders out in front of them.

It became apparent to me that there was no one individual in charge of movement in its entirety, it looked more like organized chaos to me. These militiamen were so stretched out, from first regiment to last, it was impossible to tell how far back the last group followed. And, although it is not possible to accurately measure a group's enthusiasm to fight, I calculated that all had but one goal in mind, that being to deal the British a significant defeat.

The first day's journey was not one anyone could have anticipated, for although the roads were good, driving rain forced us to set up our encampment after only a half-day march, only eighteen miles, at Bedford Hills, near the head of Cane Creek, near present day Dysartsville, North Carolina. The only saving grace for me was that it was not a full day's ride, so my unprepared bottom half suffered minimally. I did ride horses when I was younger, but that time was a "long, long time ago," whatever that phrase meant to me now.

This was the same location where several weeks before my Uncle Charles had fought Ferguson's Tories. We would remain here for two nights. I can assure you that with no tents among our gear, this was a truly miserable start to the expedition.

For the next two days, the only respite we could find from the pounding rain was felt when we could stand beneath the canopies of trees to reduce the volume of water drenching us. It was like living in a wet sock! One individual who did not seem to be affected by the bad weather was the "large" regimental commander, Colonel Benjamin Cleveland, who could very often be found, lying down, head on his saddle with a blanket covering his head.

I recalled that in the 21st Century the Army at least gave us "ponchos," which were made of some polyester-like material to keep us somewhat dryer when it was raining. I missed my poncho, that's for sure!

It was here, at Bedford Hill, sixteen miles from Gilbert Town, under the multitude of trees surrounding us, their leaves turning red and yellow and beginning to fall to the ground, that on the evening of October 2nd, 1780, a decision would be made to deprive my Uncle Charles of would have been his expected command of all of the fourteen hundred Whig militia forces.

The militiamen did their very best to start fires in this soaked, wet environment. These Overmountain Men and militiamen from several different colonies and regions no doubt lacked any measurable military discipline, for numerous fights broke out amongst them both day and night, most often without any apparent justification. It appeared to me to be the result of a general lack of centralized command structure; no one really knew who the overall commander was.

When I inquired as to why these militiamen were acting so rambunctious, Cousin Joseph offered me his own explanation. "They have been away from their families, left back across the mountains for over a week to fend for themselves, so they are anxious to find

Fergusion, defeat him and get back home to their wives and bairns. This is how they relieve themselves of the pressure they are feeling," If you are unfamiliar with the word "bairns," it is the Scottish-English word for "children."

It was time to find someone I could talk to…

CHAPTER 21

A NEW FRIEND

As I walked around the campsite the men continued to express their concerns about not finding Ferguson nor being able to put an end to him. While setting up my campfire, Captain Robert Patton, a company commander in my same Burke County Regiment, stopped by my bed site and inquired "How are you doing this night Major McDowell?"

Patton was another "taller than usual" militiaman, standing close to six feet in height, his weight distributed evenly over a long sinewy body. He had a steady, resonating voice, one that surely commanded both attention and loyalty on the part of his assigned men. He greatly impressed me with his sheer physical presence, so I remarked to him "Robert, I am very happy to meet a man so dedicated to our cause." Further, "I would be proud to fight alongside you when we meet Ferguson and his Loyalist forces."

Robert Patton identified himself as being thirty-two years of age and hailed from Alder Springs, North Carolina. Our mutually enjoyable conversation continued for about an hour, during which time we both reminisced about the families we left behind. Remarkably, and much to my surprise, my new friend Robert disclosed that he knew Elizabeth Dysart, my 18th Century "crush" back at Quaker Meadows Fort. The more he spoke, the clearer it became that he possessed a similar impression of her beauty and demeanor. The thought that I had such strong feelings for a woman I'd only known for such a brief period, after so many years of loneliness, confused me.

Quickly changing topics, I asked Robert, from this day forward, to "Address me as Davy, saving my title of "Major" for when we're in mixed company." Robert quickly replied, "Likewise, please address me as Robert or Captain under the same conditions." It was clear to me that the nickname "Bob" would not be his choice for addressing him, although I knew it was already in common use in the Carolinas in the 18th Century.

I recalled that Robert's 21st Century relative, Robert Patton IV, also preferred to be addressed as the more formal "Robert." I found it humorous to consider that "Some things never change, even in two hundred and fifty years."

Observing the look on my face, Robert spoke again, adding "Davy, there are many things we think of at times like this; families, children, sweethearts and our homes, but I have no doubt that when the bullets go to flying you will be right there beside me, killing those damn Tories!" For a moment, I was surprised that the word "damn" was used in the 18th Century vernacular. I surmised that in the days and years to come that word would often be shouted from the mouths of my fellow countrymen.

Our conversation nearing completion, Robert shared with me "I am the son of Robert Patton, born in 1715 in Northern Ireland." For all practical purposes, this identified him as an "Ulster Scot," part of a large group of former Scotsmen who departed from the same general area in Ireland as did the elder Joseph McDowell. Robert's final words to me were "I born in the city of Philadelphia in the Pennsylvania colony. I moved south to the Carolinas as an adult." Robert then got up from his seated position, gestured a good-bye and returned to tend to his company of men were camped out.

While we lower ranking militiamen (under the grade of Colonel) were tending to our rifles and muskets, in particular cleaning them in preparation for battle, Colonels Campbell, Shelby and Cleveland, along with Majors Winson and McDowell, were working on securing rations for us all. Rumors continued to spread among us, while our leaders apparently spent a considerable amount of time doing their best to locate Ferguson. They sent out scouts, while at the same time ensuring our safety by stationing pickets all around our campground.

Major McDowell saw to it that all of us in his regiment had a ration of liquor this night. He was a man who skillfully took care of those assigned to the Burke's County Regiment. The care and concern he showed for his men did not go unnoticed by either subordinates or superiors. My new friend, Robert Patton, agreed with me regarding this conclusion.

I had absolutely no idea what would come next...

CHAPTER 22

THE COUP AT BEDFORD HILL

We spent two nights at Bedford Hill, waiting for more favorable weather for our journey south. Closing in on Ferguson, who all believed was now in Gilbert Town, it was time to appoint a Commanding Officer for our forces. The most obvious choice to lead would be my Uncle, Colonel Charles McDowell, the senior officer present among the fourteen hundred on this venture. A leader's meeting will be held to confirm the Commanding Officer.

Since this entire military venture was not approved by a higher authority in the first place, I was dumbfounded when the group's leadership came up with the idea that required our forces to seek out a Continental Army officer serving at the rank of General.

There is absolutely no doubt in my mind that in this meeting Colonel Andrew Hampton would be expressing his personal mistrust of my uncle, most certainly a result of the death of his son in the months before at Earle's Ford. It was Hampton, unfortunately, who was beginning to see his venomous sabotage efforts come to fruition.

In addition, while eavesdropping at a distance in the hours before the leader's meeting that evening, I observed Hampton moving from one small group of senior officers to another, spewing his own brand of emotional and professional havoc on my uncle's fitness for command.

Hampton's voice could be clearly distinguished from among those of other militiamen in the small groups he met with throughout the day, where he could be heard insisting, time after time, "He should not command, his negligence at Earle's Ford is the reason my son Noah is dead!" He was surely referring to my uncle, Colonel Charles McDowell!

Hampton's cause apparently gained support by evening in the form of Colonel Issac Shelby, who I'd learned had such a low opinion of my Uncle Charles' leadership abilities that he hadn't hesitated to report his unvarnished disregard for him on several earlier occasions. I found that Shelby's assertion that McDowell was "too slow and too old" ridiculous, since he is well aware his own father was twenty-five years older than McDowell when he led a successful expedition against the Chickamauga Indian towns and, further, that other highly regarded leaders such as South Carolinians Francis Marion and Thomas Sumpter were, respectively, seven and four years senior to McDowell.

I concluded that if they needed a real measuring stick for "old men" they needed to consider General George Washington, Commanding Officer of the Continental Army, who was eleven years senior to McDowell. Shelby was no "youngster" either at close to age thirty I did catch wind that Shelby's final contribution to the unseating of my uncle occurred when he brought up some controversy about McDowell's allegedly indecisive conduct at the Battle of Cane Creek. I only learned about these opinions through bystanders, some of whom were also curious about the decision-making process now in place.

The assembled Colonels and their subordinate officers concluded that my uncle, Colonel Charles McDowell, should be the officer sent to General Gates at Hillsborough, North Carolina to request the appointment of a Continental general officer to lead their forces against Ferguson. The trip from Bedford Hill to Hillsborough was close to two hundred miles in distance; it would take several days to travel there on horseback.

It is documented by several sources that it was Shelby who proposed that no "precious time" should be wasted in appointing another Colonel as the overall commanding officer once McDowell was gone. I was very disappointed by the method they used to remove my uncle from command.

Private John Craig, a militiaman in the Virginia Regiment, advised me that he was physically present at a leader's meeting held in haste after Charles McDowell's departure. He described what he heard, "I was in close proximity to the meeting of Colonel Shelby, Colonel Sevier, Colonel Cleveland and the other field commanders when the decision was made for Campbell to assume command. Colonel Shelby was the first who proposed Campbell, and it was without one single dissenting voice agreed to."

I recalled that in the 21st Century I read what I considered to be the most insulting description of all regarding my uncle's decidedly unplanned departure. In that narrative it was reported that "for whatever reason, McDowell went away, leaving the army to proceed united against Ferguson." This statement is highly inaccurate.

For anyone to infer, as another source did, that Charles McDowell "gracefully submitted to what was done" is again practicing deception. This is, I admit, my personal assessment of their decision-making process, which I would rate as "flawed."

I was not included in the leadership group's decision-making that evening, which may have been due to my recognition as a member of the McDowell family. Knowing my uncle as I now do, as a member of his immediate family, I wondered if either Hampton or Shelby suspected I knew too much already, so they ensured I was kept busy, at a distance, far away from them. I was only a Major, so they had power over me. I have absolutely no doubt Shelby knew the battle with Fergusion would take place within the next few days and that McDowell's journey by horseback to Hillsborough would in effect remove him from command.

I therefore conclude that the decision to send him away was an example of overt professional sabotage, literally a "coup," originally planned by two of the Patriot Colonels, Hampton and Shelby.

Around this same time, I was shocked to hear from others that my cousin Joseph, who assumed command of his brother Charles' Burke County Regiment, did not actively defend his brother's right to command. The fact that my Uncle Charles' own brother, Joseph, joined in with the others in their unanimous vote for Campbell astounded me!

I wondered if Joseph was overwhelmed by all the animosity toward his brother and just gave in, or if he actively sought command of the Burke County Regiment for himself? I would keep asking questions.

Unfortunately, I was unable to eavesdrop on any of their conversations during that critical meeting.

I was, however, close enough to hear a conversation between Uncle Charles and his younger brother Joseph, just as Charles was pulling himself up onto his horse, moments before he rode off toward Hillsborough. It was during this brief encounter between them that Joseph, while patting the mane of Charles' horse, assured him "Brother, I will make you proud in the manner by which I lead the Burke County Regiment in your absence."

Charles seemed to be profoundly moved by these words, and calmy responded, "Joseph, my dear brother, beware of the politics afoot here, for one ear may hear one thing, the other something entirely different." With a quick wave and a command of "Get, Tom!" off he went.

By agreeing to make the trip to Hillsborough, Uncle Charles was in effect showing his personal humility, love of country and disregard for any personal gain or glory. There was one truth in reports I read after 1780, that no overall commander was appointed that evening until Charles McDowell left the encampment at Bedford Hill. I doubt they waited for his departure just to avoid hurting his feelings.

In a conversation with Joseph after Uncle Charles departed for Hillsborough, I found it very difficult to get any details of the leader's meeting from him. I was, however, able to hear enough to understand their justification for appointing Colonel Campbell as commanding officer.

Cousin Joseph mentioned that the entirety of senior officers held an unfavorable assessment of his brother, describing him as "too slow and methodical" and that his leadership style did not align with the "aggressive mountaineering tactics" they favored. Expressed in a few words, it was clear that the Patriot leaders were seeking a commanding officer who possessed a leadership style better suited to their concept of battle.

Shelby, himself the immediate subordinate to McDowell by date of rank, would not have been able to carry out this coup without the assistance of others. I found absolutely no evidence, from October 1780 on, that Colonel William Campbell participated in this backroom intrigue.

I felt lost and wondered what would happen to me next, since my primary 1780 "mentor," Charles McDowell, was no longer present? It became apparent to me that from this moment on it would be my cousin, Joseph "Quaker Meadows" McDowell, who would be my sole connection to my reality, whether here in 1780, or forward in time to my existence in the 21st Century. For your information, the correspondence Colonel Shelby sent with Uncle Charles to General Gates read as follows:

"All our Troops being Militia and but little acquainted with discipline, we could wish him (the general officer) to be a Gentleman of address and able to keep up the proper discipline without disgusting the soldiery."

No, I did not have a copy of this correspondence, but someone there that evening made a copy for me. Regarding Uncle Charles' departure from Bedford Hill, I would be remiss if I did not let you in on some other interesting information. After Charles McDowell departed that evening from Bedford Hill, his later presence is noted on only one more occasion, when he took a short sojourn at the camp of

South Carolina Colonels William Lacey and James Williams at Flint Hills, about twelve miles eastward of the head of Cane Creek.

There remains no record of Charles McDowell traveling to Hillsborough. It is acknowledged that well before he could have reached Hillsborough, the Battle of Kings Mountain had already taken place. There is no documentation that General Gates ever received the Overmountain Men's request for a general officer.

It would be left to Cousin Joseph to decide my fate from this date forward...

CHAPTER 23

ON TO GILBERT TOWN

On the next day, October 3rd, in the morning before we continued our march south, Colonel Cleveland requested a gathering of all the troops. This quite "large man" proceeded to address everyone while the force commander, Colonel Campbell, formed a circle with Shelby, Sevier, McDowell, Winston and all the other officers. I listened intently as he eloquently spoke these words:

"Now, my brave fellows, I have come to tell you the news. The enemy is at hand and we must up and at them. Now is the time for every man of you to do his country a priceless service-such as shall lead your children to exult in the fact that their fathers were the conquers of Ferguson. When the pinch comes, I shall be with you. But if you shrink from sharing in the battle and the glory, you can now have the opportunity of backing out and leaving; and you shall have a few minutes for considering the matter."

After Cleveland finished speaking, Cousin Joseph stepped forward to give an inspiring follow up challenge to those assembled:

"Well my good fellows, what kind of story will you, who back out, have to relate when you get back home, leaving your braver comrades to fight the battle and gain the victory?"

A thought struck my mind, "Maybe I need to get to know Cousin Joseph a lot better?"

Shelby was next up:

"You have all been informed of the offer, you who have declined it, will, when the word is given, march three steps to the rear, and stand, prior to which a few more minutes will be granted you for consideration."

Not even one man accepted the offer given to them by Shelby. There appeared to be no cowards among the multitude of over a thousand men assembled here. Shelby exclaimed

"I am heartily glad to see you to a man resolve to meet and fight your country's foes. When we encounter the enemy, don't wait for the word of command. Let each one of you be your own officer and do the very best you can, taking every care you can of yourselves, and availing yourselves of every advantage that chance may throw in your way. If in the woods, shelter yourselves and give them Indian play; advance from tree to tree, pressing the enemy and killing and disabling all you can. Your officers will shrink from no danger-they will be constantly with you, and the moment the enemy give way, be on the alert, and strictly obey orders."

That same evening, as I lay down and went to sleep, I dreamed about what transpired in the evening hours of October 2nd. Reviewing everything that had taken place that evening, I had to admit it was possible my Uncle Charles might not have been the leader best suited for command.

This was the first time I had remotely conceived of Uncle Charles having any leadership deficits. It had always been my belief that he was born to command the militia troops, to include the soon-to-be famous Overmountain men. My dream ended with many still unsettled questions.

Along with all the Overmountain Men, we continued south on the 3rd, frequently traversing Cane Creek on our trek toward Ferguson. We would again halt our trip that evening when we encamped at Marlin's Knob for an overnight respite, near the home of one Samuel Adams.

On October 4th our burgeoning force found itself maneuvering our way, but not yet to, Gilbert Town, where we expected to engage Ferguson's forces. Gilbert Town, which was at this time one of the larger settlements in the former Tryon County. I learned that the town was named after William Gilbert, one of the county's largest landholders.

Gilbert Town was apparently one of Ferguson's favored spots to bivouac his Loyalist troops, to include in the weeks following the Battle of Musgrove's Mill. In addition to Gilbert's residence, one could find a barn, a blacksmith's shop and some outhouses on his property. Gilbert Town seemed to be the place Ferguson would choose to fight since he was quite familiar with it. As recently as September 1, 1780, he had set up camp here.

For his headquarters, he had used William Gilbert's home, while his troops situated themselves on a high hill behind the house, which would forever thereafter be known as "Ferguson's Hill." Gilbert's farm was about three miles from the town.

As the evening went on, I could hear Colonel Hampton comment that his home was but a short distance from Gilbert Town and, furthermore, that his son Jonathan held distinct contempt for King George.

On we marched again, this time in much better weather, allowing us to travel the fifteen miles to Gilbert Town in good time. Shortly before we arrived at the outskirts of the town, Colonel Campbell stopped the troop movement and gave all the gathered militiamen another rousing speech, in which he once again offered anyone with any hesitation the option to drop out.

Not one man chose to leave. Can you imagine fourteen hundred men in possession of the same universal mindset and purpose? This is what drove these Patriots, particularly the Overmountain Men, onward toward what would have been considered as "The Turn of the Tide of Success in the American Revolution."

As I listened to Campbell's moving oratory, I concluded he was a man of truly inspiring character, one who used his superior communication skills to ensure that every single militiaman present knew both the risks and, more importantly, the glory that awaited them with a victory.

With his speech completed, each of us militiamen expressed an acute sense of anticipation, so along we went...

CHAPTER 24

FERGUSON WAS GONE

The truth was later revealed that Ferguson was never at Gilbert Town per se, but in fact eighteen miles to the south-west before later heading towards the Broad River in pursuit of a group of militiamen commanded by Colonel Elijah Clark. While encamped on the night of September 30th at Denard's Ford on the Broad River, in what was then Tryon County, Ferguson composed another inflammatory message to Whig supporters in both North and South Carolina.

It read as follows:

"Gentlemen: Unless you wish to be eat up by the inundation of barbarians, who have begun by murdering an armed son before the aged father, and afterwards lopped off his ears, and who by their shocking cruelties, and irregularities, give the best proof of their cowardice and want of discipline; I say, if you wish to be pinioned, robbed and murdered, and see

your wives and daughters, in four days, abused by the dregs of mankind-in short, if you wish or deserve to live and bear the name of men grasp your arms in a moment and tun to camp."

Furthermore, *"The Back Water men have crossed the mountains; McDowell, Hampton, Shelby and Cleveland are at their head, so that you know what you have to depend upon. If you choose to be degraded forever and ever by a set of mongrels, say so at once, and let your women turn their backs upon you, and look out for real men to protect them." The proclamation was signed.*

Pat. Ferguson, Major, 71st Regiment

Ferguson's warning certainly contained a lot of bluster and exaggeration, apparently in an attempt on put general hysteria into play. This type of rhetoric backfired on him when it encouraged many of the previously neutral or "weak kneed civilians," as he referred to them, to join the Patriot cause. Around this same time, on September 30th, Ferguson sent two messages, the first to Colonel John H. Cruger, Commanding Officer of the British garrison at Ninety-Six, requesting one hundred men to reinforce him.

Colonel Cruger turned down Ferguson's appeal, declaring he had insufficient troops at his location to provide the requested support. Cruger recommended Ferguson make this same appeal to General Cornwallis at Charlotte Town.

Ferguson was in retreat, hoping to cut the distance between his force and reinforcements. In the meantime, while waiting, he began sending out pleas to those he had recently furloughed, asking them to return to his command.

Details of this provocative challenge were passed on to me by a militiaman from Burke County, ones that had just joined our cause the day before. It would not surprise me if it was words like these, apparently already known to Cousin Joseph, that resulted in our force gaining additional militiamen as we continued to venture south, Ferguson had made specific movements with his Loyalist troops so that he was nearby any potential King-loving men that would choose to join him.

Aware that the Overmountain Men and other militia groups were attempting to over-take him on his fight toward Charlotte Town, Ferguson began his search to find a suitable place that would with-stand any Whig attack.

By Monday afternoon on October 2nd, Ferguson departed Dennard's Ford. He was delayed because he tried to intercept Colonel Elijah Clark and his Georgia men. With that no longer an option, he continued a slow march to Tate's Plantation, where he set up camp. Ferguson remained there for two days before moving again. No documentation I'd seen adequately explained why he stayed there for two days, versus moving forward after a short respite.

By October 6th Ferguson and his Loyalist army were on the move again at four in the morning. It was during this march that Ferguson temporarily halted his advance to send his second message to Cornwallis at Charlotte Town:

"My Lord: A doubt does not remain with regard to the intelligence I sent to your Lordship. They are since joined by Clarke and Sumter-of course are become an object of some consequence. Happily their leaders ae obliged to feed their followers with such hopes, and so to flatter them with accounts of our weakness and fear, that, if necessary, I should hope for success against them myself; but numbers compared, that must be doubtful.

I am on my march towards you, by a road leading to Cherokee Ford, north of King's Mountain. Three to four hundred good soldiers, part dragoons, would finish the business. Something must be done soon. This is their last push this quarter, etc.

Patrick Ferguson

It does appear that Ferguson understood that Whig troops under the command of Colonel Campbell were in pursuit of him, although this does not mean he was purposely moving to a final position on Kings Mountain. On this same date, October 6th, Ferguson eventually crossed Kings Creek through a pass in the mountain, heading in the direction of Yorkville.

A short distance after crossing the creek, about two hundred and fifty yards away from the pass, he found himself looking at what is usually referred to as a "crest on the ridge of Kings Mountain." Having transversed this area myself, I would prefer to call it a "plateau," but that is my choice of words for it.

It is here that Ferguson's ego may have overtaken his common sense. This is the place that he declared words to the effect to all present that "I am on Kings Mountain and God Almighty and all of the Rebels out of hell could not drive me from it." This is quite an egotistical boast, one that appears to suggest that as the campaign in the South continued, Ferguson's ego went out of control. His location on this "plateau" had an abundance of wood all around it, but Ferguson made the decision not have his soldiers chop any down for use as barriers on the sides of the slopes before they dropped off so sharply. Instead, he chose to set up his baggage wagons on the northeastern side of the ridge, near his headquarters.

This would turn out to be a fatal mistake on his part, a decision that surely would not have come from a well-versed tactician like Ferguson. Where was the man who attended the London Military Academy, who had the intellectual capacity to invent the "Ferguson rifle?" Ferguson spent almost an entire day there doing nothing except exposing himself to danger.

His message to Cornwallis, never received, and with his request for his furloughed soldiers rejected, Ferguson would have to fight whatever enemy showed up with the eleven hundred men he had on hand.

Ferguson's reasons for stopping at Kings Mountain instead of proceeding to Charlotte remain unknown. In respect to this same point, no one apparently knows why he made the decision to encamp there when he was aware that the Overmountain Men were in hot pursuit. Ferguson's unsound behavior upon arrival at Kings Mountain was in sharp contrast to the tactical savvy he displayed in his many prior battlefield interactions.

To make matters even worse, in what I'd classify as a gross display of poor leadership, Ferguson chose not to post guards around the perimeter of the ridge which was, as stated previously, covered with hardwood and thick foliage. By the nature of the battlefield known as Kings Mountain, Ferguson was giving up all the tactical advantages associated with being on the higher ground.

I wish to make some personal comments again, to include that I was shocked when I walked the plateau myself for the first time in the 21st Century. I could not figure out how Ferguson had been defeated so convincingly by the Patriots. Even this officer, with just a meager dose of tactical military training under his belt, could not imagine a group of soldiers, themselves outnumbered, running up a mountainside at over a twenty-degree incline, defeating an enemy in possession of the "high ground."

The more I looked at the terrain, the more baffled I became...

CHAPTER 25

ALEXANDER'S FORD

On the morning of October 5th our march south resumed. We made little progress and camped at Alexander's Ford by the Green River near the South Carolina border. This lack of progress was undoubtedly due to the condition of the militiamen themselves, for we were all sore from so many days of extremely challenging travel. The condition of our horses was also of great concern to us; they were reaching the point of exhaustion.

Colonel Campbell directed guards to be set up this night so that we militiamen could get a uninterrupted night's sleep, however the guard posts had to be relieved every two hours, so it was not an entirely restful night when taking into consideration the rotation schedule. With all of this going on, I almost forgot that not all our thousand plus force were on horseback, many of them were walking all the time we were riding.

These men who were not on horseback had to be the toughest among all of our militia force. Our leaders only came up with one solution to our wandering travel with its accompanying miseries, that was to send out more scouts in a quest to identify Ferguson's current location.

Surely believing we would be departing soon, I concluded I could now be rated as at least an "amateur horseman" for I could now ride long distances without feeling the intense displeasure my "bottom" had experienced while being on horseback for extended periods of time. Whether or not I should have felt different after riding for only five days is irrelevant; if I was indeed blessed in this way my bottom half was decidedly grateful.

Determined not to let Ferguson escape us, on this evening, October 5th, Campbell gave the order to begin the twenty-one-mile march to "Saunder's Cowpens" in South Carolina.

On to The Cowpens we went...

CHAPTER 26

THE COWPENS

Upon arrival at "The Cowpens" we were advised that the owner was a man named "Saunders," no first name known, who was a wealthy English Tory who raised large herds of cattle, which were corralled here on his property.

When Saunders was questioned by Whig officers, he claimed that Ferguson had not been in the area any time he could recall. All knew he was lying, since intelligence efforts in the area revealed that Saunders in reality, had a close relationship with Ferguson, who had undoubtedly encamped here on several occasions.

It was here, at The Cowpens, that more good fortune came upon us. We were awoken as close to five hundred horsemen suddenly appeared in our midst. Among them were both Carolinian and Georgia leaders, including James Williams, William Chronicle, Edward Lacey and William Hill, the last two protégés of the famous Thomas "Gamecock" Sumpter.

I was able to determine that Colonel Williams hailed from the Ninety-Six District in South Carolina, Major William Chronicle from Tryon County, North Carolina, Colonel Edward Lacey from Chester County, South Carolina and Colonel William Hill from York County, South Carolina.

Colonel Hill was very well known as the founder of the first iron works in the Carolinas, where he produced both cannons and ammunition for the Patriot cause. Others included Frederick Hambright and William Graham from North Carolina, along with other militia forces from South Carolina. Lieutenant Colonel Frederick Hambright was from Lincoln County, North Carolina; while both Colonel John Hardin and Captain John Hardin were South Carolinians.

I did not fail to note that seventy-five of these new recruits were from Laurens County, a short distance from my "future" South Carolina home near Greenville. I was now aware that my 21st Century home was a hotbed" for Whig activity two hundred and fifty years in my past. Statistically, our numbers here increased even more when Georgia militiamen under the command of Colonel Elijah Clarke made their way to where we were bivouacked.

With our joint force now in mind, our leaders mulled over what their next decision might be. Our own scouts finally returned with blank looks on their faces, admitting they had no idea where Ferguson was. At this same time, while everyone was congregating here en masse, our luck dramatically changed to the positive when Joseph Kerr, a "crippled" Patriot spy (this was an act on his part) unexpectedly arrived about noonday with news he had been at Ferguson's base camp at a location known to locals as Kings Mountain.

To know that Ferguson had relocated himself and about one thousand two hundred troops to a site thirty miles to the east on the road to Charlotte Town was the vital information we needed. I began to think to myself, "We are finally going to get some fighting in!" From some of my limited conversations with other militiamen present this day, it was obvious they were of the same mind.

It was early that same day that Campbell came up with the concept of having a manageable force of nine hundred of the most fit mounted horsemen disengage from the large gathering here at The Cowpens and proceed to Kings Mountain. In 21st Century military terminology Campbell's formation of troops could be characterized as a "strike force."

The stark reality of Campbell's decision was that the other well over five hundred men gathered, many of them foot or with crippled steeds, would be left behind at The Cowpens or be forced to march on their own to Kings Mountain.

The purpose of this elite group of mounted militiamen was to engage Ferguson in combat as soon as possible; before he was able to move any further east to Charlotte Town or have the time to recruit reinforcements. As Campbell and his senior officers moved around our campsite, they selected the best of both man and accompanying steed.

Campbell and his cohort were all of the same belief, that being that if we waited any longer to attack, "Bloody Ban" Tarleton and his Dragoons might have been given sufficient time to join Ferguson.

My cousin, Joseph McDowell, now Regimental Commander of the Burke County Militia in my Uncle Charles' absence, approached me and pointedly asked "Cousin Davy, would you and your horse join us in pursuing and engaging in battle Major Ferguson and his Loyalist followers?

I shouted my answer back to him in military style, "Yes, Major McDowell, I would be pleased to follow you, to hell if you so ask!" Although he was our Regimental Commander, I did not call him "Sir" since we were of similar rank. Furthermore, and what some might consider remarkable, I now "hated,' or at least felt great animosity, toward our British oppressors.

I wondered if my "real status" ever played a part in his decision for me to join him at Kings Mountain? Could he have forgotten "where" and "when" I came from? No matter, I was very proud to be among the final twelve or so chosen to meet head-to-head against Ferguson and his Loyalist traitors. I hoped my participation in the battle would turn out to be of great reward to me on both personal and professional levels.

While at The Cowpens late in the afternoon, we enjoyed our first meal of consequence since we left Quaker Meadows. Teams of militiamen shot enough of Saunder's beeves to feed us all, while others gathered up enough corn to support any additional hunger. Nine hundred men on their trustworthy horses would ride that very same evening to what Ferguson thought was his unconquerable mountain fortress.

It was while still here at The Cowpens that I met private James Collins, a youthful looking young man who had settled himself in on a nearby horse blanket. I walked over to him and politely introduced myself, "Good evening young man, I am Major McDowell from the Burke County Regiment in North Carolina. How are you this evening?"

With prior knowledge that private Collins had been chosen to ride with us to Kings Mountain, I further disclosed "I'm doing my best to better get to know the men I'll be fighting with. Could you please tell me something about yourself, like how you came to be here with us?"

His reply was almost immediate, "Sir, my name is James Peter Collins. I am of Irish descent, born on November 22, 1763, in Tryon County, North Carolina, which makes me seventeen years of age next month. My parents carried me as an infant to South Carolina, where we have our home. I joined the militia not long after the fall of Charles Town. I came into service because where I live in South Carolina the Tories were too strong for us, so the Whigs had to associate for their own safety. Before it was thought I could carry arms, I was often employed by Whig leaders, Colonel Moffett in particular, to carry and fetch news. He placed his confidence in me."

Collins reported to me that he and his fellow militiamen gathered here had been unfairly "paraded" and "harangued in short manner this morning on the prospect before us." He noted that provisions were earlier "scanty" and that "hungry men are apt to be fractious." The most significant words to come out of his mouth followed when he stated "the last stake is now up and the severity of the game must be played; everything is at stake, life, liberty, prosperity and even the fate of wife, children and friends seem to be on the issue; death or victory was the only way to escape the suffering." There is no doubt in my mind that James Collins and his family in South Carolina are prime examples of how poorly the British treated their American colonists.

I next remarked to James, "It is a pleasure to know to get to know you, young man. I hope you find enough food to fill up that stomach of yours, which may be very empty right now." Collins added his own context to the food question, "I have often thought that if a man would eat a little parched corn, which by the by I have often thought,

146

then swallow two or three spoonful of honey, then take a good drink of cold water, he could pass longer without suffering than with any other diet he could use."

Now, this was indeed a tough young man! I wondered if there could be any truth to what he was saying about his proposed diet regimen. Parched corn and water? I would take a pass on trying it out myself

The more time I spent at The Cowpens in the early evening, the more Ferguson's current location was substantiated. This came in the form of reports from released prisoners, captured Loyalist messengers and those who had very recently transported foodstuff to Ferguson's camp.

There was not much time left before we would be mounting our horses and be on our way to King's Mountain!

The tension builds...

CHAPTER 27

KNOW THINE ENEMY

When it comes to identifying the "ultimate enemy" of pro-Patriot colonists in 1780, the title and name of Major Patrick Ferguson quickly come to mind. The advantage I had over my Uncle Charles and Cousin Joseph was that I was in possession of information about Ferguson's background before he assumed General Clinton's assigned position as "Inspector of Militia" in May of 1780.

Of course, I could not reveal anything I knew to either my uncle or cousin; it was an unspoken "rule" that no such briefings could or would take place. You could consider this to be our version of "don't ask, don't tell."

Patrick Ferguson was born at Pitfor, Aberdeenshire, Scotland in 1744, the fourth son of James Ferguson of Pitfor, who served as a Senator of the College of Justice and his mother, Anne Murray, sister of Patrick Murray, 5th Lord of Elibank, which presumes that although his family was well off financially, as the fourth son, Patrick Ferguson's options in life were limited. Anne Murry's brother wrote to her and described her son with this description "He is the son of Mars and will be unworthy of his father if he does not give proofs of contempt of pain and danger."

In July 1759, Patrick Fergson's parents purchased him a commission as a Cornet in the Scots Grays after he attended the London Military Academy at age fifteen. As an active participant in battles in both Flanders and Germany in the Seven Years War, he was injured and returned home for a year of recuperation and to deal with the death of his father.

After a period of convalescing, Ferguson returned to active duty and purchased a commission as a Captain in the 70th Regiment of Foot, where he went on to serve in the West Indies. By this time, with money on hand, he was able to purchase a slave plantation called "Castara" on the Island of Tobago. His feelings about slavery remain unanswered in literature.

After a peaceful North American duty assignment in Halifax, Nova Scotia, Fergusion returned to England in 1772, where he invented the "Ferguson Rifle," a firearm weighing only seven and a half pounds versus the fourteen pounds of the "Brown Bess," the standard weapon in use by British troops. "Ferguson's Rifle" design was unique in that it did not require the use of a ramrod before firing, which greatly reduced reloading time. Not only was Ferguson an inventor, but he was recognized by one of his contemporaries, George Hanger, as "the best rifle shot in the British Army."

Ferguson presented his new rifle design to King George III in 1776 and in 1777 was sent, along with ninety hand-picked marksmen, to the American colonies in what I would define as a "military experiment." My review of available literature did not reveal why Ferguson's rifle was not officially put into general use by the British Army, although I believe it would have made sense to do so.

What happens next to Ferguson pertains to an event that has gone down in history as one to be remembered as a precautionary tale The story, as told, portrays Ferguson on a reconnaissance mission with his ninety assigned sharp shooters before the Battle of Brandywine, at which time Ferguson apparently had the opportunity to kill a high-ranking Continental Army officer, one who was in his immediate area, astride his horse.

This Continental Army officer was undoubtedly close enough to be killed by a man with Ferguson's marksmanship talents. Ferguson himself noted that both he and the officer exchanged looks during this encounter. While numerous eyewitness accounts identify this Continental Army officer as General George Washington, Commander of the Continental Army, others claim it was another Continental Army officer, Colonel Casimir Pulaski.

Regardless of the officer's true identity, Ferguson aimed, but hesitated to shoot, unwilling to commit what he saw as a dishonorable assassination, especially as the officer rode away with his back turned. If Ferguson had indeed shot and killed George Washington, the Continental Army's Commanding General and our eventual first President, our nation's history may have turned out much differently. From my personal perspective as a former military officer, to this point in his career, Ferguson was a man of indisputable honor.

It was but a few days later that a life-changing event took place for Ferguson at the Battle of Brandywine, when he took a Patriot musket ball in his right elbow, shattering it. Experiencing an injury such as this would lead most military officers to consider retirement, but not Patrick Ferguson. He made the conscious decision to find ways to deal with his disability for the rest of his life; he did not take the easy way out, which I do find praiseworthy.

While spending months recovering from his wound, Ferguson never gave up on his dream of a military career as he successfully taught himself to use his left arm for such simple tasks as writing, but, more importantly, to be able to effectively fire a weapon or deliver a death blow to his enemies while holding his saber in his non-dominant left hand.

While literature consistently notes the injury to his right arm, I feel they all grossly fail to give him the credit he is due for not giving up on either himself or his military career. By July of 1778, Ferguson was back on active duty, assisting the British as they evacuated Philadelphia, on their way to safe haven in New York.

Something must have changed in Ferguson's value system, for by October 15th of 1778 he ordered his assigned British soldiers to use their bayonets to kill sleeping Continental soldiers at what is referred to as the "Little Egg Harbor Massacre." It was reported that Ferguson and his troops paid little concern for either human lives or public property in this offensive action. His superior officer, General Clinton, was impressed with Ferguson's "successful performance of duty" at Little Egg Harbor. At this time, Ferguson's sense of morality may have displayed its first signs of inconsistency.

Ferguson was promoted to the rank of Major on October 25th, 1779, in the 71st Foot Regiment. His new assignment sent him to

Charles Town in the South Carolina colony in support of the British invasion of the South. While engaged in the submission of Charles Town, Clinton paired Ferguson with a professional rival, Lieutenant Colonel Banastre Tarleton. Reference their respective military performance at Charles Town, Ferguson was, on one hand, portrayed as being "far more humane and considerate of the principles of right and wrong than his colleague Tarleton" and as "Equally intrepid and determined as Tarleton, but cooler and more open to the impulses of humanity." Was it possible Ferguson was having second thoughts about his behavior at Little Egg Harbor?

I mention Tarleton for a specific reason, to differentiate between the two and their separate leadership styles, although both were "hated" by sympathizers to the Whig cause. Clinton's overall assessment of Patrick Ferguson's duty performance at Charles Town was sent to the home government, noting "success, under the direction of that very active and zealous officer, Ferguson." At least at this point in time, no one could accuse Patrick Ferguson of being a braggart like Tarleton, whose most famous claim to fame, upon his later return to England would be "I killed more men and ravished more women than any other man in America."

General Clinton, after suppressing any resistance in Charles Town, next sent Ferguson and his assigned one hundred and fifty Loyalist Provincial Corps to the British stronghold at Ninety-Six in South Carolina. Ferguson, along with Major George Hanger, his contemporary, were directed to recruit all the volunteer soldiers available in this part of the colony and, in addition, gather up all the grain and cattle they could possibly gain possession of.

Ferguson explained to the backcountry farmers that his aim was not to wage war on women and children, but to help relieve their difficulties. He went into more detail in a speech to Loyalist supporters when he proclaimed:

"They (the Loyalists) are strictly enjoined to offer no injury to the persons or property of those men who have been of the rebel side who remain at home and shew a disposition for peace and submission, but to afford every protection in their power to them and to women and children of every denomination…those who plunder and outrage disgrace the name of loyalists will be punished even to death as scoundrels who wish to continue to their country the miseries of war, to distress the women and children and other innocent people, to destroy all the property on both sides, and to retard the progress of His Majesty's arms."

However respectful Ferguson meant his remarks to be, they did not sit well with pro-Patriot families in the colonies. Ferguson's name quickly became associated along with worst of their other British oppressors.

Physically, Ferguson was not as short in stature at 5'8" as many apparently chose to portray him, for he was of average height for the times. He was, however, quite slender in build, which may have contributed to the feeling of disregard many had for him. On the contrary, his Loyalist soldiers felt great admiration for him with his dark straight hair framed a chiseled face.

Ferguson was approachable and able to communicate effectively with the public in civil affairs, contrary to expectations of aloofness. In these early days after his arrival in South Carolina his well-placed communication skills enabled him to recruit a considerable number of Loyalist followers to the British cause.

In this same time period, Tarleton continued to support Clinton's assessment of him as "dashing, tireless and unmerciful." He is the same thoroughly "evil" British officer that was portrayed, with another last name beginning with the letter "T," in Mel Gibson's motion picture "The Patriot."

Ferguson was, however, an Englishman through and through and was convinced it would be ruinous for anyone to be disloyal to the British government. With these beliefs in mind, he showed little compassion for the colonists he considered to be "rebels."

Ferguson eventually earned the nickname "Bulldog" as he led his contingent of three hundred American Volunteers on a rampant campaign of plundering pro-Patriot farms and property; targeting their animals, homes and even household goods. On these military excursions Ferguson did allow his soldiers to commit such ungentlemanly acts as taking rings from the fingers of women and then threatening their very existence by shooting their cattle, killing their primary food source.

When Ferguson was able to capture and identify a Whig sympathizer, he sent them to the British prison facility at Ninety-Six, where many perished due to poor sanitation and malnutrition. As a result of activities such as these, the mere mention of Fergson's name would strike a hateful chord among all who followed the Patriot cause.

It would come to pass that on September 10th, 1780, that Major Patrick Ferguson would make public one of his more famous threats to the Patriot community in the Southern colonies. It was no doubt directed toward those who identified themselves as being either from the "back-country" or "Overmountain Men."

This quite bold message he sent out threatened that "if they did not desist from opposition to British arms, he would march over the mountains, hang their leaders, and lay waste to their country with fire and sword."

Ferguson's challenge did not take into consideration the type of people he was dealing with. His attempt to intimidate them produced just the opposite effect as it served to increase the sense of anger and outrage among the majority Scots-Irish folk living in the southern colonies. Whig supporters were accustomed to being treated as less worthy than those British born, so they shook off Fergurson's insults as if they were dismissing raindrops falling from the sky.

One of my cousins, Joseph McDowell of Pleasant Gardens, held a deep personal grudge against the British for an event taking place on September 15th of this very year. One of Ferguson's officers, Lieutenant Anthony Allaire, while in charge of the ransacking of his property, made public remarks such as "Pleasant Garden is a very handsome place. I was surprised to see so beautiful a tract of land in the mountains." Allaire added "But this settlement is composed of the most violent Rebels I ever saw, particularly the young ladies." Events like this tested cousin "PG" McDowell, for he no doubt had good reason to hate the Loyalists who offended him with these remarks.

Ferguson's version of a declaration of war was in circulation before I joined my relatives at Quaker Meadows on September 30th, although talk of it continued to make the rounds as a topic of discussion on an everyday basis while I was there among the force of fourteen-hundred assembled men.

Ferguson eloquently attempted to reveal his place in life in a letter he wrote to his mother while in America, before the Battle of Kings Mountain:

"The lengths of our lives is not at our command, however, much the manner of them may be. If our Creator enable us to act the part of honour, and to conduct ourselves with spirit, probity, and humanity, the change to another world whether now or fifty years hence, will not be for the worse."

Major Patrick Ferguson's place in history would be decided at the Battle of Kings Mountain...

Chapter 28

On to Kings Mountain

It was about nine o'clock in the evening of October 6th, 1780, that Colonel William Campbell gave his orders to prepare to mount. We had no idea that it was his intent to conduct a pursuit all through the night to engage Ferguson at Kings Mountain. Once again, and to the dislike of everyone, rain began to fall as we rode off. This forced us to take off our hunting frocks and wrap up our rifles and powder to ensure they were kept dry so that we were ready to fire our weapons any time they were needed.

Traveling throughout the night in heavy rainfall had a significant impact on our group; we were already fatigued prior to mounting our horses. We did feel a sense of exaltation about what was to come and by its very nature continued to drive us forward. A major factor working against us was the lack of any decent illumination to guide us, for although it was a half-moon somewhere above us, our ride was made in large part in semi-darkness.

As an example, when I looked up while riding on the very narrow path we were traveling, most of the time I was only able to see the high foliage to the sides of the trail. It was not a comforting situation, since in my own military days, the worst thing that could happen to a soldier would be not knowing where you were on a map. That means being "lost."

The regimental commanders, including Cousin Joseph, rode up to the front of their assigned militiamen. Along the way, some of those in our large group of horsemen momentarily found themselves lost, this a result of poorly defined terrain features and the inclement weather conditions that accompanied it. It wasn't until mid-morning that we were able to ford the swollen Broad River at Cherokee Ford. The militiamen with the sturdiest horses crossed first, with several of them attempting to assist others in the crossing by bracing themselves against the current. One factor in our favor was that the sun came out at the beginning of the next day; it was quite temperate, which enabled us to dry out a bit.

We did halt for a short break along the trail, on what would end up being about a thirty-five-mile trek on our now overextended steeds. With no general instructions having been given to us, those men who had brought extra food with them ate it; while the great majority of our militia force stripped and then ate the stalks of raw corn they discovered in a nearby cornfield. I was happily surprised to find a piece of beef jerky in my saddlebag, which had earlier gone unnoticed. I quickly consumed it.

Upon discovering a second piece tucked away even further down, I became even happier. I removed it and offered it to my friend Robert Patton, who was close by, hitching his horse to a tree. Robert accepted the piece of jerky and gracefully thanked me, "Thank you so much, Sir, you may have saved me from starvation!"

"It is my pleasure," I replied, once again not knowing if that term was even used in 1780. I was indebted to whomever it was back at Quaker Meadows that had placed the jerky there in the first place. My suspicion was that it was Miss Maebell, my great aunt's enslaved servant, who had earlier treated me with such kindness. Word was that we still had some distance to go; that Kings Mountain was still a good fifteen miles away.

We rode on, until we were within two to three miles of Ferguson's location. It was here, on our way to Kings Mountain, that we captured a fourteen-year-old Tory spy named John Ponder. He was arrested for acting suspiciously while in our immediate area. I made sure I was present to hear what we were going to do with him. That said, it was Lieutenant Colonel Hambright who announced he knew Ponder's family and that he believed it likely they were now at Ferguson's camp. Hambright ordered Ponder to be searched before beginning the interrogation.

Found on Ponder was a dispatch from Ferguson to Cornwallis at Charlotte Town, noting his current strength at Kings Mountain and requesting reinforcements. Patriot leaders did not have a problem disclosing Ferguson's location to the multitude of militiamen, yet they chose not to reveal his numbers. Hambright got very specific in his questioning, to include asking how Major Patrick Ferguson was usually dressed. Ponder praised Ferguson as being "the best uniformed man on the mountain." Further, that "you could not see his military suit as he wore a checked shirt, or duster, over it."

Hambright ensured that all his men knew how Ferguson was attired. In his highly accented Pennsylvania Dutch accent, he gave his semi-official orders when he barked out "*Well poys when you see dat man mit a pig shirt on over his clothes you may know who him is and mark him mit your rifles.*"

To say that Hambright held a personal grudge against Ferguson would appear to be an understatement, he wanted to see him dead! After this short stop, we continued toward the mountain. Along the way we ran into a good Whig, George Watkins, recently imprisoned by Ferguson, who verified that Ferguson remained encamped on the plateau at Kings Mountain.

Our road to victory was now before us....

Chapter 29

Arrival At Kings Mountain

From my perspective of reporting this journey, please note I am not using the term "story" to describe it. I must admit I have no idea how many historians have previously reported on the Battle of Kings Mountain. What I do know is they were not, like me and John Crockett, father of Davy Crockett, physically present that day.

All of us, over nine hundred strong, arrived at the base of the hill below Ferguson's plateau promontory at about three o'clock in the afternoon, after a long ride through the night, the next morning and an additional three hours in the afternoon from twelve o'clock onward. We had spent close to eighteen hours in the saddle before we reached our destination.

Overall, our nine hundred ten man militia force consisted of two hundred men from Campbell; one hundred twenty from Shelby; one hundred twenty from Sevier; one hundred ten from Cleveland, ninety from McDowell; sixty from Winston; Lacey one hundred; Williams, sixty and from Graham and Hambright, fifty.

I thanked God for giving me a backside that survived the treacherous overnight ride. There is no doubt that at the beginning of this journey I was not prepared for such strenuous physical activity since I was not, by my nature, a "real horseman" like my Patriot contemporaries. As the days had gone by, I had become as "real" as possible. The skills I'd picked up while serving in the U.S. Army proved to be of great advantage to me as a militiaman. I'd long ago reached mastery level in marksmanship, command of soldiers, moving under fire and evading capture by an enemy.

After tying up our horses to nearby trees, we gathered up our rifles, shot, powder and tomahawks. We then sharpened our knives in preparation to attack. There was no doubt among any of us that we were extremely fortunate, for upon arrival we were able to dismount our horses without revealing our presence to what surely had to be pickets Ferguson stationed above us on the slopes.

Standing beside my horse, I was able to locate Cousin Joseph, who was standing about ten yards away from me in the distance. He had just dismounted his horse, who he had named "Atlas," which I felt was the perfect designation for the steed carrying this stalwart warrior. Quite bluntly, I inquired of him, "Cousin Joseph, what is our strategy for the attack?" His words to me were quite brief, and somewhat terse, "That was decided by the senior Colonels while on our way here. If I receive any additional information, I will so advise you."

His characterization of their decision-making process was becoming more familiar to me. These senior colonial officers in 1780 seemed to be in no hurry to make any decision, or was it possible that there were too many "voices" to be heard? The names of Campbell, Shelby, Sevier, and Cleveland, etc. came to mind.

That said, my intuition told me it would not be long before we would all be running up this very hill while enemy fire was focused down on us by Ferguson's Loyalist troops. It appeared that Ferguson had chosen a very practical defensive position.

One question rang out loud and clear to me; did our commanders know if they had an adequate number of troops to surround and attack the enemy on all sides? This question came to mind since I was aware they did not know the length and width of the plateau.

While waiting to hear exactly what they had determined our attack formation would be, I reinforced in my mind that no matter what their planning might entail, I was accompanying Cousin Joseph and our Burke County Regiment into battle. Within ten minutes of our arrival, I became aware that each of the regimental commanders present were gathering up their troops, each extorting them to "fight like heroes and to either conquer or die." These were indeed inspiring words!

Rather than accept that each regimental commander spontaneously came up with these same identical words, I propose these words were chosen by the senior leaders sometime before we arrived here at the battlefield. This did make sense to me.

While waiting to hear any additional directives from our leaders, I once again took note of the battlefield at Kings Mountain, which I had examined on several occasions there in "my time." When making my initial first visit here in the 21st Century, I found myself wondering how the Patriot militiamen had prevailed, instantly recognizing that the British possessed a distinct advantage by positioning themselves on the higher ground.

I knew that topographic data for Kings Mountain noted that from where we were located here at the bottom, to the plateau on top, it was but sixty to seventy feet in distance, but quite a steep climb at that. None of the accounts I had previously read accurately reflected that the grade approximates twenty-two degrees. Running uphill into gunfire (and bayonets) from troops positioned high above you is certainly not a venture for the faint of heart!

Within a minute, we received our final instructions from a voice unfamiliar to me, but still very authoritarian in nature, enthusiastically encouraging us to "fight 'till he dies." This command was quickly followed by one originating from Colonel William Campbell himself, who yelled out loudly to all within hearing distance, "We will be fighting this battle on foot, the Indian way, not on horseback!"

Cousin Joseph was up next, calling out in an iron-clad like voice to all the men in our Burke County Regiment, "Follow me lads!" By now, our over nine hundred militiamen, to include me, had left our horses at the bottom of the hill and had begun to surround the entire plateau, most of us on foot, with the intent of attacking upwards toward our sworn enemy. Those very few who made the choice to remount or remain on their horses for battle would most likely regret it; the terrain in this environment was not well suited for combat on horseback.

It was at this exact moment that I once more felt a familiar twitch in my ear, this time my left, so I looked down toward my right arm, where I carried my fully loaded Pennsylvania long rifle. Before I could say a word to anyone present, to include my friend Robert Patton or Cousin Joseph, both positioned in crouching positions behind nearby rock formations, I could see my body was in the throes of becoming transparent, which I instantly interpreted as a sign that something was amiss.

With my long rifle now laying discarded on the hillside beside me, questions began to race through my mind, like "What is happening to me?" and "Am I going home now, never to know the truth about the McDowell's and their legacy from Kings Mountain?"

I had no option but to see that another option, my new, "alternative presence" would provide me with the opportunity to personally observe and report on the actions of Cousin Joseph, other McDowell family members and the many other militia members positioned around the battlefield. I wondered if it were possible that my reporting could serve to support and/or replace some of the testimony collected from its participants many decades later, when their memories had very likely faded as the years passed by.

These fateful fifty-seven minutes of combat to come would be known from this day forward as "The Battle of Kings Mountain." I did not hesitate to follow my cousin and our Burke County militiamen as they started running from tree to tree for cover, reloading and firing as they began their ascent up the mountainside.

However, as the seconds went by, my body became totally engulfed in the sensation of floating. I was able to comprehend I was no longer on foot, but "above," observing the entire battlefield from an all-encompassing perspective, examining each combative position as it would be seen on the face of a clock.

Quite remarkably, I found I was now agile enough to move, at will, from any position on the plateau to another. I was also quite fortunate in that I could hear spontaneously expressed words and complete sentences from both our militiamen and those supporting the Loyalist cause. Miraculously, while now "floating," both my mind and body felt renewed; I was no longer experiencing the fatigue that had to be negatively impacting my fellow Patriot brothers, who were all fighting for their country's absolute right to exist.

Floating above the battlefield, I could now see...

CHAPTER 30

THE BATTLEFIELD CLOCK

From my perspective of reporting to you, please note I am not using the term "story" to describe any events that took place at the Battle of Kings Mountain. I have no idea how many historians have previously taken up the task of describing the events of October 7th, 1780.

It is my opinion that historians tend to discount or greatly minimize the significance of the battlefield topography and its influence on the eventual outcome. For that dynamic alone, topography, the Loyalist forces would likely been projected as the victors.

I am including a physical description of the battlefield that day, from my position, "hovering" above it. Please bear with me and imagine you were there, at my side, looking down at the battlefield. Your cooperation in this manner will enable you to visualize where all the fighting took place that day at Kings Mountain.

The map I've included will help you avoid some of the confusion traditionally associated with accounts of the battle. I am going to be as specific as possible about regimental troop areas of operation on the battlefield so that you may more clearly comprehend the events as they took place. Observed from twelve o'clock (midnight) to 11:59, you simply need to look at the clockface to locate the position of Patriot leaders and their regiments.

By its very nature, this battle incorporated a great myriad of military combat actions into a short fifty-seven-minute timeframe. No matter how time-limited, the historical significance of this Patriot versus British Loyalist confrontation was accurately characterized by Thomas Jefferson as "The Turning of the Tide of Success in the American Revolution."

As a point of reference, the plateau measured about six hundred yards in length and at its narrowest point only seventy to eighty yards in width, sloping downward at about a ten-degree angle. In their upward charge the Patriots found the hillsides to be both rocky and heavily wooded, covered in both mature hardwood and short-leaf pine trees. There is no doubt that this mix of trees and rocky outcrops provided the Patriots protection from enemy gunfire coming down from above, while at the same time giving them a brief respite from running non-stop up the hillsides.

The Patriot regiments may be located on the clockface as follows:

Cleveland's Regiment @12:02; Lacey's Regiment @1:00; Chronicle & Hambright's Regiments@ 2:00; Winston's Regiment @2:17; McDowell's Regiment @5:00; Campbell's Regiment @ 7:00; Sevier's Regiment @ 8:00; Shelby's Regiment @ 10:00; and Williams' Regiment @11:30

Any future comments about actions that took place on the battlefield can be referenced to the map provided…

Map of the Kings Mountain Battlefield

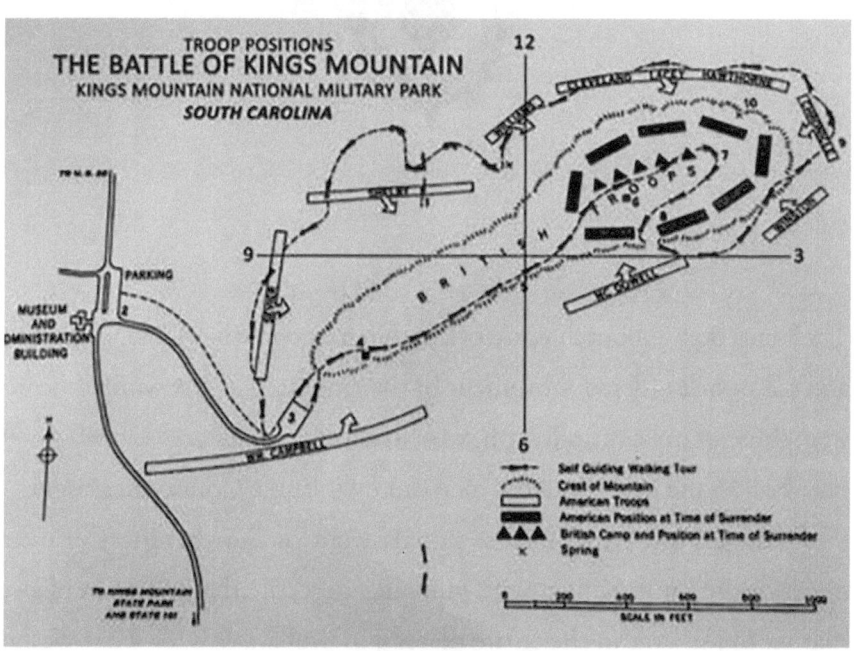

CHAPTER 31

THE BATTLE BEGINS

The attack began about three o'clock in the afternoon when Colonels Shelby and Campbell ordered movement of the troops. The first words I heard were those of my cousin Joseph, who in a forceful military voice shouted out "Follow me lads" to all the men our own Burke County Regiment.

All along the battlelines, signals went out to this mass of over nine hundred militiamen, with guidance to secure themselves in places that would surround the entire plateau in preparation for what was to come. I could hear Colonel Campbell yell out "Fresh prime your guns and every man go into battle firmly resolving to fight until he dies!"

Sevier and Campbell's men were to assault the mountain's "heel," while those led by Shelby, Williams, Lacey, Cleveland, Hambright, Winston and McDowell would attack the main Loyalist position at the other end of the plateau.

It made sense to me now as to why there was no record of a "Major David McDowell" being present at the Battle of Kings Mountain. In conjunction with this, I then remembered that on my initial 21st Century fact-finding mission to the Kings Mountain National Military Park on the South Carolina/North Carolina border, that the names of both Charles and Joseph McDowell were etched onto the battle monument.

I concluded that rather than being on the field of battle as a participant, the alternative left to me was to remain unattached and unnamed, yet in a position to accurately report, first-hand, on this historically significant event.

Remarkably, I could see the entire battlefield below, from 12:00 to 12:59; intently observing our militiamen running up the steep slopes on all sides toward the enemy encamped above. Our Patriot forces were indeed blessed, for although the Loyalist troops had the assumed advantage of shooting down at us from above, they were having a difficult time striking us, their human targets.

I could see that on the battlefield below there were over nine hundred Patriot militiamen in place against about eleven hundred Loyalist troops, each side hoping for the same outcome, the destruction of their enemy. The fact that so much was going on here in fifty-seven chaotic minutes makes it impossible for me to report to you on every individual battlefield encounter, for there were an almost infinite number of them. I will do the best I can to identify the most significant events of the day, along with the duty performance of any of my McDowell relatives, whether it be either positive or negative in nature.

THE ENEMY IS IDENTIFIED

What kind of men made up Ferguson's force on the plateau known as "Kings Mountain?" Of the eleven hundred here under Ferguson's command, one to two hundred were "Provincials," not a permanent corps, but one brought up for special service from the Kings American Regiment, which was headquartered in and around the New York and New Jersey colonies. In the early part of the war, Ferguson's Provincials wore green coats, just as Ferguson's "Rangers" did at Brandywine.

The Provincials honed one skill in particular, the use of the bayonet to charge their adversaries. Ferguson ensured that all Tory troops under his command mastered themselves in the use of this technique. Ferguson contributed to what he felt would be their success by reconfiguring their long rifles so that a blade could be secured to the muzzle of their weapon.

Kings Mountain would be, by far, an All-American battle, however, each side had one non-native-born combatant. For the Loyalists it would be their senior officer, Major Patrick Ferguson, born in Aberdeenshire, Scotland; while for the Patriots it was Lieutenant Colonel Frederick Hambright, born in the Duchy of Bavaria. Please keep in mind that some of the over two-thousand American-born colonists fighting for the British this day were there because of British intimidation.

12:02 CLEVELAND

Colonel Cleveland's Surrey County Regiment appeared at about 12:02 on The Battlefield Clock. As Campbell and Shelby's men began their attack, I could see Cleveland and his men were delayed for about ten minutes in the swampy ground they had chosen to occupy at the bottom of the rise; it was a quagmire to move through. While waiting to make his way upward, Cleveland went around his lines of anxious militiamen and addressed them:

"My brave fellows, we have beaten the Tories and we can beat them again. They are all cowards; if they had the spirit of men they would join with their fellow-citizens in supporting the independence of their country. When you are engaged you are not to wait for the word of command from me. I will show you, by my example, how to fight; I can undertake no more. Every man must consider himself an officer and act from his own judgement. Fire as quick as you can and stand your ground as long as you can. When you can do no better, get behind trees, or retreat; but I beg you not to run quite off. If we are repulsed let us make a point of returning and renewing the fight; perhaps we may have better luck in the second attempt than the first. If any of you are afraid, such shall have to leave to retire, and them are requested immediately take themselves off."

After hearing Cleveland make this offer, one I had never heard during my time as a soldier in the U.S. Army, one militiaman, John Judd of Cleveland's regiment, offered to remain behind "to hold the horses." I could see on the faces of his fellow militiamen that his words identified him as a coward. His offer made such a measurable impact on all assembled that his brother, Rowland Judd, stepped forward to save their family honor by making it clear he was prepared to give his life for the cause of freedom.

Once Cleveland's regiment began their offensive, they progressed up the hillside rapidly. While under heavy fire, I could hear Cleveland shouting in a bellowed voice "Yonder is your enemy and the enemy is mankind!" Strange phrasing, I could debate the meaning of the second part of his proclamation, but my attention continued to be focused on battlefield exploits.

As Cleveland and his troops proceeded up the slope, they used the natural habitat, consisting of trees, rocks and even bushes to protect themselves from the Loyalist musket fire. Cleveland, ducking and weaving himself, was continually yelling "A little nearer to them my brave men!" Cleveland fascinated me.

Compared to a anyone else on the battlefield this day, Cleveland would have to be seen as a "prime target" at six foot one and over three hundred pounds. Surviving the battle as he did, many would propose he had to be under God's protection for the entirety of the fifty-seven-minute battle.

There is no doubt Benjamin Cleveland, with his corpulent bodyweight, did not fit the physical profile of a "typical Revolutionary War fighting man." That said, he consistently exhibited courage under fire the many times I observed him that day. After speaking those inspiring words to his men, I saw Cleveland's horse "Roebuck" struck by two separate musket balls. This meant he would certainly be looking for a new horse right away!

Dismounting from Roebuck, Cleveland moved out on foot. He would later transition back to horse when a new mount was secured. Having his first horse shot out from under him confirmed my earlier assumption that leading from the front on horseback dramatically increased the odds of becoming the victim of a musket ball.

It was after this very event, his unmounting, that I could hear a Loyalist "story" begin to make its rounds among the troops present. According to the rumors, Charles Bowen, of Campbell's regiment, was close to the top of the plateau in search of the body of his allegedly deceased brother, Lieutenant Reece Bowen, at which time when he was abruptly confronted by Colonel Cleveland. Considering the only identifying sign to distinguish Whig from Tory was the placement of either a piece of paper or tree sprig in their hats, Cleveland demanded the countersign, which Bowen failed to produce, most likely because he was very nervous.

Believing the man in front of him was a Tory, his sworn enemy, Cleveland aimed the muzzle of his long rifle toward Bowen after he failed to speak the countersign, which was "Buford." Miraculously, Cleveland's weapon misfired, at which time Bowen went on the attack, seizing the opportunity to assault Cleveland. Within microseconds of burying his tomahawk into Cleveland's head, a soldier named Buchanan, who was familiar with both, shouted out the countersign.

Cleveland, recognizing how favored by providence he was not to have a tomahawk planted in his skull, set aside his weapon and pulled Bowen into his arms for a big hug to express his joy that both were survivors of the encounter. I continued to hear Cleveland's exhortations as men moved up the steep twenty-two-degree incline toward the top.

One of the more careless of Cleveland's officers I observed this day was Lieutenant Samuel Johnson, who led his assigned militiamen into a very untenable position on the slopes, where he not only lost several of his assigned men to weapons fire, but found himself with four bullet holes in the skirt of his coat, one of the four causing a severe wound to his stomach. Some may have characterized his movement on the battlefield this day as "adventurous," while I would prefer to use the term "risky" to describe what I consider his poor decision making. Losing any soldiers while attempting to appear either "bold" or "dashing" will never be acceptable to me.

While thinking "Oh my" about Lieutenant Johnson's behavior, I did see a thoroughly captivating example of hand-to-hand-combat in the form of another of Cleveland's young officers, Charles Gordon. Watching from above the battlefield, I observed Gordon inserting himself into proximity of the enemy, where he seized the shirt of one Tory and began dragging him down the mountainside, unaware this officer was still in possession of his pistol, which he discharged in Gordon's direction, invalidating the use of Gordon's left arm. Acting immediately being struck by this bullet. Gordon pulled out his sword and fatally dispatched the Tory soldier. I consider his actions on the battlefield to be an example of personal valor, setting a high bar for all of the soldiers under his command.

A soldier I would later identify as William Griffis was making his push upward on the hill when he was met by Loyalist soldiers moving downward, in formation of course, with their bayonets poised out in front of them. By the time this encounter ended, Griffis was not only wounded in the right shoulder by a musket ball but stabbed in his right leg by an enemy bayonet. He was among the first of many Patriot brothers to receive multiple wounds this day.

Griffis was joined on the battlefield by Joseph Philllips, who was in this regiment's first wave to attack the Loyalist picket line. He was joined by John Witherspoon of Captain John Lewis' company. It was his superior, Major Michah Lewis, who while still mounted, announced to Colonel Cleveland "We executed the order and destroyed nearly all the picket while on Light Horse." If you been there with me to see the very challenging terrain features, I believe you would have similar concerns about the viability of successfully making it to the top while riding a horse under a hail of bullets.

I observed Witherspoon actively engaged in the battle; being repulsed, retreating and then attacking again, at least once, after bayonet charges. While I was focusing on Cleveland's regiment, reports of a similar nature continued to come in from other friendly sources.

Before I could turn my attention to another location on the battlefield clock, I could hear Witherspoon comment, in an exasperated voice "Colonel Williams received a mortal would and Major Lewis was also wounded." I would have to wait to report on this event, which I knew was one of significance.

It was clear to me now that I had been blessed with yet another "special talent," one in addition to my already burgeoning repertoire. I now had both exceptional hearing and vision! This new dimension of my existence here would allow me to go both "back" and" forward" in short spurts of time for observations. Without this ability, I would be unable to accurately report on so many of the events happening that day on the battlefield at Kings Mountain.

Cleveland's men would be the first to reach the plateau, while the fighting continued elsewhere...

CHAPTER 32

LACEY, CHRONICLE, HAMBRIGHT, & WINSTON

LACEY 1:00

Colonel Edward Lacey's regiment took their places to the right of Cleveland's on some of the most challenging terrain at site. Lacey's soldiers were in large part Scots-Irish from the South Carolina counties of York and Chester Counties and were battle-hardened by a summer of continuous conflict. Lacey, a Colonel himself, was a very interesting man. While he was growing up in South Carolina, he visited a gypsy fortune teller who told him he would be a great leader, one who would never shed any blood. Lacey led a South Carolina militia force operating from Ninety-Six and rose to the rank of Colonel after the Patriot defeat at Camden.

Rumors were that one of Lacey's militiamen had a less than favorable reputation in that he would "go weak at the smell of gunpowder and immediately retreat," so I made it a point to pay close attention after he was identified by his fellow militiamen. Was this man being unveiled as nothing more than a "coward?"

As the air filled with the sounds of muskets and rifles firing, this same militiaman could be heard exclaiming "I am determined to stand my ground today, live or die;" quickly followed up by the very unpatriotic act of him grabbing the reins of his horse and retiring close to one hundred and fifty yards to the rear! This was likely the only time during the battle that I would find something "humorous." I also wondered why this soldier, with this reputation, had been chosen to join our nine-hundred-and-ten-man force here at Kings Mountain? This question would go unanswered.

Moments later, another militiaman whose name I did not know, yelled out "Lacey's gone, his fine horse has already been shot out from under him," apparently in error, the result of his misidentification of the horse's rider. While Lacey remained on the scene, his regiment suffered two probable fatalities, David Duff and William Watson. Another militiaman, Robert Miller, of Chester County, received a serious wound to his thigh.

The British forces had a rationale behind their bayonet charges, they reserved their rifle fire until their downward pursuit had concluded, at which time they retreated upward with Patriots in pursuit, when they could be picked off by Ferguson's riflemen. These "retreats" were made with purposeful intent, although no matter how much planning they had done, it could not overcome what has been called "terrestrial infraction," which can cause one to shoot over the head of those below.

Where some propose that the British forces were merely trying to save their ammunition by using this tactic, others characterize it as unreliable.

2:00 CHRONICLE & HAMBRIGHT

Major William Chronicle, born in Belmont, North Carolina, was in command of sixty to eighty men in the Lincoln County Regiment, second in command to Lieutenant Colonel Frederick Hambright. Their force consisted of men known as "The South Fork Boys." How a major came to lead a regiment is quite simple, his superior officer Colonel William Graham, was relieved by Colonel Campbell, the Commanding Officer, just before the battle, when he granted him permission to go to the bedside of his seriously ill wife.

Chronicle would then assume command of the regiment. All were from the area around the South Fork of the Catawba River."

Lieutenant Colonel Frederick Hambright, of higher rank than Chronicle, gracefully deferred his right to the leadership role because Chronicle was more familiar with the battlefield terrain at Kings Mountain. As he and his men were fast approaching the base of the ridge, I could clearly hear Chronicle shouting out "Face up the hill!" entreating them to follow him upward in that direction`

Chronicle was about twenty-five feet from a group of Loyalists formed at the top of the ridge when he was struck in the breast by a musket ball. He died almost instantly, to forever lie here, his final resting place, on the battlefield where he fought so bravely. He was indeed a very courageous young lad, really a "man," who led at the front, setting an example by making the ultimate sacrifice at twenty-five years of age. Three of his Captains, John Maddox, William Rabb and John Boyd suffered a similar fate this day, only to join Chronicle in eternal peace on the mountainside.

I read about this incident involving Chronicle multiple times. I recalled that when he fell, taking his last breath, he was still wearing the gold ring his fiancé, Miss Alexander of Mecklenburg County, North Carolina, had given him. Although my focus was somewhat limited, I was able to see the noted gold band on one of Chronicle's fingers, which greatly saddened me, bringing me close to tears, for it reminded me of my lost love, my dear Ann, who was wearing her gold wedding band when she passed away five, or over two hundred years ago.

Frederick Hambrecht was born in Moosbach, Duchy of Bavaria (later Germany) in 1727. At eleven years of age his family moved to the Pennsylvania colony in America. In 1755 he relocated to South Virginia and by 1769 was residing in Tryon County, North Carolina. Using his newly adopted and Anglicized surname "Hambright," he was a major proponent for the colonies throwing off the collar of oppression the British had imposed on them.

With the militia rank of Lieutenant Colonel in the militia, Hambright assumed command of the Lincoln County Regiment at age fifty-three. Hambright, showing little regard for his own safety, charged up the hillside on his horse and was struck by enemy fire, in this instance to his thigh, possibly cutting an artery. His boot quickly began overflowing with blood, while his hat was the recipient of three separate musket ball holes, none of which caused any injury. I wondered if he was just lucky or protected by Providence?

Hambright, still on horse, disregarded all the requests being made by his subordinates to dismount. Next, in his quite distinct Pennsylvania

Dutch accent, he called out to his troops *"Huzza my prave boys, fight on for a few minutes more and the pattle will be over!"*

I was able to identify several other heroes on this day from Chronicle and Hambright's South Fork Boys, to include sixteen-year-old Robert Henry, who could be seen taking up position behind a log, firing at the enemy and then preparing his weapon to fire another shot. At this time, the Loyalists began another of their downhill trots with their muskets, with bayonets attached. One of them found young Henry on the hillside, not yet prepared to fire his weapon.

In less time than to take a breath, I could see a Loyalist soldier lunging forward with his bayonet toward young Henry. Although striking close to its intended target, its point glanced upon contact with the rifle barrel, passed in a downward direction through one of Henry's hands and, finally, into his thigh. Henry's luck had not run out yet since one of his fellow South Fork Boys, who was cloistered behind a adjacent tree, saw what was happening.

This militiaman quickly turned and fired his weapon, putting a fatal round into the enemy soldier. William Caldwell, a fellow militiaman in his regiment, attempted to pull the bayonet out of Henry's thigh. Then, upon observing the bayonet still embedded, kicked at his leg, with the result it was finally released from his leg. Was this typical of how battlefield "medicine" was practiced in 1780? If so, I wanted no part of it!

I realized that I had spent a lot of my time with Chronicle and Hambright's troops, but could not resist watching the actions of one William Twitty, another South Fork Boy. Twitty was told his best friend had been killed by a Loyalist soldier when he was doing his best to reach the top of the plateau. After some time, Twitty believed he knew the location of the antagonist who ended his friend's life.

I watched as he waited patiently until he could see the Loyalist's head poking out from behind a tree. He aimed his weapon and fired, killing this enemy instantly. The entry wound literally "blew his brains out." These are just a few examples of heroism that were exhibited on the battlefield this day; there were far too many to accurately document them all, however hard I might try.

2:17 WINSTON

Major Joseph Winston had been detached with a portion of Surrey and Wilkes County troops to serve on the northeast right side of the battlefield close to 2:00; between McDowell and Hambright. Most of what I know about Winston's duty performance at Kings Mountain would come from my observations of his subordinate officer, Captain William Lenoir. Although holding an officer's rank, Lenior, was, at his own choice, "Serving as a common soldier and did not pretend to command anyone."

On the subject of "strategy," I believe I need to elaborate further. On our way to Kings Mountain on horseback, I overheard Lenoir speaking to some of his fellow militiamen on this very topic. Lenoir revealed that the leaders *"concluded that said detachment would be formed into four columns; two of the column should march on each side of the road, as silently as they could, and that they should govern their march by the view of each other; Colonel Winston would be placed at the head of the right hand column; Colonel Cleveland at the head of the left; and Colonel Campbell would, since he had come the greatest distanc from the State of Virginia, be complimented with the command of the whole detachment."* These instructions were about as "detailed" as they ever were.

It appeared to me that before the battle began, that no matter what his intent, Winston was identified as an "officer who could lead men." Lenoir stayed close to Winston as the battle began, noting to others, "I fell in immediately with Major Winston, in front of the right column, where no one appeared to regard their own personal safety." This comment reminded me that these were militiamen, not trained Continental Army soldiers, who were fighting this day. They were, instead, "Indian fighters."

They were within thirty paces of the Loyalists when Lenoir stopped, after seeing one of their assigned soldiers, William Roberston, fall within six feet of him. I was able to see another soldier come up quickly to his side and make the following request: "Give me your shot-bag, old fellow," acknowledging his own ammunition supply was exhausted. What a tragic scene this was to see; the fallen soldier gave him the ammunition from his own dying hands. This was a truly patriotic act on their past.

Within this same short timeframe, Lenoir was shot in both his left side and arm, while other rounds went through his hair line and clothing. Lenoir understood he was fortunate none of these musket balls caused him to suffer a fatal injury.

Although I did not see Winston's men subjected to any bayonet charges, at least two of the regiment's members (Thomas Bicknell and Daniel Siske) succumbed from Loyalist-caused wounds; while other serious injuries were incurred by Major Lewis; Captains Lewis, Smith and Lenior; and Lieutenants Johnson, Smith, Gordon and Childers.

Although men's lives were lost, I have no choice but to characterize some of my battlefield observations as "interesting," due to the battle's "back and forth" nature. After surrounding the plateau, our militia could be seen going up, down, then up again, only to be challenged each time by the Loyalists repeating these same steps.

My final view of the battlefield at 2:00 enabled me to sight Loyalist forces being encircled by militia forces on the plateau, their left wing in retreat, having no option but to move closer to their right.

It was now my Cousin Joseph McDowell's time…

CHAPTER 33

MCDOWELL

5:00 MCDOWELL

McDowell and his ninety men took their places at three o'clock. As the battle upward began, our Burke County Regiment militiamen watched as one after another Loyalist musket ball sailed over our heads. I was once again confronted with a serious question, "Were these Loyalists, the great majority of them kin to us by family ties in the Carolinas, never trained, like we all, in fighting Indian style?" This appears to be a question left unanswered by historians. This consequential question would have to remain for later consideration.

I could see that our militiamen down below had progressed less than ten yards up the hillside before we experienced our first casualty of the day, a private in our regiment, John Wilfong, who took a musket ball to his right arm, no doubt resulting in a very serious injury.

I did know that in these times the possibility of infection in a wound could have more serious consequences than the damage done by the musket ball itself. John Wilfong was the first of many casualties our men of the Burke County Regiment would suffer this day.

I was able to watch the battle upfront as the fighting erupted, with the actions of several of the Burke County men of particular interest to me: John Dobson, John Duckworth, Joseph James Rogers, Thomas Kennedy and John Wilfong, previously mentioned.

These men, while at the bottom of the hill, were among the closest to Ferguson's headquarters on the plateau above when the assault began. As a result, they were subject to some of the more serious, although not necessarily life-threatening combat injuries.

In the corner of my eye, as he was moving up toward the ridgeline at 3:00 o'clock, I could see John Dobson suddenly struck by a musket ball as it passed through his right arm near his elbow joint. Mere seconds later, before Dobson could in any way deal with this injury, another musket ball struck him on his left side, around his back, lodging itself up in his right shoulder. Considering all the weapons fire being dispersed downhill toward him, although wounded, these injuries would not take his life. A few other militiamen would not be so lucky.

I would next observe Joseph James Rogers, who like his Patriot brothers, was moving from tree to tree in an upward direction. Rogers was part of what he himself called "the right wing of the Army during battle." From his initial starting position at three o'clock, he began moving west and upward toward the center of the plateau.

I observed Rogers for a few minutes, noting he was compelled to retreat, at least once, when the British Loyalists brandished their bayonets in an attempt to push the Patriot militiamen back down the sloping mountainsides. On his second try at moving up the hill he caught a Loyalist musket ball in his calf, halting his progress, but not enough to reduce his determination to keep charging up the hillside, which he did. What a great display of grit!

In the same general area, I could see John Duckwork, whom I had met on October 6th at The Cowpens, moving very slowly, uphill, still somewhat debilitated by the wound I had heard he had received to his shoulder earlier in the year on June 20th at the Battle of Ramsour's Mill, which is near present day Lincolnton, North Carolina.

Thomas Kennedy, also assigned to our regiment, could be seen fighting on what he termed to be "the eastwardly side of the mountain," along with his regimental counterparts. Kennedy would eventually reach the summit, firing his weapon at Loyalist troops throughout his ascent. Kennedy was fortunate in that he would not sustain any injuries during the engagement.

While all of this was chaotic action taking place, with hundreds of Patriot forces running up the hill, or "acting as their own commanders," Joseph McDowell continued to fight heroically alongside his men. He could be heard yelling out words of encouragement to them as simple as "Keep moving," while fervently pointing his index finger in an upward direction toward where Ferguson claimed superiority.

As musket ball after musket ball raced downhill in his direction, McDowell kept his composure while moving rapidly, from one rocky outcrop to another, and tree to tree, while firing, reloading and firing again. Soon thereafter, I found myself well positioned above the battlefield, thrilled to observe at least three Loyalist soldiers fall after discharges from Joseph McDowell's long rifle.

Joseph was undoubtedly a great marksman at the age of twenty-four, or for that matter, at any age. Running up the mountain in what was the equivalent of a zig-zag course, he was involved in every aspect of the battle, often stopping, when timely, alongside his friend and company commander, Captain Robert Patton.

It was extremely difficult to take in the duty performance of all of the militiamen under McDowell's command due to all the chaos in play, which many would later characterize as "an uncoordinated assault" on the plateau.

McDowell's regiment, consisting of men from Burke and Rutherford Counties, were assigned to one of the flanking columns surrounding the mountain. During the battle, as Ferguson attempted to advance toward Campbell, Sevier, Winston and Hambright, he was being pursued by Cousin Joseph, Shelby, Williams and Cleveland. As the battle continued, McDowell and the other commanders were tightening their grip on Ferguson, eventually encircling him from all directions.

McDowell and his riflemen found themselves in a key position on the front lines, where they performed with distinction as the brave men they were. It will never be known how his older brother, Colonel Charles McDowell, would have performed at Kings Mountain, but Joseph McDowell did lead their regiment with great honor. Joseph had no problem working under Campbell's overall command or with Shelby, Sevier and Cleveland. Joseph received praise from his superiors for his steadfastness in the face of bayonet charges, with one other reporting that "a lesser man might have fallen apart and caused the rally upward to fail."

All taken into consideration, McDowell was one of the heroes of the day. He was undoubtedly a great leader, one who did not "toot his own horn," but let his actions speak for him. Compared to what I'd seen of his behavior in private over the past few days, on the battlefield he was an entirely different man, one who would not hesitate to shout out encouragement to his men to fight on.

Cousin Joseph would receive acclaim from both subordinates and superiors alike for ensuring his men "remained united, disciplined and courageous," for "continuing to press the attack in coordination with the other commanders" and for "sustaining Patriot resolve during counterattacks."

These comments from his superiors speak volumes about Cousin Joseph's professionalism as a leader of men. If military medals were given out in 1780 like they are in the 21st Century, Joseph would surely have received one of the highest honors.

Later, when victory was won and accolades were handed out, Joseph preferred to stay out of the limelight. He was not a boastful man. Anyone who would attempt to usurp his mantle of leadership of the Burke County Regiment that day would be seen by me in a very unfavorable light. How such a young man of only twenty-four could perform the duties of regimental commander in such an effective, truly outstanding manner is a relevant question. I wondered if he had inherited this personality trait for courage under fire from his family's warrior roots dating back in Scotland in the 15th Century, or even earlier, to the time of familial Viking raids on Ireland?

I observed one particularly colorful event on the battlefield at three on the Battlefield Clock. While my cousin Joseph was moving uphill, in the process of readying his pistol to fire at a Loyalist soldier, this same enemy soldier was doing his best to either impale Joseph on his bayonet, or at least drive him back down the incline. As the Loyalist soldier was announcing his presence with the point of his bayonet, my cousin, basically defenseless, was saved by Captain Robert Patton, who within these same few precious seconds, fired his long rifle, putting a large, instantly fatal hole in the head of this same enemy soldier. I wished I had still been physically present so that I could offer my thanks to Captain Patton for his timely intervention.

It was both amazing and eye-opening to be there to see Captain Robert Patton save the life of my cousin at the Battle of Kings Mountain. This event was never mentioned in any first-hand accounts I'd ever read about the battle, so I felt privileged to witness it in person. Moreover, I felt it possible that the calm and deliberate state of mind I routinely displayed while in the Army was a trait passed down through the centuries through the McDowell blood line.

Our Commanding Officer gets in his licks....

CHAPTER 34

CAMPBELL

7:00 CAMPBELL

Here sat Campbell and his men at 7:00. His were the first to initiate the assault after the ridge was surrounded by the nine plus hundred Patriot militiamen. There have been several different versions about the terrain features Campbell encountered when he attacked from the bottom of the hill, however from where I could see it was just as precipitous at its starting point than where the other militia regiments made their initial attempts to scale the hillside from positions in the 12:00-3:00 range. Colonel Sevier and his regiment were in close proximity at about 7:00, as both began their attack.

I can in no way discount the gallantry and tenacity on display by either Campbell or his men, for from what I could observe they were, to the man, quite courageous. After he gave instructions to the right and left wings to give the Indian war-hoop, the battle commenced prematurely when Shelby's troops were fired on by the enemy. With that first crack of sound from musket fire, the Battle of Kings Mountain had begun!

Within these next few seconds, I could see Campbell throw off his coat and lead the attack himself, yelling out "Here they are, my brave boys; shout like hell and fight like devils!" as he wielded the "Claymore of the Argyle" in his hand. The "claymore," a large sword, was a weapon traditionally wielded by Scottish legends like Rob Roy McGregor.

I could not help but look down toward Major Ferguson's second in command, Captain Abraham DePeyster, up on the plateau, cringing as he heard Campell's words; they had a similar ring to those he heard earlier this same summer at the Battle of Musgrove's Mill. DePeyster's reaction to the blood-curdling yells of these colonels seemed to unhinge him; they were simply not those expressed by gentlemen." He turned to Major Ferguson, who was standing nearby. In a frustrated voice, DePeyster shouted out "These things are ominous-These damned yelling boys?" When DePeyster looked toward Ferguson, he could see the expression of fear in his eyes. It was indeed wonderful to watch both sides as the battle moved on to the next events to take place.

Campbell would begin the battle on his sorel horse but soon realized he was presenting himself as too large a target for Loyalist muskets, so he eventually transitioned to being on foot to lead his men. Campbell's choice of horse would later bring about great controversy, in particularly inspired by his fellow Colonel and professional "rival," Isaac Shelby.

Major Benjamin Sharp, one of Campbell's subordinate officers, could be heard commenting that once they were organized for battle "We were ordered to dismount and rushed impetuously with the Colonel at our head." Paying close attention to the battlefield, I watched Campbell, on three separate occasions, ride his horse backwards and forward in front of our lines, each a very courageous act by itself.

I observed Campbell routinely moved in and out between his soldiers and the enemy while delivering exclamations such as "Boys, remember your liberty!" John Witherspoon, also in Campbell's regiment, was in awe of Campbell's leadership and praised his ability to "animate his men in defending every point that seemed necessary."

We were taking casualties of our own, often to our officers on horseback and men who were not taking their personal safety into consideration when they too readily exposed their positions. I described this battle to you as being "chaotic" and that it was, the mountain was engulfed in one gigantic volcano-like explosion of gunfire and smoke as Loyalist musket balls continued to be expelled downhill toward the Patriots below, frequently flying over their heads, while our own were sending their more skillful rifle shots uphill with measurably greater success. The point I am attempting to make is this one; no matter how outmanned we were, or disadvantaged by terrain features, God was apparently on our side this day, at least regarding the flight of our musket balls!

Campbell's two hundred men had the same experience as the other militiamen surrounding the mountain when it came to being "poked at" by "Ferguson's Rangers." Ferguson's assigned soldiers had first used this unit designation when their sharpshooting skills were featured at the Battle of Brandywine. Here, at the Battle of Kings Mountain, Ferguson's "Rangers" failed him miserably as they exhibited extremely poor marksmanship skills.

During the battle, Campbell led his troops out in front, a sign of a great leader, one who exposes himself to the same dangers facing his men. Of Campbell's assigned men, the ratio of officers to privates wounded was thirteen to one. As already stated, Campbell set the example for his officer corps by consistently leading them, while exposing himself to unrelenting Loyalist gunfire. Most likely a result of their heroism, a third of the wounded this day would come from Campbell's regiment.

After one bayonet charge after another failed to intimidate them, Campbell continued to blurt out encouraging words to his men out of concern any might suddenly take to the rear, running away repeating past behavior. Reinforcing his own instructions, to once again to regain momentum, he encouraged them with these words "Halt, return my brave fellows and you will drive the enemy immediately!" Hearing his request, his men did exactly what Campbell asked them to do, they kept fighting until they had victory in hand.

Ensign Robert Campbell. one of Colonel Campbell's subordinate officers and kin to him, was observed by me throughout the day's action. When he first arrived at Kings Mountain, I could see he was doing some reconnoitering when he found himself in a position just one quarter of a mile from the enemy sentry posts. I was astonished when I observed that his presence remained unreported by the Loyalists. To allow our militiamen to "sneak up" on Ferguson's forces in this manner provides further evidence of Fergson's personal negligence in preparing a legitimate defense.

Ensign Campbell was in Colonel Campbell's immediate vicinity when the first shots were fired. He was proud to be amongst the first to see the Loyalist sentries retreat, adding they were "leaving some of their men to crimson thee earth," which leaves little doubt they were dead.

Moreover, as the battle progressed, Ensign Campbell could be heard giving his superiors updates, such as "During the greater part of the time we were under a heavy and incessant fire coming from both sides" and that "Where the regulars fought we were obliged to give way a small distance, two or three times, but rallied and returned with additional ardor to the attack."

Ensign Campbell proved to be a hero in his own right, for while leading his men in charging up the hill he killed a Lieutenant McGinnis, an officer assigned Ferguson's Ranger Corps. As the rest of Colonel Campbell's troops began their ascent up the mountainside, the British beat their call to arms and began forming behind a chain of rocks at the top, where they had several wagons drawn up on their flanks to provide them with at least some semblance of protection.

Ensign Campbell was candid when he commented to his superiors, "the enemy has annoyed our troops very much by their advantageous position." I wonder what the average Patriot militiaman thought about what I consider to be their "makeshift" battle plan; or did they trust their leaders so much they just blindly followed their orders? Given that the Loyalists held both a numerical advantage and the high ground, most modern military experts would very likely agree that Ferguson's defeat was improbable.

In more action on the battlefield, I observed a young officer named Reece Bowen, a company commander in Campbell's regiment, making progress upward, toward the top of the plateau, when he acted haphazardly by unnecessarily exposing himself to enemy gunfire.

A militiaman in his company attempted to keep him safe by shouting out "Why Bowen, do you not take a tree, why rashly present yourself to the deliberate aim of the Provincial and Tory riflemen, concealed behind every rock and bush before you? Death will surely follow if you persist!" I was able to hear Bowen's simplistic retort, "Take to a tree, no, never shall it be said that I sought safety by hiding my person, or dodging from a Briton or Tory who opposed me in the field." Soon after uttering those words, he was struck in the chest by a Loyalist rifle round, ending his life.

Before one side could claim supremacy over the other, a tragedy would come to pass on the battlefield below. It would be Colonel Campbell himself who would be doing the suffering this time. One of his most admired junior officers, Captain William Edmundson, not satisfied with his position on the mountainside, moved up it in rapid fashion, jumping up from one secure position to another. Then, when within reach of the enemy, he launched himself upward toward them as they continued to play their game of "cat and mouse," charging with their bayonets, retreating, only to charge once again.

Captain Edmunson, upon reaching the enemy ranks, fired his weapon. After its discharge, he began swinging his rifle stock as a club, quickly disabling one of the Rangers to this front. Seizing the captured Ranger by his neck, he transported him to the bottom of the hill as a prisoner before running back where intense fighting was unceasing. While doing his best to remain unscathed, Edmondson was shot while relatively close to Campbell, his commanding officer. Found, still alive, by one of his fellow militiamen, Colonel Campbell hurried to his side, his eyes filled with tears, fearing the worst as blood was gushing from Edmundson's wound.

By the time the battle was won, as Campbell could hear proclamations of victory coming to his ears from above, I watched as he grasped one of Edmundson's hands, Edmundson grasping his in return. Sadly, but with a smile on his face, Edmundson passed away, moving on to join his militia brethren in heaven.

Right below me, in action only moments before, was Leonard Hice, of Captain James Dysart's company under Campbell, another militiaman who acted conspicuously on this day. Hirst was struck twice in the left arm by a musket balls, breaking it. However, Hice did not stop fighting, but instead continued moving toward the enemy with the assistance of an unnamed officer, who helped him load his rifle so he could continue to engage the enemy.

Acting with total disregard for his own safety, Hice, an expert marksman in his own right, was able to get off three more rounds before his luck ran out, this time when a third round struck him in his left leg and seconds later when a fourth musket ball found its target his right knee. This once and for all this ended Hice's participation in the battle. Courageous actions like those of Hice were taking place all around the battlefield while the Patriots were attacking the Loyalists under Ferguson's command.

Intense fighting was taking place all around the Battlefield Clock, making it difficult for me to take it all in as the hillside lit up with smoke from the discharge of weapons, while men were darting out from the wood line to fire at the Loyalists above them, receiving return fire from the much less accurate at long range, British muskets.

I can't continue without addressing another upcoming "controversy" on the battlefield, this time pertaining to our leader, Colonel Willliam Campbell of Virginia. Colonel Shelby seemed to promote the story that he was the recipient of the sword of surrender from Ferguson's second in command, Captain DePeyster. This confusion arose when Shelby heard reports that Campbell was not observed on the battlefield but was, instead, always located at the rear.

What I can confirm is that it was his slave, John Broddy, whose physicality greatly resembled Campbell, who was riding Campbell's normally mounted sorrel horse in the rear, while Campbell himself had at the last minute chosen a black horse to ride into battle. In reference to what I would call Shelby's "political motives," it seems that anytime he could paint a picture making him look better, he took it. There is only one word that aptly describes Colonel William Campbell's overall duty performance at Kings Mountain, that word is "outstanding." **Now, on to the other commanders...**

CHAPTER 35

SEVIER

8:15

John Sevier, himself of French Huguenot heritage, stood about five feet nine inches in height, with a hard, muscled physique and a reputation as a great frontiersman, one "who could outswear the best and worst men that followed him." His nickname "Chucky Jack," was given to him because he resided on the Nolichucky River in what is now Tennessee.

Most importantly, he was known for being able to mold a group of diverse individuals into one cohesive force. I wondered if anyone here at Kings Mountain knew that it was Sevier himself who personally pledged to repay suppliers the $12,000 to $13,000 worth of ammunition and supplies, they would consume on this trek?

I remembered that someone had summarized his leadership abilities when they revealed "He gave his commands as to equals, and, because these orders appealed to his men as being wise and practical, they gave him unquestioned obedience." The loyalty of his friends seemed to contribute greatly to his success throughout his whole career.

Sevier and his regiment started out at about 8:00 on the clock. Sevier was quite fortunate in that only a portion of his regiment was exposed to the now familiar Loyalist bayonet charges. During the fighting, his men were intermingled with those of Campbell.

While moving upward to the plateau, one of his soldiers, his son Joseph, lost contact with him. This led the young man to believe the Loyalists had killed his father. This was inaccurate information since it was Joseph's uncle, the Colonel's brother, Captain Robert Sevier, who had been seriously wounded. Young Joseph's inaccurate conception would contribute to one of the more "unpleasant" actions taken by militiamen after surrender. In this instance, peering down at young Joseph's face, I could see but one emotion enveloping his existence; plain and simple, it was a need for revenge!

Sevier lost three men in the battle, while three were wounded. One of those who died from his wounds was William Steele, which gave me some new food for thought. When I was at The Cowpens two days ago, I heard the name "Steele" come up in conversations about a local plantation near the South Carolina/North Carolina border. I made a mental note to remind me that at this point of time our country's history, the surnames of both Steele and McDowell were used by a large group of Patriots who resided in what is 21st Century Tennessee and current day Mecklenburg County, South Carolina. It became quite apparent to me that I was related to both the Steele's and McDowell's by blood.

Captain Robert Sevier would succumb to his wounds after the battle. I would see Colonel Sevier a few minutes later, on top of the plateau, unscathed, with his intense hatred for the British still intact. **Now, it was time to see what Shelby was up to…**

CHAPTER 36

SHELBY

SHELBY 10:00

As Colonel Isaac Shelby and his regiment arrived at Kings Mountain, their mission was clear; to strike the enemy in their immediate area and then move upwards toward the top of the plateau. Shelby's goal was to embarrass the British so that they "would surrender themselves at our discretion." This was a bold statement to begin with, since Shelby had already acknowledged the British maintained a defensive position high up on the plateau. Shelby went even further when he admitted "an assault on it would be almost equal to storming a battery."

I have come to the opinion that Shelby frequently used hyperbole while speaking. Fortunately, in this instance, his bluster was not passed on to his lower-ranking militiamen, but only to his officers, who were very likely aware of his predilection to boast.

Shelby would soon be heard giving instructions to his men, with the belief they might be too impulsive in their actions, requesting that they "press on to your places, and then your fire will not be lost." These words aside, Shelby could see it was Campbell and his regiment that were the first to engage the enemy on the slopes.

When I heard Campbell cry out to his own militia, I then paid attention to Shelby, who was urging his forces forward, only to see them retreat down the hill. To encourage them, Shelby shouted out "Now, boys, quickly reload your rifles and let's advance upon them and give them a hell of a fire! The words he spoke would have to fall into a category labeled "inspiring." His troops could be seen taking advantage of the overall chaos as they made steady progress upward; and after three bayonet charges, there would be no more, so up the slopes they went.

Out of the corner of my eye, I could see one of Shelby's militiamen distinguish himself through his brave actions on the battlefield. I was able to identify him as Captain Josiah Culbertson, son of Colonel John Thomas Culbertson Sr. Young Culbertson was chosen by Shelby to reach an elevated position on the mountainside so that he could attack and dispose of a Tory Captain and his soldiers who had situated themselves there in a favorable position.

From here, the Loyalists could easily shoot down at the Patriot militiamen surging upwards. Culbertson and his team of riflemen performed their assigned duties admirably, in the first phase of their operation they forced the enemy to withdraw behind some large rocks. Then, after Culbertson discovered their leader and soldiers in place there, he promptly put his rifle to his shoulder and sent a round into the Loyalist Captain's head. Viewing their Captain lying there dead, the Loyalist sharpshooters ran away as fast as they could to avoid capture.

Among those seriously wounded in the battle was Colonel Shelby's brother, Captain Moses Shelby. The more serious wound he received was the result of a musket ball striking him in the thigh and then passing through it. He was accompanied down the mountainside for medical treatment. As he lay there, Captain Shelby could not help but see one militiaman continually retreating to this location in the "rear." Suspicious he might be a coward, Shelby gave him a stern warning, letting him know that if he were to retreat downward to this area again, Shelby would personally ensure he was shot.

As the battle continued in ferocity, within ten to "fifteen minutes, the wings of the Patriot army would swing around and move upward to trap the Loyalists from all directions.

Next comes Colonel James Williams, who will be observed serving with distinction…

CHAPTER 37

WILLIAMS

WILLIAMS 11:30

Colonel James Williams was born in 1737, near the Old Fork Church in Hanover County, Virginia. His father was a Welshman. After losing both his parents at an early age, he eventually moved south to North Carolina. By 1772, he moved further south to 21st Century Laurens County, South Carolina, where he and his wife Mary became the parents of eight children.

In 1780, after overseeing the Patriot military success at the Battle of Musgrove's Mill, Williams was promoted to the rank of Brigadier General by Governor Rutledge of South Carolina. Since many of his rivals served in the rank of Colonel, Williams' promotion to a higher rank was not accepted by many; to include one of South Carolina's most respected Colonels, Thomas Sumter.

Williams' ego continued to take blow after blow as his new rank of Brigadier General was routinely disregarded by his contemporaries. It is for this reason that James Williams is referred to as "Colonel Williams" here at Kings Mountain. Williams would bolster his own group of South Carolina militiamen with twenty more from Captain Benjamin Roebuck's Spartanburg District, for a total of sixty in all under his command.

Colonel Williams had some very distinct personal characteristics; he was of average height at five feet nine inches, but was a large, "corpulent man." It was said he was very religious man, one with a dark complexion, black eyes and possessing a notably large nose, which attracted enough attention to cause some to claim it "had a possum hiding in it."

Williams came close to not being at Kings Mountain at all because of the "politics" involved in who outranked who. In making his final decision to lead his men into battle at Kings Mountain, Williams swallowed a bitter pill when he relented and assumed the lower rank of Colonel. Williams was smart enough to see he could not pass up an opportunity to participate in a major military engagement; one that might enable him to achieve personal glory.

Serving in the junior rank of Colonel as the battle began, Willliams was decidedly boisterous, hollering out, "Come on my boys, the old wagoner never yet backed out!" He and his soldiers would fight in the middle of the battlefield, down from 12:00 at the center of the clockface.

During the fighting several of Williams' men could be seen committing acts of bravery. William Giles and William Sharp were both from present-day Union County, South Carolina. I observed that as Giles was moving forward he was struck in the back of his neck by a musket ball. Believing his Giles dead, Sharp hesitated for a moment and then, with tears in his eyes, softly spoke "Poor fellow, he is dead; but if I am spared a little longer, I will avenge his fall."

Shortly thereafter, Sharp was shocked to see Giles standing upright again, firing his rifle. Fate surely on his side, Giles' neck had only been grazed by the musket ball, so he remained active for the reminder of the battle. Both Giles and Sharp fought bravely this day; their rifle shots permanently ending the lives of a significant number of Loyalist soldiers.

Thomas Young, seventeen years of age, another soldier from Williams contingent, also performed heroically. As he moved from one tree to another, under constant fire from the enemy, he continued to discharge his weapon, even when he found himself in what I'd call the "no man's land" between his own forces and those of the Loyalists, so close to the enemy he could see the pine twigs on their hats, in contrast to the piece of paper he and his fellow Patriots wore in their's.

Miraculously, when he reached the top of the plateau, Young found much flatter ground. After taking a step or two, he found himself in the presence of a Tory soldier, standing there in front of him, rifle barrel pointed directly at him. Young recognized this Tory soldier as a childhood friend, a Matthew McCray, who he knew had months earlier been compelled to join the Tory forces. Realizing he too was staring into the face of a friend, McCray dropped his weapon and embraced Young. Young advised McCray to pick up his weapon and fight alongside him; but McCray said he couldn't, and took to flight elsewhere rather than complying.

It was one Major Thomas Hammond, also from Colonel Williams' command, that was involved in an unusual battlefield event. Hammond was truly a hero in his own right at the Battle of Kings Mountain as he personally directed his men as they charged up the mountainside toward the Loyalist encampment.

On one of the many charges on this day, Hammond, with a small squad of soldiers, broke through the Loyalist lines, only to find themselves in a quandary when the enemy attempted to block a return to their own lines. With luck on their sides, Hammond and his squad adeptly made their way back down the mountainside, going from tree to tree while continuing to fire their weapons back toward the enemy.

I was happy to see Hammond make it back to safety and able to tell a story about one of his men, who just before the battle appeared to be seeking a place to hide rather than preparing to engage in the battle. When questioned by Hammond regarding his actions, the soldier explained that he had dreamed the previous night that he would be killed the following day. Hammond, believing this was just a ruse to avoid combat, dismissed this idea, making it clear to this soldier he was going to fight alongside the other men in his company.

Once the battle began, this same soldier appeared to make yet another concerted effort to conceal himself, this time behind a chestnut tree. Finally, without any further prompting from a superior officer required, he made up his mind to fight with the men in his company. Brushing some thorny bushes aside as he was making his way upward under fire, he took up behind an oak tree, peeked out to point his rifle, and took a fatal enemy musket round to his head, quickly ending his life.

When it was reported to Hammond that the soldier was dead, he felt a tinge of guilt, although he believed he acted on the best information he had at the time. Hammond, still in battle mode, did not have time to second-guess his decision making, so he fought on.

If there was anything of a "prophetic" nature to happen this day it would again be in relation to this same Colonel James Williams. When a small party of foraging Loyalists were returning to their camp, unaware that a surrender was underway, they discharged their weapons toward the Patriot militiamen. Colonel Williiams, was, at this very same moment, sitting astride his horse, heading toward the British encampment on the plateau, when he was stuck by errant Tory gunfire. Undoubtedly aware he was severely wounded, Colonel Williams yelled out to William Moore of Campbell's regiment, "I'm a gone man."

It would be Thomas Young that would again come into the picture. When he heard Wiliams had been shot, he immediately went to him to help. His fondness for Williams was recognized, when under his breath he revealed "I love him like a father, a man who had been so kind to me."

Williams was carried to a tent on the battlefield, where water was placed on his face. Williams, revived, shouted out, loudly, "For God's sake, boys, don't give up the hill!" Young left him under the supervision of his son, Daniel. The driving force behind Thomas Young's behavior from this moment on would be revenge! Williams' last words reflected his pleasure at hearing the British defeated, "I die contented, since we have gained the victory."

One of Williams' most admired soldiers was Joseph Kerr, who served him as a spy. Kerr, who was also present when Williams fell, said Williams had received numerous wounds, including a very serious one to his groin. Joseph Hughes, also assigned to Williams' command, could be heard making it clear "I received seven shots from the Tories "and that "Colonel Williams of South Carolina was killed after the British raised their flag of surrender." Hughes added "Williams was killed in the crossfire after the scouting party had returned." Without knowledge that Williams was still alive at this time, our Patriot militiamen, apparently confused, used his implied death as a justification for the random execution of Tory soldiers.

Colonel Campbell, who was nearby, acted swiftly, ordering his troops to fire on a group of about one hundred Loyalist who had been captured. They all lost their lives under the hail of Patriot gunfire! Observing the look on Campbell's face, it was obvious to me that the killing of Tory troops served two dual purposes for him: to retaliate for the alleged death of Colonel Williams and, second, to set the mood for total Loyalist submission.

These were exceptionally bitter men, these Patriots, because of all the pain and sorrow the Tories had inflicted against both them and their families while struggling for independence. Campbell had a difficult time keeping them from randomly executing any captured prisoners they came upon. The grudges they felt toward British supporters ran deep; it was time to pay them back for all their previous acts of indiscretion against their kin.

Whether or not Williams was shot from his horse before after the actual initiation of the surrender is a moot point; the militiamen used it to generate more hatred toward the British. As I listened to their anger increase in volume, I could not help but wonder how this formally disregarded "Brigadier General's" alleged demise could affect so many on such a highly charged emotional basis.

I was now on the lookout for the infamous Major Patrick Ferguson…

CHAPTER 38

FERGUSON DIES!

FERGUSON 2:17

While the battle continued, as Patriot forces forged ahead in their upward swing to the top of the plateau, Major Patrick Ferguson found himself in the unfavorable position of trying to rally his troops into some type of formation. Whereas Ferguson couldn't bring himself to accept the reality he was losing the battle, some of his Loyalist soldiers felt otherwise, with at least two white flags of surrender popping up on the battlefield.

Logistically, the Loyalists had long been exposing themselves like silhouettes against the sky, shooting downward, making them easy targets for the great majority of expert Patriot officer riflemen who had been hiding behind the trees and rocks below. From my observation point, I could see that Ferguson's major offensive measure, charging downhill with bayonets, was a failure since it did not deter the Patriots from continually moving upward to the top of the plateau.

Ferguson would have nothing of a surrender. I watched him as he rode to the location of each of the white flags, which he cut down with his sword blade, unable to suppress his primary emotion, anger. Within moments, his own second in command, Captain Abraham DePeyster, approached him and offered his proposal for capitulation, which Ferguson quickly dismissed.

DePeyster used an analogy to describe to Ferguson their current dilemma, one he believed accurately spoke of it. He portrayed their position to Ferguson as "ducks in a coop," a reference to a potential slaughter. Ferguson, however, remained his usual stoic, unaffected self, even after hearing DePeyster's dire warning.

It is possible DePeyster, himself born in the colonies, and a loyal supporter of the English King, did not fully comprehend Ferguson's extreme dislike of the Patriots, which he believed stemmed from Ferguson's anger toward their unrelenting desire to gain independence from the crown? In reality, the word "venomous" has been used to describe the mutually disrespectful relationship between the Ferguson and the pro-liberty colonists.

With knowledge of Ferguson's mindset, there appeared to be little hope he would go down gracefully, without a fight of his own. In his own words, he was never going to surrender to these "Backwater" people whom he considered to be the equivalent of "banditti."

Ferguson could be seen riding his horse, aggressively, on the sloping hillside, while leading a bayonet charge into the lines of the Patriots, who were still moving upward in droves to occupy the plateau where Ferguson's main force was situated. Ferguson was determined to keep his headquarters from falling into Patriot hands. I focused on Ferguson on the battlefield, where he was situated at about 2:00.

I cannot support any proposal that Ferguson ever tried to flee the battlefield on horseback, Ferguson would never leave his men behind. Quite simply put, he never stopped fighting at any time while I was observing him, when he was continually blowing that damn silver whistle! He was no coward, so please don't give credit to any misinformed individuals who might attempt to discredit him.

Just the opposite, Ferguson rode valiantly amongst his enemy; bravely slashing away at them, ending the life of as many Patriot militiamen as he could along the way. I had to assume few, if any of the militiamen present, failed to recognize it was Ferguson they were encountering; for while on horseback he was wearing his colorful checked shirt as he kept that whistle his mouth.

Many of the militiamen hoped they would be the one to provide the fatal shot to Ferguson, men such as one of the surname Gilleland, who was ready to shoot, but found his weapon unable to fire! Gilleland, fearing Ferguson might escape, yelled out to one of his fellow militiamen, Robert Young, "There's Ferguson, shoot him!" Young took Gilleland's demand seriously, for without hesitation he aimed his rifle named "Sweet Lips" at him, fired and watched as the round struck Ferguson, knocking him off his horse.

I suspect that several other militiamen heard Gilleland's request, for in rapid succession several of them fired at the same time, with six to eight musket balls finding their way to their easily identifiable target. In just a moment, Ferguson was dragged downhill while still on his steed, one foot caught in a stirrup, before finally he finally fell.

Ferguson's white horse miraculously survived the battlefield encounter without even a single wound.

Major Patrick Ferguson, a British officer routinely endorsed by his superiors as a leader of excellence, now lay prostrate on the ground, unconscious. I focused my attention downward, more specifically to determine what happened to Ferguson from then on, since I was aware that there were several differing accounts of his death.

Closing in, I could see Ferguson, lying there, on the ground, the recipient of numerous wounds. Ultimately defiant as Ferguson was, he continued slashing away for a few seconds before a militiaman's discharged rifle round struck him in the head, allegedly ending his life once and for all at age 36.

Within moments of his fall from his horse, I could see one of Ferguson's conscripted Tory soldiers, Elias Powell, reach down into Ferguson's vest pocket and grab his famous silver whistle as a souvenir. Sadly, there were enough other "souvenir seekers" around to warrant one Whig militiamen to inquire of them "Are you going to rob the dead?" These acts seem to support the premise that not all the Tory soldiers were avid supporters of the British cause.

While my attention was in the process of returning to the scene of the surrender, some say Ferguson remained alive for a short period of time before he died. I have no opinion as to when Ferguson passed, for even Colonel Shelby, arriving at the scene and apparently believing him still alive, clamored out to him "Colonel, the fatal blow is struck, we've Burgoyned you."

Shelby's comments surely lead one to believe he thought Ferguson was still breathing at the time. From my personal perspective, if it is true that Isaac Shelby did not offer any medical assistance to a fallen commanding officer, even one from the opposing force, I do not consider his actions to be at all "gentlemanly." I acknowledge it is possible I might feel differently had I been in the Carolinas since June of 1780, when the British first invaded South Carolina at Charles Town. I do know that war can seriously effect one's moral compass.

I apologize, for before I press on to the surrender, I'd like to provide you with further comment on Ferguson's final minutes as a British officer. Whether you liked him or despised him is irrelevant, it would be contradictory to identify his actions at Kings Mountain as anything less than heroic.

Ferguson did perform his own 18th Century version of a captain "going down with his ship." It is possible that through his behavior here in the final moments of the battle, that he was able to regain some of the family honor he appears to have lost with during the summer of 1780. There is now one overarching fact known; Major Patrick Ferguson is dead! A small cairn of stones would mark the spot where he was eventually buried.

I could hear the "talk" among the militiamen that once it was confirmed it was Ferguson's body lying there on the battlefield, it became a curiosity piece. Patriot Lieutenant Samuel Johnson, himself seriously wounded, was one of the first who insisted he view Ferguson's body, in his case as a sign of respect for his fallen adversary. Militiaman Robert Young, also wounded and of Johnson's party, on the contrary, wished to see Ferguson's corpse out of simple curiosity.

Considering everything Major Patrick Ferguson and his troops put the Patriots though during this past summer, battle after battle, their animosity toward him can be comprehended. When I later heard of some of the very distasteful acts my fellow militiamen committed against Ferguson's lifeless body, to include the purposeful urination on it, I cringed. There were rumors of even more disrespectful acts at the grave site, but I could not confirm them, since my attention was often directed elsewhere. There is more to Ferguson's burial on the mountainside and that information will be forthcoming.

I find it necessary for me to report to you about...

THE SAGA OF VIRGINIA SAL

Whether or not it is an 18th Century "urban myth," I have always wondered how one of Major Patrick Ferguson's "camp followers;" a woman known as "Virgina Sal," ended up in a grave with him on Kings Mountain. Virginia Sal was one of two women who "cared for" Ferguson when he was traveling, which was often. The other woman is "Virginia Paul." Both were originally hired to cook and clean for Ferguson. Ferguson appears to have added some other "unofficial duties" for the two women, as he saw a need for them. They were each described as young and attractive.

Virginia Sal may have been the more unique of the two women since she had red hair. Little has been written about either of these "Virginia" women, however, I will try to provide some conjecture on the part played by Virginia Sal, noting that she ended up dead well before I had an opportunity to personally confirm her story.

Ferguson's other "camp follower," Virginia Paul, mounted a horse toward the end of the battle and did her best to escape the battlefield, only later to be captured and marched north toward Burke County with other prisoners. As she rode through the tumult at the time of surrender, not a single shot was fired at her at any time. It was said that even Colonel Campbell thought she should be paroled, noting "She is only a woman, our mothers were women, we must let her go." I must admit, she avoided my scrutiny. I was unable to interview Virgina Paul to record details about her relationship with Ferguson. Virginia Paul was not in Ferguson's tent as the battle waged on.

On the other hand, I did do some "detective work" where Virginia Sal is concerned, putting together the few bits and pieces I could ascertain about her actions on the plateau. Whereas some historians may have felt it best to leave Patrick Ferguson's image as a heroic British officer intact, I prefer to examine it in more detail. Simple logic points to the fact that Ferguson's ego, which all identify as being quite large, was not satisfied by having only one "camp follower," he required two, keeping in mind that literature concludes both ladies were only "nominal cooks."

I was determined to figure out why and how Virginia Sal became the subject of so much Patriot animosity. It is acknowledged that Virginia Sal was shot, very likely while in Ferguson's tent, defending his property, very likely with a firearm in hand. Her defensive actions in Ferguson's tent apparently made it quite clear to all that she was involved with Ferguson in a "personal relationship." The Patriots hate for "anything Ferguson" was no doubt widespread among Campbell's conquering force, with the result there was no hesitation to kill her. Then, to advertise the death of Ferguson's "lady friend," they did their best to advertise her demise at their hands by parading her body around the campground in the equivalent of taking a "victory lap."

Her body was then taken, no doubt with raucous pleasure, to where Ferguson's corpse lay on the hillside, already desecrated by the overtly disrespectful acts committed by our militiamen. Quite unceremoniously, Ferguson and Virginia Sal's bodies were wrapped together, naked, in cowhide, and then thrown into a shallow grave. Some speculate they were laid face to face for even more humiliation. I was never able to substantiate this proposed positioning of their corpses.

Ferguson was proved to be correct when he proclaimed that "Only Almighty God could remove him from the mountain." Is it possible God decided this would indeed be Ferguson's final resting place?

In the meantime, up on the plateau, shots were being fired and men were screaming...

CHAPTER 39

SURRENDER

The Patriot forces had effectively surrounded the plateau and made their way up to the top with minimal casualties. With their leader Ferguson dead, panic set in among the Tory forces. Before the official surrender could take place, their second in command, Captain Abraham DePeyster, immediately sent out an emissary with a white flag of surrender.

This emissary was killed almost instantly. Our militiamen continued to swarm over the plateau, cutting off any opportunity the Tories might have had to reorganize. The enemy was now surrounded, hemmed in on all sides with no chance of escape.

Ensign Henry Dickenson, of Captain Colvill's company in Campbell's regiment, could be heard commenting that "the enemy made a firm stand for some time, but on our advancing and firing they continued to retreat to their wagons and halted behind them, which were on the summit of the mountain, from which we drove them down to the end of the mountain where I supposed they were met by the troops sent around to that quarter." The Tories were simply overwhelmed by the Whig charges coming from all sides of the mountain in one momentous push toward their baggage wagons and headquarters.

The Patriot reaction to the Loyalist raising of the "white flag" was one I did not anticipate, for instead of ceasing to fire their weapons at their enemy, the Patriots instead began yelling out "Give 'em Tarleton's Quarter" or "Give them Buford's Play," both calls of encouragement to bring about the death of every enemy soldier present.

As these executions continued, DePeyster sent out a second white flag, whose bearer was killed almost as quickly as the first. Our Patriot militiamen, not formal soldiers, did not understand that a white flag signified surrender. It certainly appeared to me that the slaughter was going to continue without pause unless a higher authority took charge of them.

A change in in this overtly uncivilized behavior, predicated on the seeking of revenge, would only be interrupted by the forthcoming presence of two of the more formally educated Patriot officers, Campbell and Sevier, who called for an immediate cease fire.

There was one glaring example of how hot the emotions became at the time of the surrender, this event involving young Joseph Sevier, son of Colonel John Sevier. On the plateau at the time the surrender was in progress, he kept on killing Tories while yelling out "The damned rascals have killed my father, and I'll keep loading and shooting till I kill every son of a bitch of them."

His father, Colonel John Sevier, suddenly appeared on horseback, at which time young Sevier came to comprehend it was his father's brother that was killed, not his father. To report accurately, Sevier's brother was not yet dead.

In almost the same breath, Colonel Campbell had to knock the rifle of one of his Virginia men who was taking aim. Campbell pled of him "For God's sake, don't shoot! It is murder to kill them now, for they have raised the flag." It would be men in Campbell's command that would suffer the greatest losses this day,

Shelby was also on hand, yelling at the Tories "Damn you, if you want quarter, lay down your arms!" Captain DePeyster informed Campbell what he thought of the uncivilized behavior of his soldiers, noting "It's damned unfair, damned unfair." Campbell chose to ignore DePeyster's comments. Campbell then directed DePeyster to get his fellow officers in rank order, take their hats off and sit down. With the Tories contained, Campbell led the assembled troops in three "Huzzas for Liberty."

Ensign Robert Campbell, of Captain Dysart's Virginia company, had seen DePeyster raise his white flag, high up into the air, at which time it was taken by a mounted Whig officer. Colonel Campbell, appearing on the scene in shirtsleeves and an open collar, had to have his rank verified by others before DePeyster would offer his formal surrender. DePeyster had a difficult time accepting the fact his enemy's commanding officer could be so informally attired.

With some sarcasm in his voice, stepped forward to receive DePeyster's sword. Campbell, the leader of the Patriot force, spoke first as he presented DePeyster with these words "I am happy to see you Sir." DePeyster, unamused, handed Campbell the hilt of his sword and reported he was not happy to see Campbell under these circumstances.

Campbell, a man of honor, turned the sword around and gave it back to DePeyster.

After the bloodshed stopped, it was determined that our Patriot forces made it through the white flag ceremony with only twenty-six killed and sixty-two wounded. Casualties on the Tory side were much higher, with around two hundred ninety killed and one hundred sixty-three wounded. More significantly, close to seven hundred Loyalists out of their total force of about eleven hundred were taken as prisoners.

Taking into consideration the noted tactical "advantage" Ferguson had on the plateau, the capture of so many of Ferguson's Loyalist soldiers does not bode well in any evaluation of his tactical acuity. Some experts have over the years proposed Kings Mountain "was more assailable by the rifle than defensible by the bayonet." Major Patrick Ferguson, a combat veteran and accomplished British officer, apparently failed to recognize this possibility.

In addition, Ferguson's lack of recognition of the plateau's terrain features no doubt contributed significantly to his defeat. At one point in the battle, as it was being lost, he ordered DePeyster to reinforce an area with a full company of British regulars. When DePeyster arrived, he found that a large majority of his men had already been killed. Those on horseback, versus those on foot, suffered the greatest losses.

The Patriot forces had effectively surrounded the plateau, scampered and ridden up its slopes, and killed a significant number of enemy soldiers. Their plan, however simple, "to surround the mountain and attack," was a total success.

On a more personal note, and with everything taking place in this still chaotic environment, I was happy to see Colonel Campbell saunter up to his kin, Ensign Campbell, take his hand in his, and express his joy in seeing that he had survived the battle without any harm.

British rule in the Carolinas was now just a pipedream of King George III. The British campaign in the South had turned sour as formally aligned Loyalist sympathizers were now more likely to view the British as "oppressors."

The Commander-in-Chief of British forces in North America, Sir Henry Clinton, said it best when he described the Battle of Kings Mountain as "an event which was immediately productive of the worst Consequences to the King's affairs in South Carolina, and unhappily proved the First Link of a Chain of Evils that followed each other in regular succession until they at last ended in the total loss of America." **An unpleasant consequence of battle would soon be confronting us....**

CHAPTER 40

AFTERMATH

The battle now won, the "dirty work" came next, what to do with the over two hundred bodies of fallen Loyalists. It should be noted that one, very important factor to consider is that the Patriots were aware that taking too long to bury the dead could result in an upcoming encounter with Lieutenant Colonel Tarleton Banastre and his dragoons.

They would therefore proceed with haste, some might characterize as "too much haste," when deciding what would be done with around two-hundred-fifty Loyalist corpses. We would also have to deal with another one hundred-fifty of their wounded. Their numbers were prolific when compared to our twenty-eight killed and sixty-two wounded.

It was on the next morning that some very unpleasant scenes appeared to me. While our militiamen knew they would be moving on the next morning, there were apparently few that were at all concerned about the dead Tories lying here on the battlefield. When wives and of the fallen showed up the next morning, and began to weep over the dead bodies, I felt their disposition should be of paramount importance to all.

Some Patriot soldiers, like James Collins, whom I met at The Cowpens, provided their own personal assessment of the situation at hand. I could hear Collins lamenting about how poorly the burial of their rivals had been addressed. According to Collins, "they were thrown into convenient piles and covered with old logs, the bark of old trees and rocks." Overall, Patriot concern for the treatment of the bodies of their vanquished enemy was minimal, if at all.

One with any sense at all could easily figure out that these bodies would go unprotected from the wild animals living on the mountain, including the apex predators, wolves. Vultures were already circling overhead in anticipation of their next meal.

I had little doubt hogs on neighborhood farms would gladly dine on the Loyalist remains that were so hastily discarded on both the slopes and plateau. I was determined not to be on this mountain again because of my knowledge of what lay there, often out in the open. Although I do not believe in ghosts, the plight of the two hundred plus men thrown into makeshift graves does directs my attention toward the wondering about the "thereafter."

The ghastly sight of so many enemy bodies being treated so impersonally aroused a feeling of guilt in my gut. In 1780, "grudges" were something to be taken seriously. I believe that if any place on earth could be haunted, this was it and if in the future anyone were to walk on this plateau it would be tantamount to walking over a "graveyard,"

I was amazed as I was presented with this example of "18th Century man's cruelty to another."

On a more positive note, our Patriot forces were fortunate that the Loyalist physician, Dr. Uzal Johnson, received no physical harm during the battle, for he was instrumental in many Patriot lives. Sadly, one physician was not nearly enough to deal with the dying and wounded on both sides. It would be Dr. Johnson who made a brave effort to save Joseph Sevier, although Sevier's suffering persisted despite his care.

Aside from the medical interventions of Dr. Johnson, the Patriots had their own physician, Dr. Joseph Dobson, who attended medical school in Scotland and Wales. After he came to America, he first lived in Virginia before moving south to North Carolina, where he became the first university-trained physician in the state. As a Patriot physician in his own right, serving with the Overmountain Men, he was there on the tree lined slopes and plateau, treating the wounded from both factions as the battle waned.

Owning property along the Catawba River in North Carolina, Dr. Dobson wasn't a high-profile character, but one who made a significant contribution to the welfare of all the combatants. From the short conversations I had with him prior to arriving at Kings Mountain, I have no doubt he will continue to serve his patients well after we depart north with our prisoners.

On the night of battle, all our militiamen found themselves extremely fatigued, only to be added to, no doubt, by the fact someone always had to be awake to guard the over seven hundred Tory prisoners we had collected. One of the Patriot soldiers admitted "The groans of the wounded and dying on the mountain were truly affecting, begging piteously for a little water; but in the hurry and confusion and exhaustion of the Whigs, these cries, when emanating from the Tories, were little heeded." There was nothing I could do to remedy this situation.

The mass of lingering and dying Loyalists did bring one of Major Chronicle's men to shed tears, asking "Great God! Is this the fate of mortals?" I propose this soldier's description of death will always warrant this same question. Apparently not all the Patriot force felt so dismissive of any attempt to demonstrate even a small degree of humanity and kindness.

Of certain interest to me was that while my Patriot friends were decidedly not interested in respectfully securing the corpses of any dead Loyalist soldiers, they were interested in the plunder now available to them, which consisted of horses, guns, articles of clothing, powder and lead.

The "everyday militiamen" who fought in the battle found at least a small degree of pleasure at the surrender when they were able to take into their possession horses or lesser valuable items that had been owned by their now-captured Loyalist prisoners. Like their lower-ranking militiamen, none of the young Whig officers were receiving any kind of pay, so they routinely rewarded themselves by taking possession of British swords, a high value item to them, as compensation.

I have already disclosed that it was Elias Powell who grabbed one of Ferguson's silver whistles earlier at his death scene. Another lower ranking soldier, Samuel Talbot, turned over Ferguson's body after he fell and secreted his pistol. After the surrender, it would be Colonel Cleveland who claimed Ferguson's white horse, since he had lost two of his own during the battle. Shelby was the recipient of another of

Ferguson's silver whistles, while Sevier took possession of Ferguson's silken sash and promotion orders to Lieutenant Colonel. Campbell came into possession of Ferguson's personal correspondence, while Lacey's men somehow came into possession of Ferguson's large silver watch.

What of my other cousin, Captain Joseph "Pleasant Gardens" McDowell, who somehow ended up with Ferguson's table service, consisting of six China dinner plates, a small coffee cup and a saucer? While "PG" McDowell served as a company commander under my cousin, Joseph "Quaker Meadows McDowell" at Kings Mountain, I did not hear even one single word spoken about his duty performance duty on October 7th.

This makes me suspicious as to how a mere militia Captain came into possession of these very personal items belonging to Ferguson. There is no documentation that he was present when the captured items were distributed in the presence of the Colonels, so when did he take possession of the China set, etc.?

I'm assuming that once Captain McDowell made it to the top of the plateau, he went to Ferguson's tent and made off for himself the aforementioned items before the "official distribution" took place. Could he be the person who fatally wounded Virginia Sal in Ferguson's tent? We'll never know, but I do admit, I'm very suspicious. I find it quite interesting that Joseph "Quaker Meadows" McDowell is not listed, anywhere, as receiving any "booty" or "spoils of war, yet he was a regimental commander in his own right.

I wondered if my cousin" Joseph "PG" McDowell, would ever attempt to claim he was the "Joseph McDowell" who was the Regimental Commander for Burke and Rutherford Counties at Kings Mountain? If he were to make this claim, it would be more evidence he was "stealing valor," which I consider to be a reprehensible act.

The family honor for one holding the name "Jose ph McDowell" at the Battle of Kings Mountain therefore goes to Joseph 'QM' McDowell, with no exceptions!

It was time to return to Quakers Meadows, but first…

CHAPTER 41

THE HANGINGS AT BICKERSTAFF'S

I watched as our militiamen dragged together seventeen of Ferguson's baggage wagons and set them on fire. We could not move our forces away from Kings Mountain at a good speed while encumbered with them, nor did we want them to be used again by our enemies.

There was concern by our leaders that our most hated adversary, Lieutenant Colonel Banastre Tarleton, might be on his way to reinforce Ferguson. Furthermore, we had no desire to fight him on the same ground we had just taken, so the decision was to move out as quickly as we could.

At eleven o'clock the following morning, October 8th, I was able to monitor conversations among Patriot leaders that were relevant to me, though only one at a time and with focused attention. I could see the Loyalist prisoners being lined up in single file and being handed two empty rifles and the rest of their kit. This was a strange sight to me, prisoners carrying weapons.

After pondering this matter for a few minutes, I concluded that this disposition made sense since these weapons were too valuable to leave on the mountain, where they could be picked up by our enemy and used against us at another time. Two hundred militiamen were left behind, along with some captured Loyalists, to bury all the dead. Whereas the corpses of our Patriots received decent burials, the dead Loyalists continued to be laid out, barely covered up and again, unfortunately, exposed to the local animal population.

As our journey north into North Carolina began, I laughed as I watched Colonel Shelby, with sword pointed down in his right hand, giving directions to one older prisoner for not properly carrying his weapon on his shoulder. After the soldier initially declined to obey him, Shelby gave him a thump with his sword, at which time the prisoner submitted to Shelby and shouldered the rifle as ordered.

We made up litters to carry our wounded, stretching tent cloth or blankets between two poles, attached to each side of a horse, who would then pull them forward. When I say "we" I am referring to the Patriot army; I remain, following "from above."

He would never be recognized by his contemporaries as a Brigadier General, but as a hero. We were no longer making timely progress, but after covering about twelve miles we halted at a "deserted plantation" owned by a Tory sympathizer. I assume he "deserted" it when he found we were moving, en masse, toward his location.

We marched on for several days, many of our militiamen close to starvation, not having had a good meal since The Cowpens. Some men were barely able to survive on a diet of fried green pumpkins. If you think this was an awful diet, you should have seen what we fed to our Loyalist prisoners; raw corn on the ear and raw pumpkins thrown into large groups of their men, like a farmer would feed their swine. With so many prisoners, we covered only forty miles. It was very slow moving while we traveled north with our Loyalist prisoners in tow.

I'm sure you know what word best describes the phenomena in effect when you have a starving group of Patriot soldiers in charge of an equally large number of underfed prisoners. This word is "mayhem." Keeping in mind that our men are not "regular" soldiers, but volunteers, maintaining any type of discipline among them was a big challenge for our leaders.

In relation to some of the bullying behavior, on our fourth day of travel from the battlefield at Kings Mountain, Colonel Campell distributed a statement requesting assistance in helping deter misbehavior. His words were "I must request the officers of all ranks in the army to endeavor to restrain the disorderly manner of slaughtering and disturbing the prisoners." These Patriot men were certainly a rowdy lot, one very difficult to manage or control.

I reminded myself that although these Loyalist men weren't Banastre Tarleton's dragoons, they were of the same breed; men who had degraded our Patriot women folk by engaging in ungentlemanly acts such as physically abusing them in the act of relieving them of their wedding rings, killing their horses and, on some occasions torturing or killing members of their family.

By Saturday, October 14th, the blood lust reached its peak when we arrived at our next destination, about ten miles northeast of Gilbert Town, at "Bickerstaff's Old Fields," also known as "Red Chimneys."

As soon as our large contingent of wardens and prisoners reached this location, I felt another twinge in my left ear, which brought me to the realization I was once again "Major Davy McDowell," in the flesh, just as I was before the battle at Kings Mountain. I didn't try, in the least, to figure out what would come next for me. I accepted the fact I had absolutely no control over my "future," whatever that meant.

The first words I would hear since this latest transitioning would be "Welcome back Davy!" from the lips of my Cousin Joseph McDowell. Uncertain how others might perceive our interactions, I continued as if nothing had happened in the past few days. My absence at the Battle of Kings Mountain never came up. Attempting to "blend in" as much as possible, I volunteered for one four-hour shift as a guard for a group of Loyalists cut out from our seven hundred prisoner population.

Joseph advised me that in addition to the ill will felt by almost all those in our command before Kings Mountain, Colonel Shelby had just moments later announced to all that eleven of our Patriot brothers had been hung at the British stronghold at Ninety-Six. This was in retribution for Colonel Elijah Clarke's failed siege of Augusta, Georgia. News of the hangings spread quickly, thoroughly enraging our already unhappy, virtually starving Patriot soldiers.

All now aware of these atrocities, our soldiers demanded revenge. Shelby stepped forward and provided our leaders with a copy of a North Carolina law authorizing magistrates to appoint a jury of twelve to determine guilt or innocence. Upon hearing of this, many of the mass of Patriot soldiers put their hands up to volunteer to serve on the jury, which was given the power to order executions. My Cousin Joseph was apparently chosen for the twelve-man jury. The once again "chaotic" nature of Patriot decision-making made it difficult for me to determine if he was, in addition, serving in the role of a magistrate.

If there ever was a "rigged trial," this was it. The guilty verdict appeared to be settled well before the assembled jurymen even deliberated. It took no time at all to find all thirty-six guilty, making all eligible for hanging. Of these thirty-six men, some were very well known by the members of the Whig community.

Their cited crimes included breaking open houses, killing men, turning women and children out of doors and burning houses. Of the Colonels present, Benjamin Cleveland, sitting as the primary magistrate, was the most ardent supporter of the mass execution of all thirty-six. For such an intelligent man, Cleveland's intensely expressed fervor for hanging these men surprised me. Cleveland's actions somewhat diminished the respect I held for him.

A small contingent of Patriot militiamen stepped forward to ask for a pardon for several of those condemned. Colonel Sevier was successful in lobbying for pardons for two of his friends, Samuel Chambers and James Crawford. Each had deserted Ferguson's army. In this same vein, my cousin, Joseph "QM" McDowell, asked and received approval for the pardon for his acquaintance, Arthur McFalls, who in years past had performed duties with him as a scout during the Cherokee War. My "other cousin, Joseph "PG" McDowell, who also knew McFall, added support for the parole.

McFall's brother, John, was not granted leniency, because at one time he had gone to Martin Davenport's farm and ordered Martin's son to feed his horse. When Martin's son refused, John McFall cut down a limb and whipped the young man. Benjamin Cleveland was adamant that this behavior could not go unpunished. From my perspective, death for beating a boy seemed excessive, however, before I said anything, I looked over to my cousin Joseph, who gave me a distinct gesture indicating it would not be wise for me to get involved in the debate. I complied with his wishes and kept my mouth shut.

A large, old oak tree was chosen as the spot where they would be hung. It was nighttime when all was ready for the executions. I can only describe the atmosphere at this time as "gleeful" among our men; it seemed like most took it as a celebration, not of life, but death.

The Overmountain Men and other Patriot soldiers gathered around the tree, holding pine-knot torches so they would better be able to observe the hangings. It was decided that they were to be hung three at a time. A rope was placed around their necks, over the tree branch above, with their feet on a bench until it was kicked out from under them. It wasn't long before I could see that there were three sets of three, for a total of nine Loyalist bodies, swinging in the wind underneath that big oak tree.

Meeting their maker tonight would be Colonel Ambrose Mills, Captain Robert Wilson, Captain James Chitwood, Captain Grimes, Captain Walter Gilkey, Captain John McFalls, Lieutenant Thomas Lafferty, Lieutenant John Bibby and Lieutenant Augustine Hobbs.

What were the cited "crimes" of these men that were hung? Colonel Mills was the Loyalist commander at both the Battle of Earle's Ford, where Andrew Hampton's son was killed and at the Battle of the Peach Orchard, where another of Hampton's friends died. Mills was also cited for encouraging the South Carolina Cherokee population to kill settlers on the frontier. I could hear many Patriots cheering as Mills' body swung under the tree branch. As the highest-ranking Loyalist officer present, he encountered significant animosity from all. Before his body dropped and the noose cracked his neck, Mill's called out "For God and Country!" Mills' wife attended his trial and later sat in the rain all night as his dead body swung from the tree.

Captain Robert Wilson, from the Ninety-Six area, commanded a group of Tories when the British captured Charles Town in June of 1780. Once again, it was Andrew Hamton that inserted himself into the conversation as an antagonist. Wilson's fate was sealed when it became known to all he was present at Ninety-Six when our eleven Patriots brothers were hung. This alone was enough to send him to the gallows this evening.

Captain James Chitwood's home was only a few miles from Bickerstaff's property. During this conflict he had confiscated the plantation of one Colonel John Walker and turned it into a hospital for wounded Loyalist soldiers. Although no further details were provided, he was convicted of murder and other illegal acts. Two young ladies, his daughters, had come to visit him, only to find out he had been hung. Chitwood had two sons, both of whom took a loyalty oath to our cause, they were paroled. His sons and daughters could later be seen transporting his body to what I suspected was a nearby family cemetery.

Captain Grimes, whose first name I did not hear, had originally settled in the Watauga settlement, later moving to North Carolina, where he organized a group of "self-proclaimed Tories" with a mission of terrorizing Whig supporters. Grimes was said to have directed the murder of several friends of Colonel John Sevier, which was certainly enough to justify sending him to the oak tree.

Lieutenant Thomas Lafferty, an Irishman by birth, now residing in Rutherford County, had joined the British cause after Ferguson ordered him either join up with him or to pay the back taxes he owed on his property. He did not have the money. Lafferty's "crime" was apparently his service with Ferguson.

Captain Walter Gilkey was another Tory from Rutherford County; his family home located on the North Carolina/South Carolina border. Gilkey's charges pertained to his visit to a Whig home, where he found the father gone and the son refusing to cooperate. For his refusal to reveal his father's hiding place, Gilkey shot the boy in the arm. Gilkey claimed self-defense, however, the boy, who attended the trial, testified Gilkey was the man "who attempted to murder him." Captain Gilkey would swing from the tree with the others.

I have already provided you with information about Captain John McFall, from our own Burke County, who was condemned after testimony was given about him abusing a young boy on Whig Martin Davenport's property.

Lieutenant John Bibby is another from Rutherford County. I did not hear any of the opening statements about the errors of his ways, only that he was also chosen to die today.

Lieutenant Augustine Hobbs, who operated out of South Carolina, was involved with Captain Robert Wilson and Tory sympathizer Alexander Chesney. These friendships were enough to doom him to the noose.

What was the general attitude of most toward the hangings, after all nine of them were swinging under the tree? This can be explained by the remarks of one militiaman, who, in a joyous voice shouted out "Would to God every tree in the wilderness bore such fruit as that!"

From this point on in history, this tree certainly earned its 'reputation as the "Gallows Oak."

Before the next two men could be executed, Cousin Joseph, himself a magistrate, and Colonel Campbell, our Commanding Officer, intervened and stopped the proceedings. The remaining twenty-seven men then received pardons. If you had been there and looked up at that tree along with me, you would have seen the bodies of nine men hanging there, swaying in the wind. I do not believe either of us would characterize the viewing as anything other than a very unpleasant sight. There was, in my mind, hope that after these hangings this punishment would no longer be a popular event among either friend or foe.

When light broke the next day, a Sunday, we prepared to march north again. Whether or not the demands for revenge had been met the night before, it was not a topic of general discussion as traveled on toward Quaker Meadows. Maybe the heavy downpour we experienced that next day took something out of those who wished more Loyalists had been hung.

As we marched away, Martha Biggerstaff, widow of Tory Aaron Bickerstaff, who was killed at Kings Mountain, went to the "Gallows Tree" on her property and cut the nine down. Eight of their bodies were buried, not necessarily in a well-done manner, in a shallow trench she dug on her own property.

Several extremely fatigued and underfed militiamen died on the long journey home. In many instances, they just fell off the roadside, never to be seen again. There did not seem to be any well-planned out effort to deal with any casualties while we were on the march north.

While still traveling, there was yet another rumor spreading that Tarleton was again planning to attack us. That rumor proved to be false, but it did give us some unsettling moments. We later learned that Tarleton was far away from us, accompanying Cornwallis as he fled back into South Carolina from Charlotte Town.

This was not our finest moment, but I needed to get home to see Miss Lizzy...

Chapter 42

Back to Quaker Meadows

Marching some thirty-two miles in the rain that next day, we arrived back at Quaker Meadows. It was unfortunate that on the trip back we lost a good number of our prisoners; some of which were trampled underfoot by our horses. Little sympathy was felt for our conquered prisoners; their lives were deemed to be of little value to us.

Cousin Joseph welcomed our army at his home at Quaker Meadows. Repeating his behavior at the initial gathering at Quaker Meadows on September 30th, he once again offered his rails to the troops so that they could build campfires around which to stay warm and dry. The great majority of our prisoners continued to suffer greatly under our supervision.

However, continuing his gentlemanly ways, Cousin Joseph offered a warm bed in the house this night to Loyalist Lieutenant Allaire and some other officers. I heard that my Aunt Margaret was not at all pleased with this gesture. Her feelings about boarding Tories became quite apparent when she remarked "Some of them were part of a party that raided the area during Ferguson's stay in the region and while they were here, they stole Charles' and Joseph's best clothes." This, she said could not be forgiven."

What I found to be really humorous was when Aunt Margaret referred to our Tory guests as "those thieving vagabond Tories." Some of our "guests" did, however, have positive experiences while the McDowells hosted them, to include the British surgeon, Dr. Uzal Johnson, who was heard remarking "we were well entertained and got a good supper, which we were in great need of." Dr. Johnson said they ate only raw turnips while marching north. I have never eaten a raw turnip, nor do I have a desire to eat one.

I heard rumors this night that my Uncle Charles was on the premises, although I never saw him with my own eyes, so, to me, he remained unaccounted for. I didn't ask even one question that evening and I was beginning to wonder if I would be living here in the 18th Century from now on. Rather than be alarmed, I immediately began to think of Ms. Mary Elizabeth Dysart, "my Lizzy," wondering how long it would take me to find her again?

From that night on, our Overmountain Men and militia began to disperse, some back to their homes and farms, while others remained to escort our prisoners to Hillsborough, North Carolina, where under the discretion of General Gates they could be used in prisoner exchanges with the British. Colonel Cleveland took another group of prisoners to Bethabara, which is modern day Winston-Salem.

I had decided, by this time, to remain here at Quaker Meadows and make my way as a true member of the North Carolina McDowell clan. Rising in the morning a day or so later, I began making inquiries about the location of Dysart's home. With this information now in my possession, I immediately mounted my horse and rode away toward Dysart's property.

Upon arrival, I tied up my horse, walked a few yards to the front of their cabin, knocked on the door and waited for someone to answer. Coming from the background, in a voice like an angel, I heard these words, "I'll be right with you." I stood there, in great anticipation of seeing "my Lizzy" again, my heart beating so fast I could barely take a breath. When the door opened it was not Lizzy, but a woman I supposed was Mary Elizabeth's mother, a fine-looking woman in her own right.

Seeing me, a young man of twenty-five years of age standing in the doorway, she knew why I was there, at which time she immediately called out "Mary Elizabeth, you have a visitor." Mrs. Dysart invited me in and I sat down on a chair in the parlor. The inside of their cabin was very nicely decorated, pointing out they were far from being "poor." Moments later, Mary Elizabeth Dysart entered the room, looking more beautiful than ever in a yellow dress with a white bow on the collar. I could sense she was just as happy to see me as I was her.

Lizzy and I spent the rest of the afternoon walking around her family's property; she showed me all the flowers growing behind their house, to include goldenrod, asters and mountain laurels. We also passed the family vegetable garden, where I saw they had cabbage, turnips, late season potatoes and winter squash growing. We then walked by their very well-maintained barn, where their horses were kept. It was wonderful to be with her, just meandering around in each other's company. There was absolutely no doubt I'd been bitten by the "love bug."

There was something very special about this young lady, she made me feel like I was once more in my youth, not a broken down, lonely, "old man" of fifty. Back at their cabin, Mrs. Dysart asked me to stay for dinner this evening. I graciously accepted, wondering how long my visit here at their house would last before I was sent packing.

This did not occur because after dinner Lizzy's father asked me to stay awhile longer, offering me his pipe to join him in a smoke. Considering I'm not a smoker, I took one quick drag, not inhaling, and gave it back to him, after which I coughed, and he laughed out loud. He asked me what my plans were for the future and all I could think of saying was "I plan on living with my family at Quaker Meadows."

I did report to him I was a college graduate but, thank God, he did not ask me what college or university I attended since none of my alma maters were founded until close to a hundred years later. Why did I offer him this information? I was very nervous, feeling as if I was being "interviewed" for my suitability for his daughter.

After an hour or so of talking with Mr. Dysart, I had more time to spend with Lizzy. We sat out on the porch in front of their cabin in the evening air and talked for almost two hours before her mother let us know it was time to end our evening. Lizzy walked with me, holding my hand, to where my horse was tied up. Every single moment of time with her was magical and my heart was pounding so fast it felt like it was about to jump out of my chest again. I looked down into her beautiful eyes, took her hand in mine and said "Lizzy, I'm not sure how you feel about me, but I feel there is something very special about you."

Lizzie squeezed my hand, looked well upward to me at my six and a half feet of height, into my eyes, and kissed me ever so gently on my left cheek. Her words that came next, flowing so beautifully from her lips, are ones I'll never forget, "Yes, Davy, I feel the same way as you, I hope to see you again soon. I want you to know I will be here, waiting for you." From her right hand she put a little sunflower in mine, which I took as a sign of her affection. I'm sure I was blushing now and knew for certain I was overcome with joy at the thought of a woman once more loving me.

We each let loose of each other's hand, and I grabbed hold of my horse's reins, pulled myself up into the saddle and watched as Ms. Mary Elizabeth Dysart, "my Lizzy," walked back to the cabin. Yes, she did look back at me once more, just before she went through the doorway; that final glance of hers so endearing I almost fell out of my saddle. There was no doubt, I was in love again!

When I arrived back at the McDowell house late that evening, several McDowells were there, apparently waiting for me, including cousins Joseph and John, along with the aristocratic matriarch of the family, Margaret O'Neill McDowell. She was interested in hearing about my trip to the Dysarts, but I kept my comments very generic in nature, doing my best not to disclose my feelings for Lizzy.

Apparently even wiser than I thought possible, my "Auntie," as I had come to call her, asked me directly, "And what do you think about Miss Lizzy?" I kept my reply short, "She is a charming and beautiful young lady." I could see it in my Auntie's eyes, she knew I was in love.

After some very enjoyable conversations with Joseph, John and Auntie Margaret, to include serious subjects like the country's future and hoped for independence from Great Britain, it was getting late and time for bed, so I went up to my room. Eventually, I got into bed and drew the covers up over me. My conscious thoughts were totally consumed by one very beautiful young lady, Miss Lizzy Dysart. I dreamed about the two of us all night; about getting married, where we could live, have children and make a home for us near my McDowell relatives. Finally, my dreams came to an end, my thoughts stilled for the night. **And then…**

I woke up the next morning and had breakfast with my McDowell family. I did notice that my Auntie was looking a bit piqued and wondered if she was getting adequate medical care. Joseph, John and I talked about some of our experiences on the journey south; the battle and the trip home, but left out the unpleasant parts, like the bodies being piled up on the plateau and the hangings. It was decided; we would push all the unpleasant memories somewhere far into the recesses of our minds. From now on, we would concentrate on the next battle we fight to gain our independence.

The weather was quite temperate for this time of the year, I'd guess it to be in the mid-seventies, so I ventured out the front door onto the porch, where I could look down into the meadow and see militiamen still camping out. My eyes were quickly focused on the road to the left of the house, where I could now see familiar figure, my uncle, Colonel Charles McDowell, walking up the hill in my direction. It had been weeks since he left that night from Bedford Hills with the mission of delivering a request to General Gates for a Continental Army general. That said, I figured he would tell me about his recent whereabouts at his leisure.

What came instead from him when he reached me was another phrase I can never forget, "Davy boy, your time here has ended." I didn't have time to say goodbye to my family here at Quaker Meadows, or even think about my newfound love, Miss Lizzy Dysart, when his lips once more unfurled and he whispered, "And now, my dear Davy, it's time to go home."

Those were the last words I would ever hear in the 18th Century...

Chapter 43

Return to My Time

I found myself once again back in the woods behind my house near Greenville, South Carolina, feeling tired and confused. I wondered why no one had accompanied me on my journey back to the 21st Century, however my immediate desire was to get into my house and take a shower since I couldn't remember when I'd last had one. As I looked to my rear, the campfire remained exactly where it was when I'd first met the McDowell brothers.

I quickly recognized I was back in my "original" 21st Century clothing and that neither my hearing or eyesight were any better than when I departed here with Uncle Charles and Cousin Joseph. And, sadly, I was fifty again.

I could feel a slight bulge in my left shirt pocket, so I reached in with my right hand and pulled out what was a crumpled flower, a sunflower. Shocked, this was confirmation to me that this journey I have described to you was not just a dream. Then things got worse, I became very sad, for I knew I'd been in love with a "real" woman.

I returned to my home, traveling through the underbrush avoiding snakes, crossed the creek, and entered my yard through the back gate. Walking across the lawn, I could see that although it looked like it had been mowed recently, there appeared to be no lights on in the house. Going up the stairs to the enclosed back deck, I pushed in the knob, opened the door and stepped inside.

I wondered how long I'd been gone; it seemed so real, not like a dream. I pulled open the unlocked sliding door and stepped inside. Everything seemed to be just like I'd left it, to include my office at the front of the house, where the tabletop light I'd left on was still on, illuminating the area over my desktop. The front door was still closed and locked, with the interior chain guard still in place. I opened the interior door and concluded the glass storm door on the outside was intact, its own locking mechanism still functioning properly.

Within a few minutes, I grabbed my car keys and drove a block away to the community mailboxes. Upon opening my mailbox, I could see it was stuffed to the limit, so I used the key secluded there by the mail delivery person to open up the overflow box below. How had this much mail gotten here in what had to be such a short period of time? I grabbed up all the mail, moved up into the driver's seat, put my seat belt on and placed the mail on the passenger seat to my right before pushing the button to restart my car.

After parking in my driveway, I went into my house to the kitchen island and placed all the mail on its quartz surface. I carefully went through it all, at which time I was able to calculate that it had been accumulating for about two weeks. I next checked the time and date on my cell phone, still plugged in and charging, just as I'd left it, and verified I had been away for twenty-two days, for it was now Monday, October 21st. I recognized I was fortunate no one had found my back door open, gone in and robbed me.

I went to bed that night, dreaming for as long as I possibly could about my journey back to 1780. I now knew how my Uncle Charles had lost his opportunity for command at the Battle of Kings Mountain; about the decision to send nine hundred ten men to fight; how heroic our American Patriot brothers were who fought there; what happened before and after the surrender; and how Virginia Sal perished and was chosen to be buried alongside Major Patrick Ferguson.

My curiosity was also resolved when I was able to determine how a mere militia Captain, another of my cousins, Joseph "PG" McDowell, could have come into possession of Ferguson's six-piece China set, cup and saucer. In addition, I could now describe the emotion-filled journey while traveling north with seven hundred Loyalist prisoners.

I must admit that the answer I sought so vigorously was now clear to me. I assert that no matter what the "real motive" was for relieving Colonel Charles McDowell of command at the Battle of Kings Mountain, Colonel James Campbell was the better choice for Commanding Officer.

If there was any one thing I kept thinking of it was Miss Lizzy Dysart. I felt a great sense of sadness in my heart for I knew she was gone from me, "lost" to time almost two hundred and fifty years ago. That is a long time to pine for a lost love. Spontaneously, a very direct thought came to the forefront of my consciousness, "Could I regain some sense of strength and redemption by meeting some of Lizzy Dysart's 21st Century relatives, if any still resided in North Carolina?"

Waking up refreshed the next morning, I put my clothes on, ate a quick breakfast and picked up my cellphone to call my Morganton contacts Robert Patton and Rebecca Heacock.

I called Robert first, who once again reaffirmed he is a direct descendant of my 1780 company commander friend, Captain Robert Patton. It was almost mind-blowing for me to comprehend that after two hundred-fifty years there were still relatives of the "original" Patton family living within a couple of miles of our Quaker Meadows home. Robert has served as President for both the Alexander Erwin Chapter of the Sons of the American Revolution (SAR) and the Historic Burke Foundation.

Rebecca Heathcock, a real, confirmed McDowell cousin of mine through Grace Greenlee Bowman McDowell, who became my Uncle Charles' wife in 1782, and even earlier back in this country's history, to Grace's father, Captain John McDowell, the Virginian. She has served as Historian for the local chapter of the Daughters of the American Revolution (DAR), America 250 Chair, docent for the Historic Burke Foundation and, most recently, is the recipient of the SAR's "Martha Washington" medal for work as SAR/DAR Liaison.

I was not done yet...

CHAPTER 44

A REMARKABLE ENDING

I had to speak to Robert and Rebecca, with the belief both might consider my "journey" a figment of my imagination. Nonetheless, no more than two hours later I was on my way on backcountry roads up to North Carolina, often transversing the same southern-bound route taken by the Overmountain Men in 1780.

These roads were fine for driving during daylight hours, however, the prospects of driving on them on a return trip at night greatly increased the odds of striking a deer in this still somewhat "wilderness" area of the state, so this was a "one-way" trip north.

Arriving in Morganton at a few minutes past noon, it had been agreed that we would meet at the Root & Vine restaurant on East Union Street, one of our mutually favorite restaurants. Once we were all together, seated at a table, I suggested a drink first. All chose iced tea.

Both Robert and Rebcca seemed to be relaxed, so I began to introduce them to my recent travels.

Robert chose the Grilled Romaine salad with Caesar dressing, followed by wood grilled Salmon and Diet Coke, while Rebcca went with Spring Salad, the Salmon option and a sweet tea. I knew exactly what I wanted, my Root & Vine favorites, a garden salad, Shrimp N' Grits, Black Angus Ribeye and sweet tea.

My now relaxed friends sat as if spellbound as I disclosed to them the details of my journey. It took a considerable amount of time to disclose all the details, from Quaker Meadows to Kings Mountain and return, but I had to tell someone who would hopefully listen to me and not immediately think I had lost my mind and "gone off the deep end."

At the conclusion of my account, both Robert and Rebecca appeared like they had reached their limits for the receipt of new information. I was pleased that through the entire afternoon neither of them told me they thought I was insane, but it was obvious they both had some serious doubts about the truthfulness of the journey I revealed to them.

Moments later, as were about to leave the restaurant, I inquired of Robert, "Do you know if there are still any Dysart's living near Morganton?" Robert brought his cell phone up to the tabletop and commented "Yes, I do have a telephone number for some Dysart's, who currently live in nearby McDowell County, which was named after another one of your cousins, Joseph "Pleasant Gardens" McDowell. They live in the town of Dysartsville, which has a population of a little over three thousand."

Robert called his contact in Dysartsville and advised them I was conducting research on their family members who lived near Morganton in the late 1700's. It was agreed that after I left the restaurant, I would drive to Dysartsville to meet them.

After saying my goodbyes, I was about to open my car door when Robert took me aside, catching me off guard, revealing to me that Mary Elizabeth Dysart, "My Lizzy," married his namesake "the original" Robert, in 1782, two years after the Battle at Kings Mountain. I was speechless.

I remembered that when my 1780's friend Robert and I first spoke about Lizzy Dysart, he had expressed the same kind of admiration for her as did I. Taking in a very deep breath and recognizing that in 1780 I was not in any position to marry anyone, I was pleased to know that Lizzy had married a man of my "old" friend Robert's high character.

Driving through the little town of Dysartsville, I finally came to an intersection where my GPS told me to turn right. Down two blocks and to the left was where I found the house noted to belong to the Dysart family. I exited my SUV and slowly walked up toward the front door.

After I'd determinably knocked twice, it opened, at which time my jaw dropped, for there, standing directly in front of me, was a more mature version of "My" Lizzy Dysart circa 1780. Before I could utter even one word, the woman standing there in front of me stated, in that same, familiar to me angelic voice. "My name is Lizzy Dysart. My name has been passed down through my family since Revolutionary War times. I understand your friend Robert has a relative who was married to my six to seven times removed great grandmother."

I just stood there, looking at her, unable to speak, like there was some immovable object stuck in my throat. My heart began to beat fast, then faster, as I continued to gaze upon her angelic face, one so remarkably akin to the Lizzy Dysart I'd met at Quaker Meadows in 1780, a woman I was totally infatuated with.

Her next words preempted any I could possibly express, "Welcome to you Major Davy McDowell Steele, my family and I are happy to meet you. Please come in." As Davy stepped through the doorway, he closed it behind him, his next journey about to begin.

ACKNOWLEDGEMENTS

I would first like to give thanks to the man who is now a dear friend of mine, Major David McDowell Steele, for without him the publication of his journal would not have been possible. Working as a "historical detective," in coordination with David's assistance, I believe you now have answers to some of the questions that have in the past has been presented as "mysteries."

These "mysteries" include the uncloaking of the personal lives of McDowell family members; how Charles McDowell lost command at Kings Mountain; how the Patriot's guerilla tactics and Ferguson's leadership failures influenced the final outcome at Kings Mountain; how Joseph "PG" McDowell" may have gained possession of Ferguson's China and; finally, how it was that Virginia Sal ended up in a grave with Major Patrick Ferguson on Kings Mountain. At least two sources were used to corroborate any conclusions.

Two local historians from Morganton, North Carolina provided invaluable assistance in the writing of this book. I first met Robert

Patton IV, current president of the Historic Burke Foundation, over two years ago. Robert and I have coordinated frequently since our first meeting about the history of the Overmountain Men and the Battle of Kings Mountain. McDowell's journal would never have been completed without Robert's assistance. Robert is carrying on the legacy of the family name of "Patton" in Morganton.

Rebecca Heacock and I share a different kind of relationship, a "blood bond," for in fact, we are cousins, going back not only to our McDowell family members in the early 1700's, but even further back to both Scotland and Ireland. Rebecca has proven to be an invaluable source of information on the McDowell's of Quaker Meadows. It is rewarding for me to know that here is at least one true descendant of the Quaker Meadows McDowell's still residing in Morganton.

My gratitude goes to Tom Lesser, also of Morganton, North Carolina, genealogist and current President of the Alexander Erwin Chapter of the Sons of the American Revolution, for so ably assisting me in preparing my application for membership in the Sons of the American Revolution. Tom is simply a "genius" when it comes to completing the paperwork required for membership. With Tom's guidance, I now have a complete set of 1780 men's clothing, which enables me to dress up like my cousins Joseph and Charles McDowell whenever the call goes out for their presence. I now proudly represent Joseph McDowell at SAR events.

William Brown III, himself a past SAR chapter president, currently serves as the chapter's sergeant-at-arms. William certainly deserves credit from me for the extensive survey work he has done on the Quaker Meadows property. It was only because of his efforts that the McDowell House and property could be accurately described.

Mr. Chivous Bradley Rutherford Gilbert of Rutherfordton, North Carolina provided me with very insightful information in reference to the hangings at Bickerstaff's Farm. In our conversation we had one day up in Rutherfordton, North Carolina, Chivous made me feel I was physically there that evening at Bickerstaff's when the nine Loyalists were hanged. In my mind, I can still see those Loyalists swinging there in the wind. Chivous is related to two of the Loyalists that were hung that night at Bickerstaff's Farm in 1780.

James Hood, owner of AJ's Family Steakhouse in Morganton, has earned my thanks for the support he has provided to me, a McDowell descendant, by employing a tree removal service to dig up the dead 1916 "Council Oak" located on his property. A new red oak tree has already been scheduled to be planted at the 1916 site. It is my hope that the SAR, DAR and all the people of Morganton also recognize James' contribution to the annual "Revolutionary War Week" held there each year in late September.

Another individual who contributed to my overall ability to complete the manuscript was Julie H. Ernstein, Ph.D. & RPA, Division Manager, Cultural Resources, Partnerships & Science, U.S. Department of the Interior, National Park Service. She provided me with guidance on the use of the troop position map originally printed by the National Park Service in 1955.

In the very beginning, it was John Hugh McDowell's book on the History of the McDowells that inspired me to keep searching for more information about their lives. McDowell's book, first published in 1918, provided me with a tremendous amount of background information. The staff at Forgotten Books in London, United Kingdom, were very gracious in allowing me to "borrow" extensively from their publication.

Whereas customer service in the United States appears to be ebbing, it is apparently alive and thriving in the U.K.

My wife, Larissa, deserves kudos for putting up with me and my "disappearances" over the past two and a half years while I worked on my manuscript, most definitely on the many occasions I advised her "I'm going back to 1780," while on my way to my office for the many hours it took to bring McDowell's journal into the light of day.

In conclusion, I am still waiting to hear from my friend, David McDowell Steele, to let me how things are going with the current "Miss Lizzy Dysart."

SOURCES

A Component Volume of Who in America 1607-1896, Bently Historical Library, University of Michigan, Marquis (1968)

A History of Gilbert Town, North Carolina, NC Home, www,overmountainvictory,org/ Gtown.htm

Analysis of the Disparate Accounts About the Battle of Kings Mountain, www.carolana.com

A Re-telling of the Story of Kings Mountain, 242nd Anniversary Ceremonies, National Park Service, Department of the Interior, https://nps.gov

Autobiography of a Revolutionary War Soldier, Feliciana Democrat (1859)

Bailey, J.D., *Commanders at Kings Mountain*, A Press, Inc. (A Press, 1980)

Battle of Cane Creek and Major Ferguson's Fatal Proclamation, Revolutionary War Journal, revolutionarywarjour-nal.com

Battle of King's Mountain, Final Stop for Major Ferguson, https://amrevnc.com

Battle of Kings Mountain, en.m.wikipedia.org/wiki/battle-of-kings-mountain

Biography of Peter Potter Collins, Sons of American Patriotism, History and Biography, Texas Sons of the American Revolution. www/texassar.org/collins-biography

Black & Black, Consultants, *Quaker Meadows, The McDowell House, Preliminary Documentaries, Research Repor*t, Raleigh, North Carolina (1987)

Black Patriots in Army at Kings Mountain, www.over mountainvictory.org /blacks.htm #KingsMountain

Burke County Regiment of Militia Cast May 9, 1777, www.carolona.com/nc/revolution /ncpatriot-military-colonels.html

Caldwell, W., *Hunting for Loyalists: The Overmountain Men and the Journey to Kings Mountain,* Victory National Historical Trail, Hallowed Ground Magazine (December 2022)

Campbell, Robert, *Description by Robert Campbell of the Battle of Kings Mountain*, Volume 15, pages 100-104, Documenting the American South: Colonial and State Records of North Carolina (1848)

Chronicle, William, *The American Battlefield Trust*, www.battlefields .org

Chronicle, William, *North Carolina Daughters of the American Revolution*, www.ncdar.org

Cleghorn Plantation/Living in the Blue Ridge Moun-tains, A Press June 2014

Cockrell, William, *Hunting for Loyalists-The Over-mountain Men and the Journey to Kings Mountain, Over-mountain Victory* National

Historical Trail, Hallowed Ground Magazine, American Battlefield Trust, December 2022

Collins, James P., *Account of The Battle of Kings Mountain, What So Proudly We Hail*, www.whatsoproudlywe-hail.org/authors-james-p-collins

Collins, James P. & John H. Roberts, *Autography of a Revolutionary Wary Soldier*, Clinton, LA Feliciana Democrat, 1859

Dragging Canoe, *The American Revolution in North Carolina*, amrevnc.com/biographies/ draggin-canoe

Draper, Lyman C., *Kings Mountain and Its Heroes, October 7, 1780* (Peter G.

Thomson, 1881)

Dunkerly, Robert M., *The Battle of Kings Mountain Eyewitness Accounts* (History Press, 2012)

Durham, Lloyd J., *Outfitting an American Revolutionary Soldier*, Tar Heel Historian, Fall 1992

Dykeman, Wilma, *The Battle of Kings Mountain 1780: With Fire and Sword* (National Park Service, U.S. Depart-ment of the Interior, 1991)

Erwin, Sam Jr., *The Battle of Kings Mountain: An Appraisal of its Historical Significance, Burke County Historical Society*, September 1980

Erwin, Sam Jr., *Some Heroes of the American Revolution in the South Carolina Upper Country*, Literary Licensing, LLC, (2011)

Ferguson, Patrick, British Inciter of the Overmountain Men, The American Revolution in North Carolina, amrevnc.com/biographies/ patrick-ferguson

Ferguson, Patrick, Ferguson at Gilbert Town and Vicinity, Gilbert Town, Its' Place in North Carolina and Revolutionary War History, www.overmountainvictory.org/ Gtown.htm

Field Trip Friday, *The History of the Battle of Kings Mountain*, Explore York County Blog, October 7, 2020

Footsteps for Freedom, Major Patrick Ferguson, Michell County Historical Trail, Mitchell County Historical Society, Podcast 2019

Footsteps for Freedom Podcasts, Episodes 22-30, Mitchell County Historical Society Podcasts, www.mitchellhis-tory.org

Foundation Document Overview: Overmountain Victory National Historical Trail, North Carolina, South Carolina, Tennessee, Virginia, National Park Service, Department of the Interior, https://www.nps.gov

General Griffith Rutherford, Gilbert Town: Its' Place in North Carolina and Revolutionary War,

Gilbert Town, Rutherford County, North Carolina Highway History Historical Marker, www.ncped.org/ media/image/ gilbert-town-rutherford

Hambright Family History, *Colonel Frederick Hambright, The Batte of Kings Mountain*, hambrightfamily-history.com

Hambright, Frederick, *Battle of Kings Mountain*, https://ncdar.org

Hamnet, C., *The Battle of Kings Mountain*, Tennesseans in the Revolutionary War, www.tngenweb.org/revwae/ kingsmountain.htm

Henry, Robert & Vance, David, *Narrative of the Battle of Cowan's Ford, and Narrative of the Battle of Kings Mountain*, Outlook Publishing Verlag Gmbh, Germany, (2020)

Hill, William, *Colonel William Hills Memoirs*, South Carolina Historical Commission, (1921)

Jones, Randall, *Before They Were Heroes at Kings Mountain*, Daniel Boone Footsteps (2010)

Kings Mountain, Lessons for Today's Leaders, Battlefield Digest, www.battledigest.com

Kings Mountain, American Battlefield Trust, www.battlefields.org

Kings Mountain National Military Park, Cultural Landscape Report, Cultural Resources Division, Southeast Regional Offices, National Park Services, Department of the Interior (2003)

Kings Mountain National Military Park Research Study, Cultural Resources Planning Division, Southeast Regional Offices, National Park Services, Department of the Interior (May 1995)

Kings Mountain National Military Park Visitor Study, National Park Service, Department of the Interior (May 2006)

Kings Mountain, Pamphlet, U.S. Department of the Interior (2010)

Kings Mountain, October 7, 1780, The American Revolution in South Carolina, www.carolana.com/sc/revolution/battle-of-kings-mountain.html

Kings Mountain National Military Park, National Register of Historic Places, OMB 1024-0018, U.S. Department of the Interior

Kings Mountain Virtual Tour, Revolutionary War 360 Degree Tour, American Battle Trust, https://battlefields.org

Letter from Joseph McDowell, Sr. to George Washington, July 17, 1758, U.S. Library of Congress, Washington, D.C

MacDowell, Dorothy Kelly, *McDowells in America, A Genealogy,* Gateway Press, Inc. (1981)

McCorkle, M.L., *The McDowells of Burke County Divided Over Who Commanded at Kings Mountain, A Sketch,* Charlotte Democrat, July 8, 1894.

McDowell, Charles, Burke County, *Stepping Aside for the Overmountain Men,* The American Revolution in North Carolina, https://amrevnc.com/biograhies/charles-mcdowell

McDowell, John Hugh, *History of the McDowells, Irwins and Connections*, Forgotten Books (2018)

McDowell, Joseph, *Burke County Militia Leader*, The American Revolution in North Carolina, https://amrevnc. com/biographies/joseph-mcdowell

McKenzie, George C., *Kings Mountain National Military Park South Carolina*, National Park Service Historical Handbook Series, No. 22 (1955)

Overmountain Victory, A Storied Tale, National Park Service, Gaffney, SC, https://nps.gov

Overmountain Victory, *National Historic Trail Lesson Plans*, National Park Service, www. nps.gov

Pancake, John S., *The Destructive War: The British Campaign in the Carolinas, 1780-1782*, University of Alabama (1985)

Parker, John C. Jr., *Parker's Guide to the Revolutionary War in South Carolina: Battles, Skirmishes and Murders*, Hem Branch Publishing (2009)

Patrick Ferguson at Gilbert Town and Vicinity, Gilbert Town: Its Place in North Caroline and Revolutionary War History, www. overmontainvictory.org/Gtown.htm

Overmountain Victory, National Historic Trail North Carolina, South Carolina, Tennessee and Virginia, https:// nichistory.com/publications/ovvi/ index.htm & www.up-countrysc.com/explore/revolutionary-war-history-south-ern-campaign

Philbrick, Hope S., *Turning to Victory, The Revolutionary War Was Won Here*, https://upcountrysc.com/ explore/revolutionary-war-history-southern-campaign

Quaker Meadows, Gathering Point for the Overmountain Men, www.amrevnc.com

Rutherford, Griffith, *The American Revolution in North Carolina*, https://amrevnc.com/ biographies/ griffith-rutherford

Revolutionary Wars Soldiers of Western North Carolina, Vol 2., Southern Historical Press Inc., Greenville, SC 1991)

Sons of American Patriotism, History and Biography, *Biography of James Potter Collins*, Sons of the American Revolution, www/texassr. org/collins-biography

St. Germain, Edward, *Major Patrick Ferguson, 1744-1780.*, www. american revolution.org/Patrick-Ferguson

The American Revolution Moves South, National Park Service, Historical Electronic Library, https://https:npshistory.com

The Battle of Earle's Ford, Encyclopedia of North Carolina Press (2025)

The Battle of Earle's Ford, Encyclopedia of North Carolina Press (2025) www.ncpedia.org/ earles-ford-battle

The Battle of Kings Mountain: A Story of Memories, American Battlefield Trust, battlfields.org

The Hated Major James Dunlap, Gilbert Town, Its' Place in North Carolina and Revolutionary War History, www.overmountainvictory. org/Gtown.htm

The Heritage of Burke Country, Burke County Historical Society, Morganton, North Carolina (1981)

The Overmountain Men & The Battle of Kings Mountain, Anchor Digital Textbook, www.ncpedia.org

The Liberty Trail: An Unforgettable Journey Through Place and Time, The American Battlefield Trust, https:// www.battlefields.org

The Heritage of Burke County, Burke Country Historical Society, Morganton, North Carolina, Hunter Publishing (1981)

The Revolutionary War's Largest All-American Fight, podcast, History on the Net, December 20, 2020

The Village at Gilbert Town, Its Place in North Carolina and Revolutionary War History, www.overmountainvicto-ry.org/GTown.htm

U.S. Army War College, Historical Statements Concerning The Battle of Kings Mountain and The Battle of Cowpens, 70th Congress, 1st Session, House Document No. 328 (U.S. Government Printing Office, 1928)

Walker, Melissa, *The Battles of Kings Mountain and Cowpens-The American Revolution in the Southern Back-country* (Rutledge, 2013)

ChatGPT5 (only used for grammar, not for research)

Wikipedia

Wikitree

YouTube Videos - The following videos were used for research purposes, available on YouTube.com

America History 101. (August 8, 2014), *The Battle of Kings Mountain: The Turning Point in the American Revolution*

America History. (April 8, 2024). The Battle of Kings Mountain, The Turning Point of the American Revolution

American Battlefield Trust. (December 3, 2023). *Kings Mountain: The Revolutionary War in Four Minutes*

Americana Corner. (September 1, 2023). *American Victory at Kings Mountain*

Appalachia's Homestead. (2024). *The Overmountain Men and the Battle of Kings Mountain*

Battle History. (April 2025). *Decisive Battle of Kings Mountain, Part of American Revolution*

Dean, Philip. (April 8, 2015). *The Battle of Kings Mountain*

CPT Gatway, (April 8, 2012). *Decisive Battles, Episode 1, Kings Mountain*

Histodat. (January 4, 3023). *The Truth of the Battle of Kings Mountain in the Revolutionary War*

History Heroes. (November 13, 2023). Battle of Kings Mountain. (1780). *Small Battle with Big Consequences*

History Rebels. (April 2025). *American Revolution: Camden and Kings Mountain*

Holmes, Barton. (May 6, 2012*), The Battle of Kings Mountain, Laurens County Museum of the Revolutionary War, Lecture Series 4K*

Lemhouse, Zack. (September 9, 2021*). Historyman Presents: The South Carolina Revolutionary War Battle of Kings Mountain with Zack Lemhouse*

SouthCarolinaTV. (March 30, 2013). *Kings Mountain: The Turning Point to the Tide of Success/the Southern Campaign*

Southern Campaign National Park Service. (September 23, 2020). *Kings Mountain 240th: The Story of the Battle of Kings Mountain and the Overmountain Men by the OVTA*

Stories of the South. (August 2021), *What Was the Significance of the Battle of Kings Mountain?*

Stories of South. (August 2025). *Where Was the Battle-of Kings Mountain Fought?*

The Adventure Channel. (2022), *Kings Mountain National Battlefield*

Truthbehindhistory. (June 18, 2024*). Truth Behind History: The Battle of Kings Mountain, a Fierce Fight for Freedom*

WBTV News (July 2021*). How the Battle of Kings Mountain Marked a Turning Point in the American Revolution*

WTVIPBSCLT (January 9, 2011). The Battle of Kings Mountain, Trails of History

www.ingramcontent.com/pod-product-compliance
Lightning Source LLC
Chambersburg PA
CBHW020609110726
47899CB00002B/433